MUSLIM
WRITERS

PUBLISHING

Many Voices, One Faith II - Islamic Fiction Stories
© 2009 Islamic Writers Alliance

Muslim Writers Publishing
PO Box 27362
Tempe, Arizona 85285

www.MuslimWritersPublishing.com

ISBN: 987-0-9819770-1-0

Cover Art by Uzma Mirza
Interior Art by Brandy AZ Chase
Book Design by Leila Joiner
Editing by Mollie Brewsaugh-Shamma

Manufactured and Printed in the United States of America

Many Voices, One Faith II

Islamic Fiction Stories

We Write What We Believe...
and We Believe in What We Write!

Introduction by S. E. Jihad Levine,
Director, Islamic Writers' Alliance

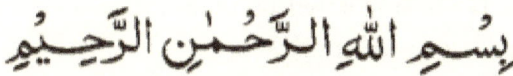

AS SALAAMU ALAIKUM AND GREETINGS OF PEACE:

The Islamic Writers Alliance (IWA) is a USA-based professional Muslim organization with an international membership. We are Muslim men and women who are published authors, unpublished writers seeking publication, poets, editors, illustrators, publishers, journalists, book reviewers, play-wrights, web designers, retailers, wholesalers, and marketing consultants. We network with each other and promote the work of the membership.

The IWA's goals are to promote literacy, and each year the organiza-tion awards fiction and nonfiction Islamic books to Islamic school libraries. We also sponsor creative writing contests in Islamic schools. The IWA also sponsors a public annual poetry contest and a public annual Islamic Fiction story contest. We also publish a quarterly online magazine, *Islamic Ink*.

In 2004, the IWA published its first anthology, *Many Voices, One Faith – Islamic Writers Alliance Anthology I*. It included poetry, short fiction, essays, and works for children.

As the Director of the Islamic Writers Alliance, I am pleased to introduce to you our second anthology, *Many Voices, One Faith II – Islamic Fiction Stories*.

Every Islamic culture enjoys stories. Those in *Many Voices, One Faith II – Islamic Fiction Stories* have been written by IWA members from all over the world, and they reflect the unique diversity and skill of our membership.

The anthology is also a result of the IWA's first short fiction contest held in 2009. The IWA's fiction and poetry contests are important tools for reach-ing our organization's goals and, as well, advance the public purpose of the organization—to promote literacy, reading, and creative writing among Muslims.

Many Voices, One Faith II – Islamic Fiction Stories introduces a new sub-category of fiction called Islamic Fiction (IF). Many genres are included in IF, but the most critical feature is a positive portrayal of Islam and Islamic values in the story. IF stories also highlight how the Muslim characters deal with everyday issues and problems within an Islamic framework. For Muslim parents, IF offers a blessed alternative to the books for children and teens offered in today's secular market.

The IWA will also be publishing its first poetry anthology, *Many Poetic Voices, One Faith*, in 2009.

The IWA gives thanks to Allah (swt) for all of the gifts He has bestowed upon our membership. We also thank Linda Delgado, award-winning author and owner of Muslim Writers Publishing, for making this anthology a reality.

For more information about Islamic Fiction, visit:

http://www.islamicfictionbooks.com and
http://muslimwriterspublishing.com

Also visit the Islamic Writers Alliance online at:

http://www.islamicwritersalliance.net

Acknowledgments

NON-IWA MEMBER PANEL OF JUDGES:

The Islamic Writers Alliance would like to thank the judges of the 2009 Islamic Fiction (IF) Contest for their generosity of time and expertise given when reading all the IF stories submitted to the contest and selecting the first place winners of the contest.

Patricia Dunn (M.F.A., Sarah Lawrence College) was managing editor of *Muslim Wakeup!*, America's most popular Muslim online magazine with over 200,000 monthly readers. Her work has appeared in *Global City Review, Salon.com, Women's eNews, The Christian Science Monitor, The Village Voice, The Nation,* and *L.A. Weekly,* among other publications. Her work is anthologized in *Stories of Illness and Healing: Women Write Their Bodies,* Kent State University Press. She has an upcoming piece in *MotherVerse,* issue number 9. She teaches creative writing at Sarah Lawrence College's Writing Institute and Summer Writer's Workshop for High School Students. She lives in Westchester County with her nine-year-old son, Ali, who wants to be President of the United States when he grows up.

Mollie Brewsaugh-Shamma received a BA degree in English with emphasis in Honors Studies from Northern Kentucky University. She also has a dual MA degree in English Creative Writing and Editing/Publishing from the University of Cincinnati. She is currently teaching music, art, and writing for The International Academy of Cincinnati. Ms. Brewsaugh is a well-known writer and author. Her work has been widely published, and some places you can read her work are: *Azizah Magazine: Stolen Names-Stolen Lives* - Having your personal information stolen can turn into a nightmare, and *Islamic Horizons: The Challenges Muslim Women Encounter.* She is a contributing author and editor in the anthology, *Between Love, Hope & Fear,* An-Najm Publishers.

Pamela Taylor is a former director of the Islamic Writers Alliance and co-founder of Muslims for Progressive Values. She can be found on the web at pamelaktaylor.com, newsweek.washingtonpost.com, and Facebook.

*IWA Panel of Judges:

IWA Board of Director, *Balqees Mohammed*
IWA Board of Director, *Mahasin D. Shamsid-Deen*
IWA Board of Director, *Linda D. Delgado*

*Biographical information is available with the judges' contributions to this anthology. The judges' stories included in this anthology were not considered for judging or contest winner selection.

Special Thanks to *Safiyyah E. J. Levine* for editing the first place winning contest stories.

TABLE OF CONTENTS

2009 IWA

Islamic Fiction Story Contest Winner

You Jist Never Know

by

Judy Nelson Eldawy

Judy Nelson Eldawy

Judy Nelson Eldawy, or Ummcamelia, winters in Egypt with her daughter and husband and spends summers in the USA. Judy earned a BSN from George Mason University. She is a member of the Islamic Writers Alliance.

Judy writes, "I remember my Mom saying I should be a writer when I was little but I wanted to be an anthropologist and an archeologist. Then reality reared its ugly head and I became an RN, mostly because housing and groceries are two of my favorite things. Alhumdulilah as it turned out, I love nursing. I have worked with HIV/AIDS patients in medical/surgical, psychological/mental health, and home health.

I married and ended up moving to and migrating between Small Town, USA and Small Village, Egypt. Allah Alim-Margaret Mead of the Delta fellaheen, that's me. I try to maintain a serene and tranquil home for my darlings in both places. In between tutoring and domestic engineering, I surf the Web, read, and research – especially herbal medicines and alternative treatments – and do some freelance writing."

You Jist Never Know by Judy Nelson Eldawy

"Howdy, darling! Get me some coffee, would ya?" the trucker bellowed, flashing the waitress a roguish grin and allowing one lid to droop over a bloodshot blue eye. VA to El Paso wasn't the easiest haul, especially closer to El Paso, when the sameness of the desert got to you. One of the perks, though, was Maisie's TA – an open secret to the savvy driver. Some of the best grub in the country plus clean, homey shower facilities and double fill-up points redeemable for not just drinks, but wireless service or goods – you'd be stupid not to stop. Most all truckers did.

The trucker, one "Grizzly" Devine by name, scanned the room for an empty table when he was hailed from the counter.

"Griz! Grizzly! Over here!" called his friend, an older stick-thin fellow going by the unfortunate nickname Biscuit, owing to his love of the same. Get a group of men together and, once past the posturing and jockeying for position, nicknaming seemed to be an essential part of the male bonding experience.

Grizzly ambled on over, a big, slow-moving man sharing a physical as well as temperamental resemblance to his namesake.

"Hey, Biscuit! Ain't this a surprise? I thought I'd be having just a screen for company. How's the missus and that boy of yours? Where you heading? And what's good on the menu?" asked Grizzly as he sat down on the stool, dropping his computer bag at his feet.

The waitress set down the coffee and a menu. Biscuit, having finished his meal, politely waited while Griz got himself settled and made his selection.

"Ok, darling, I'll have the meatloaf special with mashed potatoes, collards, and cornbread. How 'bout keeping me company with some dessert, Biscuit?" asked Grizzly.

"Well, in the interest of being neighborly, I suppose I could choke down a piece of lemon chess," grinned Biscuit, who'd just eaten two. "And keep the coffee coming."

The waitress trudged off with the order and the friends got down to the serious business of swapping gossip, though both preferred the term "information exchange."

Truckers were the 21st century's cowboys – lone rangers riding the wide open highways instead of prairies, wrangling freight instead of cattle, and dealing with lowdown, thieving rustlers who tried to hijack the loads.

Running into a friend was a rare treat. The waitress brought the food and the next couple hours were pleasantly occupied in railing against company pay cuts, mapping locations of speed traps and sleep spots, and the doings of mutual acquaintances and family.

"Biscuit, I got a situation I wanna run by ya," said Grizzly soberly. "I've been thinking on it lots lately. You might remember me telling you 'bout Travis, my baby brother? I'm kind of worried 'bout him."

"Whoa, I ain't seen you look this serious since that letter from the IRS. Is Travis sick?" sympathized Biscuit.

"No, he ain't precisely sick. He got into this new religion, and he started changing. Not changing bad, mind you, just he's gotten weird. I've been thinking 'bout talking to one of those brainwashing guys. I saw a show about them after that disaster at Waco."

"Weird how, Griz? Did he join the Harry Krisnas and start panhandling in the airports or take to wearing hair shirts and beating himself bloody?" asked Biscuit.

"No – he became a Mooslim," said Griz glumly. "We were all upset at first cuz of those suicide bombings and stuff. But he swears up and down that those guys are terrorists and have nuthin' to do with real Islam. He took out that Ko-ron and showed us where it said that their god, Allah, said not to do things like that. Not to be aggressive, but just to protect yourself and stuff and not fighting women and kids and old people. I can respect that. I mean, defending yourself is a Constitutional right; blowing up innocent people is just murder. He's not a terrorist or anything – I'd stomp his tail into next week, if I thought that."

"Ok – so what's the issue here?" asked Biscuit.

"He's different. He doesn't want ta watch the game and toss back a few with me anymore or go shoot pool. He doesn't come over for supper – says he doesn't eat pork or drink and doesn't want to make things hard for me. Says he doesn't do birthdays anymore or holiday celebrations.

"When he does come over, he starts talking kinda funny. I say, 'Trav, let's go fishing tomorrow – whadya say to that?' 'Inshell-lah,' he says. Or when I told him 'bout Charlie breaking his leg, he says 'Hum-doo-lah it wasn't his neck.' Huh?" Grizzly sighed gustily, shaking his head.

"Oh, and he wants to be called Abdool Ramen now. What's wrong with Travis? Momma'd take a switch to his britches if she were still with us, God rest her soul. I feel like I'm losing my brother, Biscuit, and I ain't got a lot of family to lose. I think burying Momma shook a screw loose, ya know?"

He shifted uncomfortably on the seat and twisted away from his friend, stretching hugely and popping his spine in the process. Biscuit signaled the waitress to freshen the cups and thought about how to reply.

"Death makes a lot of people reflect on their lives, Griz. How old's the kid, anyway?"

"Thirty," said Griz.

"So he is not a kid then. Sounds like he's making a lot of cosmetic changes, but he's still talking with you, right?"

"Yeah – he keeps throwing his religion in and talks lots about straight paths and Allah and saying Jesus is a man and a prophet." He ran his fingers through his thinning blond curls and scrubbed his face with his paws.

"I'm afraid he's gonna fry like a trout," murmured Grizzly so softly as to be almost inaudible.

Ignoring that, Biscuit clarified, "So what's wrong is he's not Christian anymore, and he changed the relationship between you two."

"That's 'bout the sum of it," agreed Grizzly.

"Do you know any Muslims other than your brother, Grizzly? Or anything about Islam other than what Travis told you?" asked Biscuit.

"Not really. That pizza joint in Claysville is run by an Egyptian fellow who might could be Mooslim. He's seems decent enough for a furr'ner. Why ya asking?" said Griz.

"Sometimes it's easier to see things and learn about things from people who aren't so close to us. I don't think I ever told you, but my sister married a Muslim. He's a real good guy and treats Cindy and the kids well. Mom thinks he can do no wrong. Anyway, some years ago, Cindy ups and becomes Muslim, too," said Biscuit.

"NO! You don't say!" exclaimed Grizzly. "Goes to show, you jist never know of folks' troubles. I'm real sorry, Biscuit."

Biscuit nodded his appreciation of the sympathy and continued on. "It was a shock, and I'll allow as how I was hopping mad for awhile. Becky made an appointment with a therapist cuz she couldn't deal with me. The doc said part of my anger was due to thinking Cindy was rejecting us and of her changing how we all relate," Biscuit paused a moment and smiled. "Also, it was downright embarrassing to be seen with her looking like a giant crow in black from head to toe," he reminisced. "Worse was her acting like she was a foreigner who'd never grown up right in Norlina, NC." He shook his head over the strangeness of it all and continued, "She's still a bit odd with the scarves and long skirts, but she's back to having some color and sass. It's not so bad now."

Grizzly guffawed. "Travis don't wear no scarf, but he'd fit right in with ZZ Top with that beard he's growing. So you think talking to some other Mooslims would be good?" asked Grizzly.

"I do," affirmed Biscuit. "It helped me, especially when I visited with Ahmed's kin in Egypt. They're just regular people muddlin' along like the rest of us. Once I got that and realized Islam really isn't all that strange from Christianity, things got lots better.

"Hey, you want to talk with Cindy? She can answer your questions and give you web sites and whatnot."

"Well, I don't want to be a bother," hedged Grizzly.

"No bother," said Biscuit, taking out his cell phone and punching the speed dial. "She won't mind…Hey Sissy, how's it going?"

Biscuit paused a minute to listen before replying.

"Fine. Listen, I have a buddy here who needs to know about Islam. You got a couple minutes?…Great. His name's Grizzly," said Biscuit as he handed over the phone. He signaled for more coffee and thought what a good thing it was that minutes after 9 PM were free.

2009 IWA Members

Islamic Fiction Stories

In Loving Memory

Amatullah Al-Marwani penned herself The Mad Rhyming Woman. She was one of the founding members of the IWA organization. She was married to Mohamed and the mother of a son, Zaahir, and a daughter, Amirah. Sister Amatullah authored the Zaahir and the Camel children's book series, wrote extensive poetry, created newsletters for her masjid and community, and served Allah with a heart full of love. She died April 29, 2005 from leukemia. I was honored to be her writing buddy for over four years, and she was my dearest friend. For those she left behind, her work is still a great pleasure to read and learn from. – Linda D. Delgado

Adam by Amatullah Al-Marwani

"Isn't that beautiful, honey?"

Caught off guard, she quickly turns her head to take in the scene before them. Laughing children with sandy feet and sunny smiles spin themselves dizzy on the merry-go-round. Even the crusty souls taking up residence on the benches lining the playground wear faces less etched by frowns of displeasure and more softened by fleeting memories of joyful youth.

"Mmm…yes, yes, beautiful," she replies, her reverie lingering in wisps and tatters. She brushes a hand across her face, deftly tucking loose strands of hair back into her hijab. If only she could whisk away her interrupted thoughts as easily!

Her gaze scans the park, zeroing in without fail on their own addition to the festivities of this summer's day. He is busy pulling the petals off the bushy flowers potted within kid-friendly reach.

"Adam! Adam, stop hurting the flowers, love, and come here to Mama!"

The toddler looks up, eyes engaged in finding the known voice, hands engaged in exploring the unknown dirt under his grubby touch. His grin requires an antidote, it is so infectious. She catches it and spreads it to her husband.

"That's our boy!" Expressing emotion doesn't come easy to this man, but he is overflowing with it now. "Masha'Allah, Aminah, that's our boy!"

She averts her eyes, unable to bear his contentment, his peace. She continues to carry the smile, but now it is the heavy weight of mere reflex, automatic defense mechanism. Her thoughts sweep her away once more as they did when she answered the phone that morning...

"Yes, this is Aminah, Adam's mother. Who's calling, please?"

Her palm grips the receiver in a hold that would leave tell-tale marks long after Adam is gone. As she listens in disbelief to the droning voice of the doctor on the other end, she could not know how often she will finger those marks in the future, tracing and re-tracing the imprints left on the day she learned her life didn't stop just because her heart did.

But that was yet to come, and she is here now, with her adoring and blissfully unaware husband. And, of course, with her heart. With Adam.

It would be eight months before his smile faded, before the colors of the world dimmed for her. Eight months of learning to let go, to cry in the shower so the tears would melt away with the water, to impart hope from her meager supply, to trust in Allah's plans of mercy and eternal beauty...eight months to say good-bye and a lifetime to wait.

It would be eight months before his tears would no longer need soothing by her gentle shushing, eight months before his bed would stay made the whole day...and the whole night. It would be until her own last moment before she would forget cradling him in her arms, willing with all her might to disbelieve so she could rant and rave and tear at her empty chest in searing grief. A lifetime to beg forgiveness from the One who must surely know her heart was being ripped from her soul while she still drew breath.

It would be eight months of beauty, the kind one only knows from pain – the more intense the latter, the more lasting the former.

Memories of Adam's 'I'm awake, I'm really awake!' grin every time his dad took him out for the Fajr prayer would overcome those of the distant hollowness his eyes later took and held.

Memories of Adam's tiny nursling coos, gently drawing life from her life would overcome those of the drug-induced coma neither cuddles nor cries could pierce.

Memories of the baby-fresh smell of Adam's skin would overcome those of the hospital disinfectant wrapping him in its silent shroud.

Memories of the eager to go-go-go little man would overcome those of the swaddled and intubated lifeless form she kissed for the final time.

The son she'd cherished for the immemorial span of two years would overcome the loss no human effort could sate.

Beauty is eternal, but only fools and the blind wait that long before appreciating it. A lesson she learned in eight months. A lesson she learned in one phone call. A lesson she needs to share with her husband and with her son. Adam.

"Aminah? Honey? Would you look at that kid! Isn't he something? Isn't he? Have you ever seen anything more beautiful than our son, Subhan'Allah?"

On some level, Allah grants wisdom and surety of passage to every soul in need. She is a vessel, filling up and pouring out this strength. "No, my dearest. I haven't. And I won't again until we reach Jennah."

Adam loses interest in the dirt and comes toward them, weaving and waving muddy fingers. The breeze catches his curls and lifts them in a quirky dance. He stops and looks intently at his parents, his lifelines. The tableau freezes in her mind, every detail captured, right down to the untied double-knotted shoestring he is always managing to undo. He places his chubby hand on his lips and blows them a kiss, his most recent and endearing baby 'trick'. It doesn't miss and is big enough for both of them to share forever. If this isn't beauty, what is?

"Adam..." her voice breaks slightly. "Adam, come on, honey. Let's get you ready to go, sweetheart. We all have to go home soon."

❧

In November of 2004, Sister Amatullah wrote, "As-Salaamu Alaikum, This is the saddest piece I've ever written because, at one time, it seemed to bear the ring of truth for me and my family. I am thankful that is no longer true."

DELETE BY AMATULLAH AL-MARWANI

Confessions of an E-Bay shopper: I'm a late payer. Yep, I bought exactly one item a year ago, and I have exactly one negative comment right up there next to my name: "Late Payer". Frantic to remove the shadow cast upon my money-spending reputation (ahh, the purchase power of the Net), my fingers seek out the delete button.

I find everything from "Buy Now" (a command that resonates with my pocketbook) to "Click Here to See a Bigger Picture" (wonder if I can have that framed for the living room?) to "Exit the System". While I'm all for pulling the e-covers over my head and pretending to sleep my way out of trouble, the latter choice sounds kind of final.

There is no delete button.

I don't want the whole world to know me as "Alp" (Amatullah, Late Payer)! How can I ever whip out my Pay-Pal Account in front of others again? How will the sellers of stuff I need (like that hijab with the bull's eye on it – a must have!) know I can find my way to the mailbox with a check? I am awash with frustration and shame (does that come in a travel size with matching crème rinse?). One simple, obscure, and forgotten transaction done in haste (well, maybe not hastily enough) is haunting me to this shopping day.

Hang on a second! What's this? "Feedback Disputes"? Aha! Fingers shaking, I click away, hope springing eternal. I knew I could smudge the edges and get that pesky remark removed! I quickly scan the first option available to me: "Leave a comment of 80 characters or less in response to the negative feedback." I'll be out of space before I'm done typing my name! Who on earth makes up these steely limitations? Note to self: Ask the inventor of the Internet what's the big idea with the small input boxes! Hmmm... where did I put Al's email anyway?

Moving on to option two, "Have the buyer add a comment to their original negative feedback." Well, what are they going to say? "Just kidding!"? Or "Alp's a great gal who sometimes mixes up the large blue postal mailboxes on every corner with 'street art'. She'll ooh and ahh over them, point them out to tourists, exclaim with pride over her city's increasing commitment to educating the masses with such bold projects, and then move on, never entering the 'touch-zone' because anyone who's ever seen fine art knows you're not supposed to lay hands on it. Let alone actually open it and place a check inside!" Oops. They can't say that – it's 380 characters too long. (Wonder if the seller would be good enough to shorten it up to "Alp's a great gal"? Why, that tidy 17-character count even includes spaces between the words and plenty of room for smiley faces!)

I know, I know. I did the crime. I have to do the time...but I can still try to find that delete button, can't I? If word gets out I'm a late payer, my shopping days may have come to a crashing end (is that my husband applauding?!).

Does this story scare you? I know my husband got all jittery when I mentioned it to him. With a quaking beard, he said, "You were shopping on-line? So that's where the new throw rug made out of recycled plastic and woven in the pattern of the solar system came from!" To which I smartly replied, "It's a learning tool for our son. And look, it even includes the asteroid belt!" (Husbands just don't understand bargains.)

Okay, you may not lose sleep over this little tale. But maybe thinking about the feedback on file with Allah will keep you awake nights in worship to our Lord and Sustainer:

"Then, as for him who is given his record in his right hand, he will say: Take, read my book! Surely I knew that I should have to meet my reckoning." Holy Qur'an 69:19-20

Short of a court order, I will never be able to delete the E-Bay record decrying me as a late payer (I know, I read all the fine print – there's no way out). Alhamdulilah, unlike the rigid human systems we pride ourselves on creating, The Most Merciful provided us with a delete button long before Bill Gates moved into his garage. Not only does Allah's delete button erase our faults, it turns them into merits. Take that, E-Bay!

But...we have to press the button by pressing ourselves into service for His Sake:

"Except him who repents and believes and does a good deed; so these are they of whom Allah changes the evil deeds to good ones; and Allah is Forgiving, Merciful." Holy Qur'an 25:70

Repent. Believe. Do a good deed. It ain't rocket science. It's ISLAM.

I'm embarrassed to buy anything on-line now (is that my husband still clapping?!). Imagine the shame and loss we'll feel if we stand before Allah with the words "Late Prayer" still in our books? Or "Stingy in the charity department"? Or "Turned the other cheek so he wouldn't have to see what was happening in front of him"?

I want to be given my book in my right hand, I want to turn and say, "Read! I *knew* I would meet up with my record! And I prepared for it by deleting everything I didn't want in here!" And how did I do that? How can you do that? How can *we* do that?

Do a good deed.

Try one on for size (can I get that in an extra large to go?). You'll love how it makes you look!

Final Destination by Amatullah Al-Marwani

This is the story of Salinah, a headstrong newly reverted Muslim American and AbdurRahman, the man who would change her heart and her faith.

Linah and Rammie struggle to overcome cultural clashes as she takes on a deeper understanding of what it means to live in Islam…to reach the "Final Destination" which is the goal of every Muslim. Along her way, she'll pass by many roadblocks and detours, believing she has arrived at that destination simply by marrying the man she loves. She will ultimately discover the greatest love of her life…Love for Allah.

"A Bee in Her Hood"

Slowly and with great deliberation, Salinah raised her right, stylishly clad foot and took the first step toward her destiny. She had planned this decision with excruciating precision, marking the pros and the cons as carefully as a miser counting pennies.

Pro: Being in a Muslim country.

Con: Being away from family.

Pro: Marrying the man of her dreams.

Con: Marrying the man of her dreams!

She grabbed her valise tighter and continued down the walkway connecting Flight #234 from America to this new soil, *her* new soil, Jordan. AbdurRahman didn't know she was arriving – he would be heartsick with worry to think of her traveling on her own (not to mention upset she refused to follow the example of the Prophet who forbade it, but that was an argument for a day not as fine as this). Foreign tongues slipped over her head, filtered by the hijab she was now glad she had worn. Entering the main promenade, she wiped the traces of tears from her face. It wouldn't do to have all these stalwart Arabs see an American cry, now, would it?

Hours later, safely ensconced in her hotel room in the fashionable district of downtown Amman – who would've thought a girl from Hagerstown, Maryland, would ever put her aching feet up on a stool here? – she rang the operator.

"*Na'am, sayyiditee?*" the deep voice on the other end inquired.

"Do you speak English?" Salinah had grown up with the cadence of 'soonest begun, soonest done' ringing through her ears, thanks to a military dad and his strict codes of discipline. Best to cut to the chase and not waste time with frivolities or even, on occasion, niceties.

"*Na'am*, Madam. I do indeed speak English." His tone indicated a familiar weariness and natural offense at being questioned by strangers in his own country. But, then again, she felt a pang of bitterness herself when recalling all the times dark-skinned Muslims had inquired into her faith, into her belief in Allah. Some even asked if she made prayers, as if it were *they* she owed them to. And God help her if they met Salinah without her hijab on! It was the hellfire for sure and no passing GO or collecting $200 on the way.

"I would like to be connected to 555-4282."

"Of course, Madam. One moment, if you please."

Her palms grew sweaty, and the receiver slipped down in her grasp as an older woman answered the phone. The voice, crackled with age and suspicion (*or maybe that's my own suspicion*, Salinah thought) didn't invite warmth and didn't extend it. *Mother-in-law* flashed in neon lights against the screen of her mind. *Future* mother-in-law.

"Ah...Salaam. AbdurRahman, please?" Salinah waited. And waited.

Apparently, the woman had long ago cornered the market on how to make potential mates for her son squirm in silence. But Salinah was no ordinary, timid thing – she was an American and, by God, she'd come all the way to Jordan to marry AbdurRahman, and both sides of both families had better start getting used to it. *And pronto*, she added to herself, flipping back her hair in the coltish mannerism of a woman who didn't take no for an answer (though she frequently gave it as one).

"Um...Hajji? AbdurRahman, okay? *Aaab ... durr ... rah ... maaan?*" she dragged the word out slowly, rolling the r's with a trill of her tongue as Rammie had taught her.

Clunk.

Just when Salinah began to press the disconnect button, she heard the resonant voice of the man whose arms she would soon fill. Rammie was in harried – and loud – dialogue with his mother. Salinah sat numb, sensing anger in the responses and was surprised when mingled laughter filled the line.

"As-Salaamu Alaikum, habibti!" Rammie's voice fairly boomed into her heart.

"Salaam, Rammie!" Saying his name lifted her like a kite taking off to float deliciously and lazily in the wind. "Oh, Rammie! I've missed you so!"

"And I've missed you, habibti. What time is it in San Francisco now? You're calling me very early for the girl who doesn't like to see the sun break the sky in the mornings."

"I don't know, but it's 8:30 PM in Jordan."

"Yeah, we were sitting down to a late dinner when – hey! How do you know what time it is here?"

"Because I'm looking at my watch, which I set on the plane, and the hotel clerk informed me I was indeed in the right time zone."

"Linah, you're losing me here. Plane? Hotel? What's up? Oh, hang on, hang on – " he interrupted himself to speak a few more words to his mother. Salinah waited (she was getting good at it by now) until his voice caressed her again.

"Sorry 'bout that. Mom's got a bee in her hood and won't settle down."

Salinah laughed. Rammie often confused colloquiums with an endearing charm that brought a smile to her English Master's degreed heart. "You mean a bee in her bonnet. And besides, doesn't your mom wear hijab?" she teased.

"Don't go picking on my English now, missy!" His easy fluency with her native tongue always amazed and pleased her. Spoken with the lilt of the British occupiers his family had lived under, and then the London headmasters he had studied under, AbdurRahman's command of the English language was superb – mixed metaphors notwithstanding.

"Anyway, Linah. What's going on? I wasn't expecting to hear from you for another week."

"I couldn't wait that long, Rammie. So I took a shortcut by way of Amsterdam."

"Linah, on the best of days you confuse me, but now I'm lost. Help me find my way. Speak English, would you?!"

"Rammie, I'm in Jordan. In the *Hotel Al-Harb*, to be exact."

More silence. And she thought these people were famous for their verbosity!

"Uh, Linah? First things first. I highly doubt you are in the Hotel Al-Harb, since that would mean 'Hotel of War'. And while us Arabs can be hotheads, we like our gentrified visitors to feel at home. I believe you must be staying in the Hotel *Ad-darb*, the 'Hotel of the Path' and speaking of paths…" he paused, collecting either his thoughts or his voice, she wasn't sure.

"Linah, *what are you doing here?!*"

Voice. Now she was sure.

"Oh, Rammie! Don't be mad. I simply could not live another day without you. Is that so hard to accept? Don't you love me?" She tossed the latter in for good measure, knowing full well he adored her to bits and pieces, and even those he would gather up until nothing remained of her own self when she was with him.

"Linah, you exasperate and excite me, by Allah, you do. Now, we have to figure out what comes next. You know I can't see you on my own until we're married, and you, my dear bold woman, traveled here with no mahram. Both situations are untenable to me, so – "

"Let's get married today!" they chimed in unison.

Ar-Rihana by Bayan

The author has requested to remain anonymous.

"...and this is why we are gathered here today, by the will of Allah Jalla Jallaluhu, to continue to support the foundation of this masjid. With your help, my dear and respected brothers and sisters, we can reach our fundraising goal for the night." A caller roared from nearby the podium, "Takbir!" – the crowd joined in unison, "Allahu Akbar!"

Yet I was neither impressed nor inspired by the sheikh's talk. No doubt, his recitation of Qur'an could have made stones shed tears and shattered the hesitation of those questioning their faith. No doubt, his calling to donate from what Allah bestowed on us to cover the expenses of running the local masjid was noble and sublime. No doubt, his charisma, sense of humor, and exemplar Islamic appearance could have mistaken him for a divine worshipper. But there I was, unmoved.

You see, I knew what others didn't in that ballroom. The brother being praised for his beautiful recitation, inspirational speech, and noteworthy fundraising skills was my ex-husband.

As the crowd grew excited and donations began to flow, I let myself be transported to that October morning years ago. A call from an unfamiliar number appeared on my caller ID and, against my will, I answered it. "Assalaamu-alaikum," the timid voice said, immediately adding, "Is this sister Umm Jihad?" I had no idea who could be calling, especially since I could count the number of people who knew my number in one hand. "Alaikum salaam," I replied, coming across a bit forceful, unintentionally. "Sister," she proceeded, without being fazed by my curtness, "I think we have something in common."

I knew instantly this call would forever change my perception of so-called muslims.

So I asked the sister to explain. She proceeded to say her name was Umm Isa, from Texas, mother of five, recently married and already bordering on divorce. In my mind, I refused to admit I knew exactly where this conversation was heading. She continued to explain nonchalantly that her husband, a sheik, had proposed a secret (public-to-be, in the near future) marriage to avoid hurting his wife, who vehemently opposed polygamy. Umm Isa, blinded by his Qur'anic recitation, Islamic knowledge, beard, and thaub, had consented to marry him this way, swearing an oath to never disclose their marriage if they ever got divorced, and agreeing to see him infrequently, when he could manage to be away from home at night, while he supposedly performed itikaf. To hear the sister tell her story was painful enough without the realization that my story, from years past, sounded exactly the same and included the same man.

The sister paused, caught her breath, and then continued: "Sister, I heard you were married to him and wanted to ask you what happened. He said you committed zina, and that is why he divorced you. But I heard from others that the truth is different."

"Oh, yes, it is," I mused, as I noticed that calling each other "sister" dissolved any animosity we might have had toward each other. After all, we were talking about the same man: my ex, her ex-to-be.

"Well, sister, where to begin? Yes, I was married to him, but no, audhu billah, I did not commit zina. The story goes something like this, more or less. We married in secret to avoid disrupting his family life and dealing with the community gossip, since he was the imam of the local masjid. However, a few days after consummating the marriage, he said he would be unable to be fair to me, did not want to hurt me, and would rather let me go (a.k.a. divorce).

Astonished, I could not believe I had been played, used and abused, and would soon join the divorcee ranks once again. So I gathered all my pain and shame and, without a second thought, headed to his house to expose him in front of his wife. To my surprise, when I arrived she already knew what I was coming for. She was hurt, no doubt, but also ruthless, and at once asked him to divorce me in front of her. Right then, it dawned on me this was not an isolated incident. I was not his first 'victim,' nor would be his last. Hearing from you, my sister, corroborates that."

The cacophony in the room brought me back temporarily from the memories of that call in time to hear him recite the ayah of Qur'an that translates:

"And He has united their hearts; had you spent all that is in the earth, you could not have united their hearts, but Allah united them; surely He is Mighty, Wise." – *Surah Al-Anfal 8: Verse 63*

"So even though you are not all from this locality, you should love your brothers and sisters who are, and help them to keep the masjid running. Open your hearts, brothers and sisters, and donate generously in Allah Az'awajal's cause," he implored.

I instantly thought of the hadith of the prophet (saw) that reads: "The example of a believer who recites the Qur'an is that of a citron (a citrus fruit), which is good in taste and good in smell. And the believer who does not recite the Qur'an is like a date, which has a good taste but no smell. And the example of an impious person who recites the Qur'an is that of Ar-Rihana (an aromatic plant), which smells good but is bitter in taste. And the example of an impious person who does not recite the Qur'an is that of a colocynth, which is bitter in taste and has no smell."

Umm Isa, in all shyness, began to weep. How could I console her? "Umm Jihad," she asked, "why didn't you say anything so he wouldn't hurt anyone else?"

Defensively, I blurted out, "I did, sister, but it seems my message didn't reach you." So I proceeded to recount that year of agony, when my secret marriage transitioned from a full-blown community affair to detrimental emotional abuse to a seemingly never-ending cycle of iddah and being taken back, finally culminating in divorce. During those intolerable months, I almost lost all faith in Muslims, as my children and I were shunned from the community while the Sheikh continued to deliver the Friday sermons and lead the pious followers in prayer. Fortunately, alhamdulillah, a group of brothers who stood for justice, as Allah commands, had set the record straight, and the Sheikh had been quietly let go, only to end up as imam in another state. He had also been asked to resign from his teaching duties at the Salaam Online University when the director found out about the fiasco and didn't want to provide a forum for unchecked behavior to flourish. I mean, really, who would doubt a sheik who knows the whole Qur'an by heart, has a Ph.D. in Islamic studies, and has been imam for the past fifteen years?

Although suspicion in some cases is a sin, I revisited a fair warning I had had before our marriage. A friend with strong connections had run a moral background check on the Sheikh, only to find out he had been expelled from his country of origin for secretly marrying and divorcing an innocent sister in less than a week. Her family, of high social rank and with powerful strings in government, had immediately pulled on those strings and had had him expelled from the country. Ergo, the migration to the US, now from state to state, a trail of abused sisters in his wake. Like a serial killer, he had used charm and intelligence with a mask of sanity, to lure divorced, vulnerable sisters who reached out to the imam for advice. With promises of a fulfilling life, and an opportunity to learn about deen from a pro, along with Islamic references on the permissibility of a secret marriage, he had managed to marry and divorce sisters for over a decade without being "caught."

I realized then that sisters, like victims of serial murderers, usually fit a general profile. They were either poor, living on public assistance, such that a promise of an extra $200 a month seemed fair and charitable, or they were wealthy, independent sisters, without need of financial support, who could afford expensive gifts. Most sisters had children from a previous marriage, but were either incapable of bearing children anymore, or were asked to observe rigid birth control measures to prevent unwanted pregnancies. Knowledge of Islam was always absent, so that the oppression could take strong roots justified with distorted interpretations of Islamic sources. Once the secret marriage took place, sisters were asked to please Allah by observing the face veil. What a sophisticated and vile plot! No one could really tell how many wives there were without being able to distinguish between one veiled sister and another.

In the ballroom, my eyes turned to his wife and nine children sitting in the audience. I thought of the constant heartache this sister felt, as her husband, held in such high regard, secretly transgressed. I used to blame her for allowing his misdeeds complacently, selfishly turning a blind eye on the evil of it all. However, looking at their children, I felt only pity, thinking of how many stepmothers and stepsiblings they unknowingly had.

"Sister," I resumed, "I know this must all seem like a fictional tale to you, and that what you are going through is extremely disturbing and surreal, but have no doubts that Allah is Just, All-Aware. He healed my heart long ago and blessed me with a wonderful mate, who fears Him and obeys Him, and I am certain that, with prayer and patience as He has promised us in Qur'an, you will emerge from this a stronger, more faithful sister."

Then sister Karen, amicable and energetic as always, interrupted my reverie. For the past three years we had been tirelessly working together, along with sheik Ali Nasr and other pious, hard-working brothers and sisters, to form and run the Muslims Coalition Against Abuse (MCAA).

"Sister Umm Jihad," she said, "it's time!" I quickly composed myself from the journey back in time to tackle the task at hand. Outside the ballroom, our table was already set up with brochures about MCAA and the list of services we provided. As I arrived, sister Karen was already lively in educating a group of young sisters.

"MCAA," she said, "it's not only a support system for victims of domestic abuse and violence, but a coalition to teach sisters about Islam, to avoid abuse to take place unknowingly."

Our respected colleague and mentor, Sheikh Ali Nasr, proceeded to add, "MCAA is as much about preventing as it is about healing. We have a network of fifteen MCAA sites, all throughout the US, and local efforts are being focused on stepping over the Atlantic and establishing a presence overseas. The coalition has grown dramatically as sisters come forward, finding solace and empowerment to help other sisters."

In retrospect, I could not feel happier that Allah had tested me and helped me endure. Stemming from the injustice we experienced, a group of pious brothers and sisters, including Umm Isa in Texas, were now battling abuse in all its forms within the Islamic community. To stand there, in the hallway, and see all the tears shed years ago come to fruition through MCAA was enough to feed my soul for years to come.

Saaleha Bhamjee began her writing career as a columnist for the South African print magazine, *The Muslim Woman*. Her writings have appeared in Islam Online, *An Nisaa* magazine, *The Straight Path Magazine*, *Al Qalam* newspaper, the New Orleans-based *IQRA* newspaper, as well as the UK-based *Muslim Weekly*. She has had poems appear in the *Muslim Voices Anthology 2006*. She worked as a reviewer for the Islamic Poetry website and was a judge in their Praise the Prophet Competition.

Her first book, *The Beautiful Names*, has been published by Muslim Writers Publishing. It is available online and is due for release in South Africa in 2009.

She is working on a few novels and has completed a collection of short stories, which she hopes to have published. A few of these stories appear on the prestigious South African literary website, LitNet.

She blogs sporadically on http://afrocentric-muslimah.blogspot.com/, which serves as a showcase of sorts for her writing. Saaleha is a member of the Islamic Writers Alliance and is also the owner of Lazeeza's Bakery and Confectionery.

Mrs. Patel's Farewell by Saaleha Bhamjee

"Ouch," Haroon hissed. He had just stubbed his toe on one of the bricks that were used to support his mother's bed. His mother, Mrs. Patel, was fast asleep. She slept a lot these days. Her long walks were a thing of the past, since her legs couldn't carry her any longer. Arthritis had claimed her completely. So had heart disease and high blood pressure.

He sighed. He had seen this coming. It had all begun to unravel the day Munira ran off with Farouk. And now it was too late. The anger and shame had eaten away at her; the regret, too. He wondered about Samiha, Farouk's first wife, his neighbour. Was it consuming her, too?

He sucked in his breath, momentarily releasing the stranglehold his expansive *boep* had on his shirt buttons. He was steeling himself for an important discussion, one that would take all his wit, all his tact, the kind of tact that he had employed all his life to wheedle information out of reluctant snitches.

He thought of his meeting with Munira earlier that day. It was a Saturday morning. She sat on the balcony, brushing her hair in the sun. Her joy at his visit had made him cringe. It shot holes in his unflappable armour, allowing that nasty poison, guilt, to seep in.

"*Assalaamu alaikum Bhai*," Munira gushed. "Come inside, please. Here, sit down. I'll get you something to drink. It's really hot today, isn't it?" People had the habit of doing that, didn't they? Talk about the weather when you had nothing else to say?

He entered the house, feeling momentarily disoriented as his eyes adjusted to the gloom.

"*Wa alaikum salaam*, Munira. I won't be long, so don't worry about getting me anything," Haroon responded, as he lowered his bulk into the seat. A discomfited silence fell, during which Munira sat down on the opposite couch and studied the tips of her hair. He couldn't help but marvel at the change in his little sister. She had put on a bit more weight and looked radiant. Maybe there was something to this whole marriage gig after all. But definitely not for him, especially not with Ma in her current state.

"You look well, I see," Haroon continued, struggling to keep his voice neutral, steer clear of sarcasm. Munira met his gaze.

"Farouk is a good man," she responded simply. "How is Ma?"

Time to bite the proverbial bullet. "Well, you see, I came to see you about Ma."

"Why, what's wrong? Is she sick?" The panic in her voice was glaring.

Haroon fiddled with a button on his shirt. "Yes," he droned.

"What's wrong? Since when has she—" Munira broke off and began to weep, her shoulders shaking.

Haroon sat on the couch, watching her awkwardly. He rose and went to sit beside her. He patted her shoulder, his hands beginning to feel unnaturally large and ungainly, even more so than normally.

"Don't cry, Munira. Don't cry. I came to tell you that I want you to speak to Ma. I want her to let you into the house again. I want the two of you to make peace. Will you come if she agrees?" His voice was low, and empathy oozed from each word. A tone that was at odds with the voice of the Dadaville Gazette.

"Yes, yes, I'll come. I must. Ma needs me." A fresh wave of sobs claimed her. Haroon stood up, feeling shame – was it? – by what he had just witnessed. He took his leave and drove back home. The thoughts that ate away at his conscience in the car were much the same as the ones that constricted his chest now, as he sat at Mrs. Patel's bedside. Why hadn't he done something sooner? Why had he left it all these years? Three years was a long time for two people to avoid one another.

But Mrs. Patel, in her stubbornness, had refused to see Munira, even when she had her stroke. He had felt tears prickling at his round eyes, but not daring to venture beyond the thick frames of his magnifying glass spectacles, the day Munira had come to see Mrs. Patel after her stroke. Tears for Haroon were a novelty. He could picture the scene. Mrs. Patel had thrown her out of the house. A tear-stained Munira, scarf bunched over her mouth to stifle the sobs. A raging Ma, grey hair fleeing her *chotli*, beard hairs looking more menacing than ever.

"You'll cry over my *janaazah*. And then, too, don't enter this house. You left it for a man, didn't you? Go back to your man."

Naturally, all the alert ears of Lambat Street had heard the exchange. They had seen Munira's tears, and no doubt they had exchanged smug smiles. In a moment of rare introspection, Haroon had been obliged to admit that this was his reaction, too, when families struggled to keep it together, or when their smelly linen was given a public airing.

In the months after Munira's scandalous elopement, her marriage to a married man ten years younger than herself, a man who happened to be her neighbour's husband, Haroon had felt shame for the first time in his life. Normally, he was responsible for much of the shaming that happened in Dadaville. But he had lived it down. He was too good a gossip monger to be dismissed.

Munira had tried thrice in the two months that followed to ask Mrs. Patel for *Maafy*, forgiveness, but then, too, she had shouted her out of the house. The entire street had enjoyed ringside seats to the incident. Exactly as Mrs. Patel had intended it. Munira deserved the shame after the disgrace she had brought upon the family. But when the stroke happened, and Mrs. Patel still hadn't softened, Haroon couldn't help but question whether three years was not too harsh a sentence, especially when the judge was now staring death in the face.

He hoped to succeed in pleading Munira's case before it was too late. Life was really so short these days.

Mrs. Patel's eyes fluttered open. Her gaze was intent, solemn. "*Bhai*, I had a dream. I dreamt of Papa. He was calling me. I'm going *Bhai*, I'm going. Papa is calling me. He held my hand." She sighed deeply, with all the theatrical flair of a Bollywood actress, minus the shovel loads of makeup, plus a few bristly hairs on her bony chin.

"Na, Ma, don't say this. You're fine—" Haroon broke down, sobs racking his chest.

"*No rar*, don't cry, *Bhai*. You'll be fine. I have had a good life. You have been a good son, unlike—" She began to wail. A true Bollywood moment, the kind where the camera would swing from face to face, up close, showing trembling, lipsticked lips and eyelashes so long you could sweep the floor with them. Except in the Patels' case, it showed Haroon, all wobbly chinned and coke bottle bottom glasses and Mrs. Patel, wrinkly, grey-haired and shrewd-eyed.

"Ma," Haroon began between sobs, "I need to speak to you." He sniffed – except that it came out like a giant grunt – and stuck his podgy fingers under the glasses to wipe his eyes.

Mrs. Patel's strident wails stopped. She eyed Haroon from one surprisingly dry eye. "What about?" she demanded.

"Promise you won't get cross, Ma. Promise me that." Haroon's sobbing had petered out, and he wiped the snot and tears from his face with his shirt sleeve.

"But how can I promise if I don't know what you're going to say?"

"Just promise, Ma. It's important."

Mrs. Patel fixed him with a trenchant stare. "This had better not be about Munira."

"But Ma," Haroon moaned.

"It is about her the *ghaderi, sali*. I'll never forgive her. She has brought disgrace on our family."

Haroon decided on a new approach. "Ma, I went to see Munira today."

"What? You went to that…that *nangi kutti*?" she sputtered.

"Ma!" Haroon was astounded. Had his mother actually called her that?

"But that's what she is, isn't she? Think of what she did?"

The bedroom walls were closing in on Haroon .He could see Munira's tear-stained face, her pleading earnest eyes; he could hear her sobs and the agony that turned her words brittle. He needed to get through to Ma. Time was running out. This Papa business was an omen. He could feel it in his bones, which hid somewhere beneath the skin, though he couldn't be sure, since he hadn't felt them in an age, save for his knuckles.

"Ma, what did you say when you woke up?"

"What? When?"

"Just now."

"Umm. What was it now?"

"Ma, please, you know exactly what I am speaking of here. Don't play games. Now isn't the time."

"Okay, okay *Bhai*. I spoke of Papa."

"Did you really see him in a dream?"

"Er, well…"

"Ma!"

"Okay, I made it up, but it could be true, couldn't it? Papa is calling me. I'm going now, any day." Haroon could almost hear the mournful *basoori* tune in the background, that flute tune that accompanies all emotional scenes in Bollywood. All very filmi.

"What do you expect from Allah, Ma, when you do go?"

She looked perplexed by the question. "Well, His Mercy and Forgiveness. Isn't that what we all hope for? We are all sinners, aren't we? But that doesn't mean…" her eyes narrowed as comprehension dawned on her.

"Yes, it does, Ma," Haroon cut in. "It does mean that if we want mercy, we have to show mercy. Forgive her, Ma; she is really sorry. And, what's more, Ma, she is happy." Haroon finished his sentence. His words hung in the air between them like the garlicky aroma of Mrs. Patel's parathas

"But she was wrong, she was wrong." Ma was crying now, softly. Tears traced a path down her wrinkled cheeks like a rivulet in a dry sand bed. She wiped them away with the corner of her scarf.

"Ma, we all make mistakes. Every day. But we expect His mercy, don't we? We hope that He will forgive, and He does. Think of Kaloo. He gambled at Emperors and died in the Mosque on a Jumu'ah, Ma. Could anyone have wished for a better *maut*? She's your blood, Ma, your daughter. Please, Ma, please…She's my sister…" Haroon broke down once more. He took the roll of toilet paper from Mrs. Patel's bedside, rolled off a wad and blew noisily into it, a sound not unlike a trumpeting elephant.

"*Bhai*, phone her. Tell her to come."

Munira arrived with Farouk at her side. Her eyes were puffy and red. The ginger sun drooped in the flawless, indigo sky. A pall of smoke from the Thembuville fires had already settled over the dingy street. She saw Haroon's hand on the curtain, caught a glimpse of his bespectacled eyes just before he pulled the curtain back into place. She could feel more eyes from many other windows, all trained on her, expectant, zealous. Her intestines knotted tightly as the memory of her last visit to the house came to mind.

She stepped onto the *stoep* that had served as Haroon's lookout for as long as she could remember. She saw Samiha's eyes spitting fire from behind the curtain on her side of the house. When would she learn to accept the union? Farouk loved her, too. She was the mother of his children. Surely, that meant something. She sighed heavily. Farouk took her hand into his, gave her a gentle squeeze and stood by her side while she knocked sharply on the door.

Haroon opened.

"*Assalaamu alaikum, Bhai*." She trained her voice into a state of calm that belied the conflict that raged within. His face broke into a wide smile.

"*Wa alaikum salaam*, Munira, come, come in. You, too, Farouk. *Beho*, please sit."

Farouk shuffled past Haroon's paunch and sat on the edge of the seat that Haroon had proffered. Haroon wordlessly indicated the room that Munira had once shared with Mrs. Patel. She approached cautiously.

Mrs. Patel lay on the bed, propped up by a few pillows. Her scarf was draped loosely on her head, and her eyes were closed. Haroon poked his head around the door.

"Is she sleeping?" Munira mouthed.

"No, I don't think so," Haroon murmured.

She stood at Mrs. Patel's bedside, took her papery hand into her own and called her. She twitched, but she did not stir. Munira began to weep.

"Ma, Ma, please look at me. It's me, your Munira. *Taru poyri…*" She twitched again. Tears squeezed their way past Haroon's eyelids and escaped the rims of his magnifying glass spectacles. He came over, held Mrs. Patel's shoulder and shook her gently.

"Ma, Ma…" his voice was urgent.

Munira threw herself onto Mrs. Patel's body and began sobbing hysterically. Farouk entered the room and prised Munira free. She flung her arms around his neck and wept into his shoulder.

"Shameless girl! In your mothers' house, and you're in that man's arms. Have you no respect?" Mrs. Patel's eyes were round with reproach – the same look that she had often given to her children when they moved around too much in their seats, or took a second biscuit when they were out visiting with family.

Munira jumped back, away from Farouk, took the roll of toilet paper, tore off a chunk and blew her nose.

"Ma," she gushed. You had us so worried."

Haroon trumpeted into his tissue once more. His face broke into a smile.

Farouk wiped at the wet patch on his shoulder, his eyes shifting nervously between Mrs. Patel, Haroon, and Munira.

Mrs. Patel shot him angry looks every now and then, until he was obliged to retreat to the lounge through Haroon's bedroom.

"What can I do for you, Ma?" Munira was eager, nervous, and very relieved.

"Make me some *chaai, masala* tea. Then you can tell me all about your new life, *dikri*. You look well, *masha Allah*."

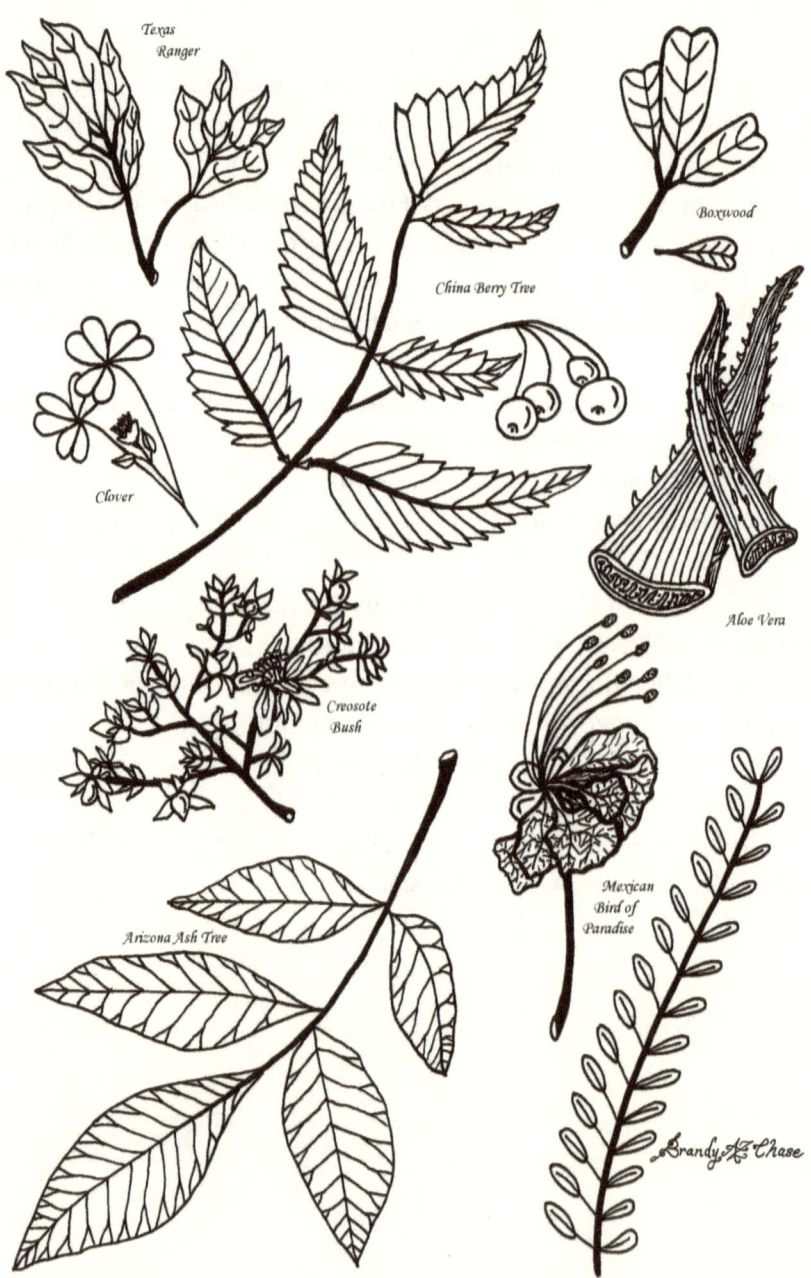

Texas Ranger

Boxwood

China Berry Tree

Clover

Aloe Vera

Creosote Bush

Arizona Ash Tree

Mexican Bird of Paradise

Brandy A. Chase

BRANDY AZ CHASE

Brandy AZ Chase was born and raised in sunny Tucson, Arizona, USA. She converted to Islam at seventeen from Atheism and goes by the Islamic name of Aminah-Zahira. She lived in Lebanon for four years before moving to Al-Ain, United Arab Emirates, where she currently resides with her Lebanese husband and two children.

She has been writing poetry, sci-fi, fantasy, romance, and historical novels since she was twelve. Also, she has been studying art and drawing with different mediums. Having recently discovered the genre of Islamic Fiction, she has written many short stories and poems. In addition to writing she does home schooling, artwork, interior and landscape designing, and blogging at http://www.brandyachase.blogspot.com/.

She created an All Muslimah Blog Directory at http://www.allmuslimah. blogspot.com/ and can be reached through her e-mail: BrandyAZChase@ gmail.com.

Of the things in life she loves are books, sword fighting, wooden ships, tiger lilies, delving into the realms of imagination, and, above all, Allah and all the great things Islam has brought to her life.

PIRATE'S PEACE BY BRANDY AZ CHASE

Alessandro twirled his thin moustache, keeping half an eye on the Italian ship. His slender hand clutched the hilt of his sword, flicking it in irritation at having to stand guard. As the sharpest blade in all of Italy, *he* deserved to board the Libyan merchant vessel caught off the coast.

A sudden flood of Libyans surging from the merchant hold turned the tide against the bold Italian pirates. Alessandro's keen brown eyes spied Capitano Drago starboard, battling three dark men single-handedly. Looking aft, he saw his best shipmate, Bonafacio, fall to Libyan steel. With a deep roar of rage, Alessandro grabbed a line and swung over, landing on the port side of the vessel, where the Libyans had a stronghold. His blade was a blur. Six men fell to avenge Bonafacio.

"Ao! They're taking our ship!" Jacopo bellowed in outrage. Alessandro cast a guilty look over his shoulder. Five dark figures were lopping off the

Italian hold lines. Scrambling to his rope and swinging across, his sword reached its target. Seeing themselves surrounded by pirates, the four remaining held up their hands in surrender, swords clanging to the deck. With the revolt checked, Alessandro took survey of the other vessel.

Capitano Drago had three Libyans remaining, kneeling in surrender, as the pirates freely plundered their booty. Feeling Alessandro's scrutiny, Capitano whirled around, scowling fiercely, his dark heavy eyes glinting. Sailing his beefy mass over the gap, Capitano landed directly in front of his underling, seizing him by the shirt.

"If you weren't so handy with that sword, I'd cut you down myself, you filthy mongrel, for dereliction," Capitano spat. "We almost lost our own ship! Your incompetence deserves a reward! You'll serve to scour the hold and brig 'til we reach shore. Get on with it, you pestilent sea bile!" Capitano barked as he released Alessandro with a shove that landed him on his back. Cursing his fate, punishment, and, above all, Capitano Drago, Alessandro muttered his way down to the brig, followed by the seven remaining Libyans.

"A man who chooses to do wrong has no one to curse but himself," one of the Libyan men said in jerky Italian, leaning against the brig bars. Alessandro caught the man by his homely green shirt and glared into his dark eyes. Their noses, one pointy, the other flat, almost touched. Cursing him with a long stream of Italian, Alessandro released the prisoner to tend to his duties.

All week, Alessandro was worked to the bone. Capitano descended daily to the brig for inspection. The Cat-O'-Nine-Tails was not spared if anything was found wanting. After meting out lashings, he'd return top deck to gorge his already widthsome girth. Alessandro joined his sea mates for their meal. Often, he was too late for first choice and had to make do with scraps. He made up for his hunger by eating some of the scraps offered to the prisoners.

One afternoon, as he swabbed the lower deck, he spied the flat-nosed man sharing his portion with his friends. "Why split your meager means?" Alessandro called out, leaning on his mop handle.

"Allah has given me this food from His Mercy," the flat-nosed man explained. "I'm showing my gratitude to Him. By returning the favor to my Brothers, they may in turn thank Him for His Benevolence."

"Allah, eh? Some heathen god is he?" Alessandro sneered and spat on the brig's bars. The dark man stood slowly and came cautiously near, but not too near, the bars.

"No. Our Lord is Lord and Creator of All. He is One. There is nothing like Him. He is God over you as well and *Knows All*," he said with his voice so full of certainty, his smooth face so serene and his eyes at peace that, for a moment, Alessandro could only stare. After realizing a length of time had passed, he shook himself and snorted dismissively at the man. He resumed working, but continued watching the dark, pious man. Alessandro's heart fluttered in his chest like a caged butterfly. He had never known peace like that. He never valued his mate's welfare as his own. If this God, Allah, *knew everything*, then He knew how he longed for a spit of land to call his own. Land on which to work and raise a family.

That evening, he walked numbly up the stairs to the top deck, his crew celebrating with rum and bawdy sea songs. He half joined them before sinking to lean against a rail with his close friend, Reno. The songs quieted down while he studied the stars glimmering above like candles leading him through the night. A warm breeze caressed his cheek and threaded through his curly chestnut hair, hanging from the tight red bandana, like a mother soothing a child's troubled mind. Reno guzzled his rum and took his mate's share as well. Alessandro's eyes flickered over the empty cup in annoyance.

"What think you of God?" he asked Reno.

"As long as me have rum in me cup, a bella by me side, and a tip of gold in me pocket, I have no need for gods," he slurred, standing and hobbling down the rail. Alessandro had an overwhelming urge to knock the buffoon overboard at his crass remark. He needed to speak with someone possessing more brains.

Creeping down to the brig, he peered through the bars at the seven Libyans lying neatly in a row. Spotting the green-clad, flat-nosed man, he sat cross-legged in front of him.

"Psst, you there! Wake with you!" Alessandro hissed through the bars. The man woke and copied his pose. The moon showed half full through the porthole, lending its surreal light. Alessandro propped his elbow against the black cannon and twirled his moustache thoughtfully.

"Tell me your name and more about what this Allah wants from us lowly men. How do we gain His favor?" he mused in an undertone.

"I am Munashe," the Libyan replied leaning forward, his thick lips lifting in the corners with a gentle smile. Speaking softly of the Power and Attributes of Allah, and our purpose of worshipping Him in this fleeting world, he answered Alessandro's unspoken questions. "We are united in Peace. These brothers would give each other the shirt off their backs. We honor ourselves, men and women. Even formal criminals, like pirates, we respect, for once they enter Islam, their past sins are forgiven," Munashe elaborated.

With the sky lightening in the East, Munashe excused himself and made ablutions with sea water, then prayed. Alessandro's heart beat rapidly in his chest; he could feel it saying Allah, Allah, Allah. The Libyan returned, sitting, and Alessandro nervously licked his lips. "How do I join you in your path to peace?" Munashe woke his companions by whispering in their ears. They sat crowding around Munashe and Alessandro.

"Just say after me…" Speaking slowly, Alessandro repeated the Testimony of Faith, *the Shahadah,* after the Libyan leader. He felt like a king, newly crowned, as the beaming Libyans silently shook his hand through the bars.

"I want to free you. If I do, will you arrange a way for me to remain safe from Capitano Drago in Libya and even come to own some land?" Alessandro whispered fervently, hardly believing his own ears, only feeling the pull of giving to them, as if his new heart was directing his mouth without asking his brain. Their eyes shining with hope firmed his resolve.

"I swear by Allah the All Hearing, if we escape safely, we will provide you with a good life, including fertile land, a good wife, and a means of earning an honest living," Munashe promised, placing his hand upon his heart.

Alessandro, beaming, added lowly, "Then keep a weather eye for my signal. Tomorrow night I have last watch." He heard Capitano Drago stomping around above, cursing at the pirates, and rushed to his duties. His body was so elated by his new faith and promise of a future that it didn't notice the lack of sleep.

Alessandro slid on his recently shined black boots and admired the flow of his best livery. In a few hours he would assume the last watch of the night. While Capitano was taking his lunch earlier, he had snagged the brig keys and a stash of valuable goods and concealed them close to the tow line, still pulling along the Libyan vessel behind them.

Waiting patiently for the last third of the night to fall, Alessandro eyed the sky warily. The sea was smooth as glass without a breeze. If Allah didn't send them a wind to aid their escape, they would be doomed. Capitano had no mercy for treachery. He would first be lashed, then tortured. He had seen it done to others. Shivering at the thought, Alessandro raised his palms to the sky whispering, "Oh, Allah, grant us safe passage from those who deny You and mock You. Bring us strong winds to carry us far to safety, where I may start life anew, striving to please You." He lowered his hands, taking a few deep breaths, feeling the calm flow through him.

Alessandro assessed there were only three awake now. No one further would rise until first light. So if he and the Libyans were long gone by then, it would probably be well after sunup before anyone raised the alarm. He had to take these three out. Creeping up behind the first, who was leaning on a rum barrel, Alessandro used the butt of his pistol to gently lay him down.

"What happened to him?" one of the remaining asked, seeing him kneeling next to the man.

"Couldn't hold one more drop. Better cart him below." Alessandro grinned, hiding his pistol. The two men strode over to lift their fallen mate. He moved swiftly behind them, pretending to assist, when they, too, fell, leaving only Alessandro standing. He listened for a further challenge, then stealthily stepped down to the brig and slid the key into the lock, gently turning it. With every click he winced, but no calls rose from the dark.

Seven dark men silently slid to the aft of the ship, taking the offered sacks of supplies and climbing along the taut tow line to their vessel. Running to their stations, they prepared to cast off. Tense minutes passed wordlessly, with everyone looking over their shoulders, until Munashe signaled. They lined up on the deck in a row and began praying.

Alessandro, so taken by the sight, ran to join them, though he knew not the words and knew not the rituals. Up and down, four times his face touched the rough deck; the wood imprinting on his forehead in his earnest desire to please Allah. Like a true miracle, the limp sail began to billow and stretch with a gust of wind filling it. Alessandro cut the tow line.

The Italian pirate ship shrank into the horizon with the sky lightening. Clasping Alessandro on the shoulder, Munashe proclaimed, "You have kept your promise, my new brother, and so we give you the new name of Unathi, meaning 'God is with us'. We will fulfill our promise to you. You will be staying in my home until I have satisfied it." Alessandro clasped Munashe back in affirmation, then moved to stand alone by the rail, looking out at the blue sea glimmering.

As the sun woke and climbed out of its watery blanket, bathing the sails golden, Alessandro Unathi could feel it well up inside him and settle in his bones: peace within. The beauty of the feeling brought a tear to his eye. He had gone from killing seven of these good men to saving seven. The tear ran down his rugged cheek, and he quietly praised Allah for the beginning of his new life.

REAL MEANING OF RAMADAN BY BRANDY AZ CHASE

The mouth-watering aroma of roasting chicken wafts across the room, filling my nose, making me unconsciously lick my lips, as I say my final two salams to end 'Asr prayer. My green eyes snap to the large wooden clock on the periwinkle living room wall and read the time – 5:45 PM – shattering the peace prayer gives me. Pushing my hands against the floor for balance, I hop to my feet, flip off my pale pink prayer hijab, and shimmy out of its matching skirt. I roll them together and throw them in the general direction of my bedroom on my way to the kitchen. With only eight minutes to Maghrib athan, on the first day of fasting for Ramadan, there certainly isn't time to waste on folding them. In my rush, I nearly trip over my daughter, Rana, who is coloring a picture on the floor of the kitchen doorway.

"Mama, can you draw me tiger ears?" she begs, holding up her orange crayon. I don't even look at her, focusing instead on the stove full of boiling pots.

"Not now, honey. Just draw two triangles," I reply, opening the first pot of a creamy Turkish lentil soup. Wafting the steam toward my nose, I inhale deeply, recognizing the need for more seasonings. I attack the spice rack, gathering five glass bottles in my arms.

"Mama! Look! I drew two ears!" Rana crows in triumph. I exhale noisily, and then dutifully murmur my enthusiasm as I concentrate on the spices. A pinch of salt, dash of cumin, three shakes of paprika, half a teaspoon of garlic powder, and a dab of cinnamon – just for fun, swirl into the depths of the large soup pot. Another waft of steam assures me of delicious perfection.

"Mama! Draw me stripes! I don't know how." Rana stands, holding a black crayon and her paper. I move her gently aside to kneel down and rummage in the under cupboards for the yellow glass bowl. My mother-in-law gave it to me, to ensure I never disgrace a table again by placing the soup pot directly on it. I quickly empty the soup into the deep bowl, admiring the way the yellow lentils match it. A perfect fit! Gently setting the pot back on the stove and lifting the rice lid, I move some aside with a spoon to check the water level. Good, it's done! I flip off the burner and carry the heavy pot to a waiting oval platter. A tug on my sleeve nearly unbalances me as I spread the yellow rice evenly over the plate.

"Rana, careful! This is hot. Get out of the kitchen!" I reprimand, turning to put the rice pot back on the stove. Kneeling to check the chicken in the oven, I test it with the tip of a knife. Tender! I begin muttering to myself in my angst to hurry. "Okay, hot pads…put the chicken just so on the rice…add mint leaves on top for decoration…slash the radishes and slice to make flowers…will have to write Hana a thank-you note for the radish tutorial." I spread the radish flowers along the edge of the platter. Just needs pine nuts and almonds now. I shake some out of a bag into a little frying pan of oil and put it on medium heat on the sixth burner. Oh, no! The cheese rolls! The color rapidly turns from tan to brown, and I flip them over in the hot oil, and then shake the frying pan of nuts.

"Mama! Come on! I really need stripes! And a tail! A tiger has to have a tail!" Rana says from behind me, startling me, as I thought she'd left, almost knocking the frying pan off the stove.

"Rana! Please, for the love of Allah! Go to your play room and color a coloring book with pictures already made. I don't have time to color for you now," I yell, and flip my head around just enough to show her my anxious face. Her green eyes fill with tears, and she runs off in a huff. I swallow my guilt, reminding myself she isn't the one who has to cook a perfect Ramadan dinner. Tapping the homemade French fries, I see they are perfect, and the cheese rolls are ready to be drained. I turn off all the burners and drain the nuts, then scatter them artistically over the chicken and rice. Also, I drain the fries and cheese rolls and dash salt across them. Standing back and surveying the counters full of dishes, I mentally go through my checklist: chicken and rice, French fries, cheese rolls and spinach triangles, creamy Turkish soup, hummus and baba ganoush with fresh pita bread, tabbouli salad, handmade baklawa, home-blended cocktail fruit juice, kibbe in yogurt sauce…check, check, check! Alhamdulillah, all complete after a good twelve hours of working. It could have been done in less time with more hands, but as we are now across the world from our families, it is up to me to make our first Ramadan alone special. Zayed already complains he won't get to taste his mother's perfect cooking this Ramadan, so I have to strive to fill that void, too.

"Rana, come set the table darling," I call out, knowing she can't resist this fun chore, no matter how mad at me she is. She appears quickly, her golden curls bobbing, and thrusts a picture into my hands.

"See the tiger I made?" I glance down at it. It is good for a five-year old. Basic geometry shapes and straight black stripes everywhere.

"Excellent! Now, set the table. Baba will be home in literally one minute!" I order, as I put her drawing on the fridge, then spread out the plastic mat on the floor of the living room, just like back home. Rana places the four plates, bowls, spoons, and cups for each person. I hand her the water bottle, instructing, "Fill the cups carefully while I get the food."

A furtive glance at the clock shows 5:51 PM as I rush back to the kitchen to grab the platter of chicken and rice and set it in the middle of the mat. As I stand back up to get the kibbe wa laban, a desperate shrill wail fills the house. My son has the worst timing ever! I rush to the bedroom, picking up my four-month old son, and rock him automatically as I move back to the kitchen. Shifting him to one arm as I grab the heavy bowl of kibbe wa laban, I use my entire strength to carry it one-handed to the mat. I manage to set it gently, but my son nearly wiggles out of my arm at the last second. I rise again as the front door opens, and my husband, Zayed, steps in, smiling. He looks amazed at the paper lanterns and Ramadan Kareem signs Rana and I painted last week and strung up this morning across the ceiling. His smile falls, though, looking down at the floor table.

"Amirah! My boss is five minutes behind me! Why isn't the food on the table? Do you want him to think I have an incompetent wife?" he hollers, rubbing his forehead. Mahmoud continues howling in my arms.

"Oopsies!" Rana squeals, over-filling the water in one of the cups, spilling it onto the tile floor.

"Get a rag and clean it up," I order brusquely. "Zayed, take Mahmoud. He's the one keeping food from being delivered to the table, and 'Assalamu alaikum' to you, too!" I snap to my husband, handing him our son as I go into the kitchen once again.

I run back and forth as Zayed sits on the couch with Mahmoud and gets him calm and even gurgling coos. Bringing the cocktail fruit juice last, I survey what my day of hard work has rendered. It looks picturesque – except the shiny spot glinting on the tiles.

"Rana, you missed some water! Quick! Half a minute to athan! Zayed, turn on the TV. Sister Hana said after athan calls, and they announce Maghrib on TV, they will put a Ramadan children's song to commemorate the occasion. It will make Rana excited about Ramadan's iftar, just like back home," I exclaim, as I toss Zayed the remote and Rana runs off for the floor rag.

"Ugh! Take him! Change his diaper – now. He smells! Put your hijab on. My boss will be here any minute," Zayed replies, wrinkling his nose in disgust, and passes a squirming boy to me. He leans back on the couch and flicks on the TV. Truly a heavy responsibility for him, I sigh. "Dates! I cannot believe you forgot the first thing needed! My mother never, ever put anything on the table unless the dates were there first. Run, grab the bowl, Amirah!" Zayed scolds, waving his arm in the air for emphasis. I glance at the table to be sure I haven't forgotten such a gross error, and then mentally smack my head. The dates are indeed missing.

I spring quickly into action, holding Mahmoud lightly in a mighty effort not to squish his full diaper as I race to the kitchen. My bare footsteps are slapping the tiles until one step makes a splat. Before I can register the source of the sound, I am screaming and slipping forward, my precious son flying literally out of my hands as my mind realizes I am falling. His head level with mine, his green eyes open in shock, and I think quickly, if his soft head strikes the tiles from this height and speed, he is doomed. He most likely will die. His head must *not* hit those tiles!

My left arm instinctively snakes out to grab his chubby knee, pulling his body toward mine as my knees hit the ground. My right arm comes around trying to catch his head, still free falling, but it seems like it can't move fast enough and will miss. It *cannot* miss! My left elbow smashes into the floor, and my right elbow tucks in just in time to land under my son's back, but his head is still dropping. At the last micro second, my outstretched arm follows the motion of the tucked elbow and manages to get under him. My wrist smashes between skull and tile. Excruciating pain shoots up my arm, but I don't even twitch. I don't even blink. He is *alive!*

Alive. My *son!* Mahmoud. I realize then Zayed has reached my side as I remain kneeling over my son's cradled body. He is trying to help me up. Jerkily, I rise to my aching knees, still cradling my son on my throbbing wrist. *Alive!* My body trembles uncontrollably as the stress of the day seems too much to bear. My beautiful son has almost died in the split of a second. The first call of the athan begins echoing off the city, "Allaaaaahu Akbar..." My son almost didn't hear that athan. As the realization of the preciousness of life and the swiftness of death sinks in, I can't stop the tears from running down my face, and sobs quickly follow, racking my body. The fear-laced adrenaline releases itself with cold waves of nausea. I clutch Mahmoud to my chest staring into his large innocent eyes.

"You're okay, Amirah. It is just a fall. Don't cry. Are you hurt? What's wrong?" Zayed asks, his voice soft, yet unable to understand the level of my hysteria. I'm not able to speak as I realize I am the only one who knew my son's life was in danger, and Allah allowed me to be the one to save him. I hold Mahmoud tighter and sob harder. I can't even stand, and Zayed gives up trying to help me do so. He cradles us against his chest and murmurs reassurances. Slowly, as the athan finishes, I grow calmer. I relay what really happened tearfully to Zayed, so he can properly understand my emotions.

As the shock flows through him, he hugs us tighter. Having overheard the commotion, Rana wiggles her way into the mix, not to be left out. We all huddle there silently in our own thoughts, food ignored, hunger forgotten, for the first full minute of iftar. We understand the true meaning of Ramadan and are truly thanking Allah for all He gives us and realizing how easily it can vanish without warning.

A knock on the door breaks our reprieve, and I groan. Zayed merely cups my chin and lets his thanks and love for me shine through his eyes for saving our son. I give a watery smile and let him help me to my feet. My severely bruised knees protest the movement.

The ache in my wrist pulses stronger as I finally glance at it. A swollen purple bump is expanding rapidly. Shifting Mahmoud to my left arm, I twist my wrist around, carefully checking for breakage; alhamdulillah just a bruise. I'll gladly break every bone in my body to save my family, I realize, and told Zayed so. He gives me another firm hug, and then I take Mahmoud to the bedroom to change his diaper and put on my hijab. Rana wipes the floor where I slid in the patch of water, and Zayed fetches the dates and sets them on the table before opening the door and cheerfully greeting his boss.

Once everyone is sitting and eating from their full plates, I can't help but feel like it's a charade to act so normal. The cheese rolls, perfectly golden brown, taste like sandpaper, and I try to keep the tears back as I stare into my children's eyes. Zayed, seeing my lackluster eating, passes me another cheese roll with a smile to cheer me up. He doesn't even mention how unhealthy it is compared to tabbouli salad. I eat more heartily for his sake, but nothing can ever vanquish my memory of how swiftly Allah can take back His creation.

Linda D. Delgado

Linda D. Delgado is a mother, grandmother, and great grandmother. She graduated from the University of Phoenix and is a retired Arizona DPS Sergeant. Linda is the author of the award-winning children's book series, Islamic Rose Books, co-authored *Grandma & Hijab Family Activity Book*, and authored two non-fiction books: *Halal Food, Fun and Laughter* and *A Muslim's Guide to Publishing and Marketing*. Linda is also the creator of the Grandma & Hijab-Ez comic strip series and the owner-publisher of *Muslim Writers Publishing*: a traditional Muslim publishing house: www.MuslimWritersPublishing.com and www.widad-lld.com

Don't Look Back by Linda D. Delgado

Sarah walked as quickly as she could. As quickly as a 5-foot 2-inch, 105-pound woman could while carrying a heavy suitcase in one hand, holding the hand of her frightened and crying son with the other hand, and her slight body bent forward from the weight of her 18-month-old daughter strapped to her back in the sling made just for her youngest child.

"He's coming Mommy. I can hear him," her frightened son whispered and began to turn his head to look behind their hurrying figures.

"Don't look back, son." Sarah whispered back as she lightly pulled on his arm, urging his small feet to move more quickly.

Five years ago, Sarah was a laughing and not the least bit nervous bride. That afternoon she was to marry Yousef and begin the life she had dreamed of since she was a young child. She would be a good Muslim wife and, Allah willing, in the future – hopefully, not too distant – a new mother and servant of Allah. Their home was ready and waiting. So much planning and work by both families had already been done. Yousef had a wonderful job at the University, teaching English, and he already had tenure. Sarah paused as she waited for her mother to come and get her for the best day in her life to begin.

∾

"Saaarah! Saaarah!" The screaming voice shouted as his running foot-falls seemed to be getting closer and closer.

"Mommy, Mommy, he's coming," shrieked her son. Sarah's daughter let out a plaintive wail from being roused from her sleep by her brother's shrieks and the shouting from the man just one half block behind them.

When had things changed? The abuse was gradual…an insidious, evil snake that wove itself into the fabric of Sarah's life. First, it was the name-calling and ridicule. She was a terrible mother. She didn't know how to cook. The house was dirty. She was boring. Then came the shoving. At first, not hard. Just something to get her attention, so Yousef told her. "Pay attention, Sarah, and do what you're told. Don't ask questions. Shut up. Learn your place, you stupid woman!" Then came the threats when he saw her talking to some sisters at the masjid. They were just talking about their children. But Yousef would not believe her. He accused her of telling the sisters lies about him. That night, when they returned home, he beat her so badly that when he stormed out of the house she barely managed to call her mother to come get her and her six-month-old son.

Then came the tears, the words of regret by Yousef. The promises not to ever harm her again. The presents and pleadings. Her mother told her not to be so hard on poor Yousef. Yousef needed patience, and she needed to try harder. Sarah's father shook his head in disapproval every time Sarah sought refuge at her parent's home after a beating. Every time her parents, the Imam, and the "good sisters" talked and talked and talked until she felt she had no choice but to return to her husband's home.

The home was not Sarah's, Yousef said. She should feel fortunate to live in his grand house and be grateful for the food he provided and clothes she wore. But Sarah was ungrateful, so Yousef told his brothers in Islam, and they told their wives. It was Sarah who was sent, time after time, to the Imam at the masjid for counseling on how to learn to become a better wife. A dutiful wife that did not make her husband have to beat her for her own good! The Imam talked to her parents. He talked to Yousef's parents. He talked to Yousef. Nothing she ever said to the Imam was held in confi-dence. Before long, people in her community were looking away from her and barely mumbling salaams. She knew what they were saying about her and the pity they had for Yousef to be saddled with such a poor excuse for a wife. That is what her parents and in-laws said. That is what the backbiters said. Sarah was alone and for five years lived in isolation and suffered the verbal and physical abuse.

"Hurry!" Sarah gasped. Sarah saw the yellow light ahead and knew that the traffic light would change. She could not be stopped on this side of the street waiting for the traffic light to change again. The pain in her side was slowing her down. Her son's small feet could not keep up, and she realized she was half dragging him along. Sarah dropped the suitcase that contained all the worldly possessions belonging to her and her two children. The broken latch gave way, and the suitcase lid flew open as it hit the cement behind Sarah. The winter wind swirled and blew, and the clothes in the suitcase were grabbed by the wind and tossed onto the pavement. Sarah reached down, picked up her son and, as her feet seemed to fly off the street curb, she could hear the screeching tires and horns honking as she darted across the busy roadway.

"Saaarah! Those are my kids! Stop or you will pay for this with your life...by Allah!" Yousef continued to rant. Her son was crying quietly with his head buried in his mother's shoulder.

"Don't look back." Sarah managed to gasp several time, as she kept a tight grip on her purse that held the bus tickets that would take her and her children to safety.

Sarah sat in her garden and bounced her youngest daughter on her knee while waiting anxiously for the telephone to ring. Adnan should have already picked up sis Julie and her three children. Why hadn't he called to let her know they were safe? Each time Julie and Adnan planned and executed a rescue mission for a sister in Islam...a victim of domestic violence...Sarah couldn't help but be drawn back to the memory of the night she escaped from Yousef after he had tried to choke the life from her. Sarah shuddered, then, looking down at the smiling face of her daughter, she hugged her tight.

That was ten years ago. She was safe and so were her two elder children. Allah had helped her and blessed her with a wonderful Muslim husband who shared her passion for helping victims of domestic violence and verbal abuse. He was a part of the rescue team that had met Sarah and her two children when they made that wild dash across the busy intersection…running in fear for her life. She and Adnan had been married for eight years now, and they had three children besides Sarah's two eldest children. They were a close family and Adnan and Sarah worked hard to show their children the true teachings and beliefs of Islam.

Sarah had struggled through many trials to get a divorce that Allah had made legal for Muslim women and not just Muslim men. She had prayed hard and stayed focused on the truth of Islam and, by Allah's will, she had prevailed against the corruption and sickness within the community and husband she had fled so many years ago.

"Mama, Mama! We're here!" Joseph came rushing though the back gate lugging a battered suitcase ahead of Adnan, two small children, and sister Julie. "Don't look back," her 14-year-old son told the young boy, who held tightly to Joseph's hand as they reached Sarah.

Sis Julie looked scared and fearfully looked back over her shoulder, momentarily, and then Joseph's words seemed to register. Adnan motioned her to move ahead of him as he closed the back gate and locked it.

"Why didn't you call? I have been waiting and worrying," Sarah exclaimed. Adnan just gave her a gentle smile and nodded his head toward the three children huddled around sis Julie, their hands clutching her skirts. Sarah sighed inwardly. Another cell phone lost to the cause.

Sarah paused and smiled back at her beautiful husband, and then turned her attention to their temporary guests. Adnan would be making phone calls to brothers and sisters to get them organized to transport sis Julie and children to a safe house. There she could relax, get counseling, pray, and begin to make plans for a new life without pain and suffering from a man who did not love her but only wanted to exert his control over her. Sarah silently said a dua to Allah for helping them to get Julie and her children out of harm's way. She said a second dua for the Muslim Ummah that the terrible suffering of the victims of domestic violence be recognized by Muslim communities for what it is and no longer remain hidden and ignored.

Later that night, as Sarah looked in and saw Julie and her children sleeping peacefully in their makeshift beds, she once again recalled the words she said repeatedly to her eldest son the night Allah helped her change her life: "Don't look back!" These words now had new meaning for Sarah…they were the words that had transformed in meaning to trust and hope.

No Roses for Grandma by Linda D. Delgado

Susan eased back onto her knees and tipped the wide-brimmed straw hat back from her forehead. She wiped the sweat from her brow with the back of her long-sleeved shirt.

It was 7:00 AM and already the Arizona sun beat down on the rose garden Susan was weeding. Grandma's rose garden. Grandma had died three years ago, but Susan would always think of the rose garden as her grandmother's. Her grandma and great-grandmother had planted the roses together, with her grandma learning how to care for the many rose bushes that were planted some thirty years ago. Today, each bush still bloomed twice annually.

Susan put her spade down and fingered the rim of the straw hat. She loved the old thing. Her grandmother had worn it for years, and Susan had just naturally begun wearing it once her grandma was no longer in need of it.

Susan turned slightly to see her grandpa across the yard from her. He was watering the shrubs. Susan grinned. Grandma had finally convinced him to wear the matching straw hat she had bought for him, but she was never able to convince him that he should water the plants just before sundown. Her grandpa could be a tad stubborn when he got an idea in his head. Susan's smile disappeared when she thought of how lonely it would be once her grandpa was gone. He was approaching eighty years now and had slowed down considerably. He fussed and fumed when Susan insisted he take his cane with him whenever they went to the grocery store. Yes, Grandpa still insisted on buying his own groceries. He also refused to wear the hearing aids that Grandma had insisted he get just a year before she died.

"Grandpa. Grandpa!" Susan yelled. No response. Susan got to her feet and walked across the front lawn to touch her grandpa's shoulder.

"What? What?" Grandpa said in an irritable tone of voice.

Susan grinned at him and said, "I think the tribe is stirring. Want to go to Denny's for breakfast and escape the family for a little while?"

Grandpa grinned back at Susan, reached into his pocket, and tossed the car keys to her. "Let's get going," was his reply.

The ride to Denny's was silent, but companionable. Susan's thoughts drifted to the ending of her junior year at university and the decision she had made. Now would be a good time to tell Grandpa...away from the family.

She knew he would support her decision, just as he had been a support for Grandma all those many years before she died. Susan had made another decision. She was transferring to the local university so she could be at home every day instead of weekends and summers. She worried too much about her grandpa living alone while she was away at the university, 120 miles away. He wasn't the kind of person to have asked her to make either decision, but she knew he would be happy with both of her decisions.

When Susan and Grandpa got back to the house, the family had gathered in the dining room. Susan's father and her two aunts were seated around the dining room table, talking. When Susan and her grandpa entered the room, Susan's Aunt Lena and Aunt Marie stopped talking and glared at her. Her father looked anywhere but at Susan. Susan knew what they had been talking about – the same thing they talked about each year on this date for the last three years – Grandma's gravesite visit.

This was the reason for their annual visit with their own families each year. It was never a happy occasion for Susan and Grandpa. In fact, her relatives did nothing but upset Grandpa and make Susan mad. They knew from the get-go that Grandma would have disliked this "family ritual," yet they insisted. *They're selfish*, that's what Susan thought.

"Where have you been?" Aunt Lena angrily asked. "We have been sitting here waiting for over two hours. You know we are supposed to leave for the cemetery, and you take our Dad and just up and do a disappearing act!"

"You know we all have airline flights scheduled, and delaying the visit could just make problems for us. We all have to go home today, and your delaying tactics are not going to keep us from going to the cemetery. We made this clear to you over the phone before we left home, didn't we?" Aunt Marie's voice was calm, but had a hint of steel in her tone. *If Grandma were alive, my aunts wouldn't dare talk like this*, Susan thought.

Susan waited to see if her Dad would come to her defense. No such luck. He was staring out the window, trying to pretend he wasn't sitting in that chair and didn't hear his sisters yelling at her. *Why did he even bother to show up?* Privately, he had told Susan he wanted Grandma's wishes honored, but he had always allowed his sisters to bully him. Maybe he was just too nice, like Grandpa?

Susan looked at her grandpa and noticed he had raised his right hand in a motion for everyone to be quiet. "Get me a chair, Grubbie." Grandpa had started calling Susan this nickname when, at the age of two, she had started digging around with Grandma in the rose garden. Susan pulled out a chair, and her grandpa sat down and leaned forward, resting on his cane.

"Tom! Marie! Lena! I had a heart attack when your mother died, and I was in hospital when the three of you decided to give your mother a Christian burial. Susan, here, read you your Mother's Muslim will, and all three of you ignored it. You were plain selfish back then, thinking only of yourselves, and each year you show up here and are selfish all over again!"

"But Dad…" Marie sputtered.

Susan's grandfather said loudly, "Enough! I am doing the talking."

Susan remembered sitting in this same room more than three years ago, arguing with her two aunts and her Dad sitting there, as usual, saying nothing. She had opened the will her grandmother had given to her for safekeeping and read it to them. Her grandmother had requested a Muslim funeral and burial. All the contact names and even the plot of land in the Muslim cemetery had been paid for and reserved. Her aunts had refused to pay any heed to their Mother's will and requests. Susan's dad had made a weak effort to reason with his sisters, but they had shouted him down, and he'd done the usual, just clammed up and didn't say anything else. Susan hadn't been able to do anything to stop their plans then, and the Christian funeral had taken place while Grandpa was still in the hospital.

For the last two years, her relatives had come back to the family home for the ritual visit to Grandma's grave. Each year, her aunts had cut roses from Grandma's rose garden and taken them to the cemetery. Each year, Susan got angrier and angrier with them.

"Years before your Mother died, you were all too busy to come and visit her. Her grandchildren married and had babies, and not one of you had the decency to bring those babies here for her to hold and love. Knowing she was too ill to travel, yet you still went about your lives not thinking of your Mother. Did you think she would live forever in her state of poor health? Now that she is gone, you want to bring her roses. Roses from her own garden, which she never cut and put on any grave. Yet you come to my home, and it is still my home, and cut her roses and take them to that cemetery, where you know she didn't want to be buried!" Grandpa paused to catch his breath.

Susan looked at her aunts and Dad. Her aunts sat with their heads bowed and silent tears rolling down their cheeks. *My Gosh*! Susan silently exclaimed. There were tears in her dad's eyes, too!

Grandpa continued, "Last year and the year before, I should have spoken up. I wanted you all to visit and tried to avoid unpleasantness. It was wrong of me to stay silent. This is your home always, and I want you all to come and visit, but do not expect Susan and me to join you at the cemetery. The time for bringing your mother roses was while she lived."

Grandpa looked over at Susan and spoke to her directly, "There won't be any roses for your grandma today."

He got up slowly from his chair, looked at each of his children and said, "I'm going to take a nap until lunch. We can talk then if you want." His children nodded their heads and murmured their apologies.

Susan sat in Grandma's recliner reading aloud to Grandpa one of the storybooks Grandma had written so many years ago. Grandpa sat in his recliner opposite her and chuckled now and then at the antics of the book characters. "Your grandma sure could write some good stories for kids, even big kids like your old Grandpa."

"I know. I think I've read these books a hundred times, and I still enjoy them," Susan paused in her reading to reply, and then smiled at her Grandpa.

"Have you decided yet about wearing a head covering?" Grandpa asked Susan.

"I was thinking I'd try it out this summer. Kinda of get used to it before school starts in the Fall."

."You know, your Grandma prayed every day for you. For all of us. I think she knew you were Muslim before you knew you were Muslim, Susan."

"I think so, too" Susan replied with a catch in her voice.

"I have a surprise for you." Grandpa handed Susan a square bundle wrapped in tissue paper.

Susan took the bundle and carefully opened the layers of tissue. Inside was Grandma's very first hijab scarf…the one she wore the day she said Shahada.

"Your Grandma asked me to save this for you."

"Oh, Grandpa! Dearest Grandma!" were the only words Susan could manage, as her heart was too full of joy to say more.

The Flying Horse by Linda D. Delgado

Sarah stepped outside and gazed to her left at a lamppost two houses down from her house. A tiny little butterfly fluttered in her stomach each school day until she saw her son, James, get off the school bus and race as fast as his ten-year-old legs would carry him to her open arms greeting each late afternoon. Only then did that flutter stop. James was home safe and sound.

"Mom! Mom! Guess what? Today we had a real author at school. I mean a really real author at school, and she told us all about writing stories, showed us her books and…"

"Slow down, James," Sarah interrupted with a wide grin at her excited son.

"But look, Mom. I am gonna write my own Islamic fiction story, and I am gonna win first prize, and it's gonna be the best story of all stories! Look." James waved a handful of papers gripped tightly in his right hand as he opened the screen door and walked back to the kitchen, where he began spreading the papers across the kitchen table. He didn't even snag one of his favorite chocolate chip cookies from a plate on the table.

Sarah had her back to James as she poured a glass of milk from the container in the refrigerator. Her eyebrows rose as she heard the words Islamic and fiction. James did not see the look of concern on his mother's face, but continued his excited retelling of the big event of his day. James had outgrown the color picture story books of Islamic persons and events at an early age, and he had begun reading Qur'an and hadith during his first grade year of school. *Fiction? For older children? What was the school teaching her son? Islamic Fiction?* Sarah thought as James continued to describe his day's big excitement at school.

Sarah pulled out a chair and sat down at the table. She smiled at her son's animated face and accepted from James the first of the four papers spread out across the kitchen table.

"I'm gonna write about a super hero and his flying horse. He helps people and even reminds them to be kind or if they almost forget to say prayers or even wash their hands before supper. He races to the people on his flying horse. My super hero's name is James!" He beamed his beautiful smile at his mother and waited for her to tell him what a great story idea he had.

Sarah looked at her son's face, and then down at the paper in her hands. Not wanting to wipe that look off his face or dampen his enthusiasm, Sarah stalled for time. She asked, "What does Islamic fiction mean, son?"

"Read that paper, Mom. It explains all about it." James made a motion with his hand to indicate he had zippered his mouth closed, and he sat quietly waiting for his Mom to read the paper.

Sarah cleared her throat, peeked over the top of the paper, and saw that her son was not going to budge until she read the paper. Sarah looked down at the paper in her hands and began to read.

As Salaam'Alaykum
Dear Parents,

Today the school had a guest speaker talk to the Language Arts students in grade levels 4 through 8. The topic was writing creative Islamic fiction stories. The speaker was Sister Maryam Walker, who is a published author of six Islamic fiction books for older youth and teens. Sister Maryam is sponsoring a writing contest approved by the principal, teachers, and school board members. We hope you will be supportive of your student's efforts to participate and write a creative and imaginative Islamic story to enter into this school-approved contest. The attached pages explain Islamic fiction and the contest rules.

Br. Yusuf Erving
Principal, West End Islamic School

Sarah looked up and saw the second page held out to her and a very serious James making another zipper-his-mouth motion with his other hand. Sarah took the second page and began reading:

Islamic Fiction books: This refers to creative, imaginative, non-preachy fiction books written by Muslims and marketed primarily to Muslims. Islamic Fiction may be marketed to secular markets, too. The content of these books incorporates some religious content and themes, and may include non-fictionalized historical or factual Islamic content with or without direct reference to the Qur'an or the Sunnah of the Prophet (pbuh). The stories may also include modern, real life situations and moral dilemmas. Islamic Fiction may be written in many languages.

Harmful Content

Islamic Fiction and Secular Fiction books will not be approved if they include any of the following Harmful Content:

- vulgar language
- sexually explicit content
- unIslamic practices that are not identified as unIslamic
- content that portrays Islam in a negative way

Islamic Reminder

Determining the accuracy and permissibility of Islamic content is the responsibility of every adult Muslim reader. This may differ according to individual differences in madhab and practice. All Muslim parents, guardians, teachers, and school administrators must determine whether a book's content is halal for their children and students. This Islamic Reminder holds true for all materials a Muslim reads.

Differences in Islamic Practices and Teachings

While Islamic knowledge presented in Islamic Fiction may be taken directly from the Holy Qur'an and traditions of the Prophet Muhammad (peace be upon him), as well as from Islamic history, not all of the Islamic content in these books will be considered factual or acceptable by all Muslim readers. This is due to differences between a Muslim reader and the writers, editors, and publishers with respect to personal practices, beliefs, and knowledge, as well as the influence of his mathab, culture, and tradition.

Reference: www.IslamicFictionBooks.com

Sarah was ready for the third page, which spelled out all the contest rules. The last page James handed her was a parental permission signature form, which would allow James to enter the writing contest or not participate in it.

Sarah looked up after reading the last page, and James made the motion to unzip his mouth and immediately started his "sales" pitch.

"Br. Yusuf said that some Muslims do not understand what Islamic fiction is and think it is haram, but it's not. It's halal, and it's much better reading about Muslims like me and you. It's better than reading all those fiction books by non-Muslims. And my story is gonna be halal because, remember, when the Prophet's young wife had a flying horse, and she told the Prophet all about her flying horse and its adventures? Remember, Mom? So writing fiction stories that include good stuff about Islam is good, don't you think?" James finished his sales pitch in a rush and waited expectantly for Sarah to speak.

"I'd like to discuss this with your father, and then pray on it tonight before I give you an answer. Does that seem fair to you, James?"

James's smile slipped for a moment, but then quickly reappeared. "That's a good idea, Mom. I am gonna pray, too. Oh, and Sister Maryam said there is a web site that has scholars' opinions approving Islamic fiction stories and a list of lots of Islamic fiction books already written and published by Muslims. Look, Mom, it's at the bottom of the second page."

Sarah looked at the place on the page James was pointing at. She smiled at her son and agreed to visit the web site and have his father look at it, too.

James jumped up from his chair and wrapped his arms about his mother's waist. "Thanks, Mom. Thanks for listening to me and reading the papers."

That night, James dreamed of his silver-winged horse flying through the air, soaring over roof tops and racing to save Muslims from harm or wrongdoing. He clutched a handful of mane and leaned into the neck of his magnificent friend as they flew from one good deed to another.

The next morning James hurried to gather his school books and get to the breakfast table. It was all he could do not to have blurted out his question before Fajar prayer. His Mom and Dad were already seated at the table, drinking their morning cup of coffee, and his dad had his face buried behind the morning newspaper. James sat down after greeting his parents, and it was then he noticed the paper turned face down across his breakfast bowl. James's heart began beating a mile a minute, and it seemed like he couldn't breathe. He wanted to turn over the paper, but hesitated. *What if my parents said "No"? I am not gonna argue or cry like a baby,* he told himself. *I'm too big to cry…*but he wasn't so sure his eyes would cooperate with his big boy brave words.

James turned over the paper and saw both his mother's and father's signatures giving permission for him to enter the writing contest!

"Boy, am I hungry. I'm so hungry I could eat a horse," James exclaimed and grinned from ear to ear.

His father looked over the top of his newspaper and said, "Just be sure that flying horse of yours doesn't hear you say that, James."

Yahiya Emerick

Yahiya Emerick is a convert to Islam who has worked to bridge the gap between traditional knowledge and modern needs. He has authored 25 books on Islam directed toward students, converts and the wider interfaith community. His recently completed translation of the Holy Qur'an into modern English is widely anticipated and is designed to fill the needs of both Muslims and non-Muslims in understanding the historical context of the revelation. He has also been an active speaker and promoter of Islamic values.

Hakim and the Special Letter by Yahiya Emerick

A breeze as sharp as a razor grazed past Hakim's forehead. Startled, he stopped to catch his breath. He had been running off and on for over four hours now and needed a break. But it wasn't the running that bothered him so much. It was trying to keep from tripping over roots and ruts on the slim mountain trail he had to travel over. At dusk, when he left his little mountain village, he hadn't suspected that his journey would be this hard. He had to travel by night so his parents wouldn't know he had left.

After the umpteenth bruise, he began to question the wisdom of that decision. Three weeks ago, a fire damaged one of the houses in the village. But not just any person's house; it was the home of the Sheikh and teacher of the town. The fire was not a bad one, but it had burned up the only real treasure the people had, an old copy of the Holy Qur'an – the Qur'an that the Sheikh would read to the people in the morning after Fajr prayer. He would translate the meaning as he went and, although his Arabic wasn't perfect, he could get the basic meaning across to the brothers and sisters. Many people would have gladly traded places in the burning hut to save that special book, the only one they had.

Hakim, who loved Allah dearly, cried when he first heard what happened. He had learned so many *surahs*, or chapters, and was the Sheikh's favorite student. After the shock wore off, Hakim made the secret promise to Allah that if He would help him bring another Qur'an to the village, then he would memorize the whole book and become a hafiz!

So Hakim secretly asked the Sheikh's wife to write a letter requesting a Qur'an from whomever Hakim could find outside their mountain home. It was this letter that Hakim carried in his pocket and this mission that burned in his heart like liquid steel.

The close of night definitely affected his progress. Twice, he slid down slippery trails that at times felt more like wet sheepskin than rock. He had never been away from home so far before and wondered what the world was really like. The older men, who sometimes left for trade, told stories of a world of fantastic machines and huge villages, but Hakim was never sure if he should believe them or not. Now, he would find out for himself if what they said was true.

He had brought several shirts along with him to protect against the cold, but Hakim found that the farther he descended, the less chilly he felt. He stopped for a moment, looked up into the night sky, and saw the stars as bright as mini-suns flung across a ceiling. Not a cloud passed over to ruin his spectacular view of Allah's universe. He stood captivated, wondering if he would see a comet chasing away some Jinns in the sky.

Although he stared intently, he couldn't see any streaks of light this time. Instead, the sounds of walking and rocks moving from far below him startled him from his daydreaming. Someone was coming up the trail toward him! Quickly, Hakim scrambled off the trail and hid behind an outcropping of rock. One could never be too safe on the trail, for bandits were well known in this part of the world.

The stranger approached slowly, for the trail was so strewn with small rocks and jagged ruts that one really had to move carefully. As he moved closer in the dim starlight, Hakim made out the figure of a man holding the reigns of a pack mule laden with supplies. The man appeared to be middle-aged and wore a large leather shirt of some sort. He was humming something, though Hakim couldn't quite make it out.

As the man passed by the portion of the trail where Hakim was hiding, he stopped abruptly and poked around in front of him with his foot. *What is he doing?* thought Hakim. Then to his horror, Hakim saw the man pick up one of the shirts he had brought to keep him warm. He must have dropped it when he scampered off the trail. The man held it up, turned it around and examined it. Then he shouted, "Okay, who's out there? Come on, come out! I won't hurt you."

Hakim's heart pounded. There was no feeling in his hands, and his body felt heavy. *This must be a bandit*, he thought. *What will he do to me?* raced his frightened mind. *Will he kill me and take my clothes? Will they find my body in a hole like they did poor old Azim's last year?* Hakim was terrified. He held onto the rock so tightly that he broke a small piece off, which fell with a sharp *ping* on the ground near him.

The man turned his face in Hakim's direction and peered into the dim shadows of stone. "Come out of there," the man said. "I know there's someone there!" Hakim called out in a weak voice, *"Asalamu alaikum."* The man paused a moment and replied in an overly-sweet voice, *"Wa alaikum assalam."* Hakim then stood up from his shelter and explained, "My name is Hakim. I was unsure about who you were, so I hid myself."

"Come here, boy," the man growled. "Don't you know that you must respect your elders?" Hakim obeyed automatically, as respect for his elders was ingrained in him like his nervous system. He straddled the few obstacles between him and the trail and approached the man. Hakim began to feel more at ease and relaxed his tense body.

What should he fear from another Muslim brother, anyway?

But suddenly the man pulled out a long knife and snarled, "And don't you know that these hills are filled with...bandits!" Hakim nearly lost his footing and flung his arms in the air. He turned to run, but tripped over the leg of the man who lunged forward to grab him. The man took Hakim by his shirt and put the tip of the knife into Hakim's back and said, "Now, get up slowly." Hakim regained his feet cautiously and raised himself up, a little at a time.

"Now empty your pockets," the man then ordered. Hakim proceeded to pull out everything he had brought with him: a few coins, a small cloth, a tiny pocket blade, a wrapped piece of goat's-milk cheese, and the letter. "Is that all?" the man grumbled.

"Yes. I'm just a mountain boy on my way to the place of the big villages. Please don't hurt me. I have an important mission."

"A *mission!*" laughed the cruel bandit, "What can a mountain boy have to do that is so important? I might just kill you for fun!"

Hakim flinched his right shoulder and felt fear rising up in him like a hand trying to squeeze the air out of his lungs. Silently, he said to himself, *Allah protect me.*

Hakim stood there and watched as the bandit deftly took out some kind of a flint and candle and lit it with one hand. The other hand held the long knife, pointed threateningly at Hakim. The bandit then proceeded to inspect the sum of Hakim's possessions with a very disappointed look on his face.

Slowly, Hakim sat down when the bandit did so as well. The bandit opened the cheese and started to munch on it as he held the pocket-blade up to the light. He dropped it carelessly to the ground and picked up Hakim's folded letter.

"What's this?" he demanded. "A treasure map or something?"

Hakim hesitated for a moment and replied, "Well, yes, in a way."

"What do you mean...*in a way*?" demanded the bandit. "Here. Read it to me, because I can't read."

He flung the paper to Hakim, who caught it carefully. Hakim opened the letter and shifted his body closer to the bandit, so he could take advantage of the candlelight. Hakim started to read. At first, his voice quivered, but as the words of the letter recalled to his mind why he was there, his tone steadied and gained strength.

May the peace of Allah fill the dark corners of all our lives.

Where there is hope in Allah, there is happiness. Where there is no hope in Allah, there is pain and sadness. And even though we still hope in Allah, we are yet a little sad, for the one treasure of our village has been taken in a fire to test our faith. We declare our faith is true and will remain strong. All we ask is that the light of our lives be returned to us. We ask that Allah bring joy to our hearts once more as we recite His words anew.

O please, anyone who receives this letter, please allow the boy to return to us with a copy of the Book of Light – that same Book which can change a person's life forever. We will hold forever in our hearts the name of the person who bestows upon us this gift. We pray for the reward and love of Allah upon the one who returns to us this treasure which lights our hearts and shows us the way in the darkness.

May Allah guide you, always.
A simple villager.

When Hakim finished the letter, he looked up to find tears streaming down the bandit's face. The candlelight made his weeping seem as if rivers of silver ran from his eyes. Dropping his knife, he lowered his head into his hands and cried and cried and cried.

Hakim was puzzled at the sight, but felt moved by his sorrow and let fall a few tears of his own. He slowly shifted closer to the bandit and placed his arm around his shoulder. The bandit tilted his head into Hakim's chest and continued to weep as if he had lost someone he loved very much.

After some moments, under the stars and in the light of a tiny candle, the bandit began to speak, but this time in softer tones, with no harshness. "My father..." He paused. "My father called the Qur'an the book which brought him peace. He was the finest man. He always was good to me, but I wanted to go my own way, to be my own man. I did so many bad things." The bandit paused a moment and pushed back his sobs.

"I made him feel so bad. He thought he failed with me. He used to read the Qur'an when I came home late after getting into fights and stealing. He was so calm. He never told me to get out or to leave. He just kept reading his Qur'an and telling me he still loved me." More tears poured out from the bandit's eyes, and he rubbed his face with his hand. Then he pulled away from Hakim and sat upright.

"When he became sick, he asked me to bring him his Qur'an in bed, so he could read it. I told him I would, but then went away looking for trouble again. When I got home, I went to check on my father, but I found my father dead...*he was dead!* He died, and I didn't bring him the only thing that brought *joy* to his life. I failed him after he was so patient with me. I felt like the worst animal on the surface of the earth. I couldn't face my relatives. I couldn't stand at his funeral prayer. I had to *get away*. The one thing I took was his Qur'an. I made a promise to myself that, one day, I would honor my father's spirit. That, one day, somehow, I would make up for my miserable little life."

The bandit was silent for a moment. He gazed into Hakim's face and saw the boy that he once was. The boy he could have been so long ago. Hakim stared back into the aged and worn eyes. Eyes that had been too long from peace, too troubled by an inner pain of the worst kind: the pain of betrayal. Abruptly, the bandit rose to his feet. He walked over to his pack mule and rummaged through his bags for a moment.

When he returned to where Hakim sat, he lowered himself on his knees and handed a worn-out old copy of the Qur'an to Hakim. Hakim took it in his hands but, for an instant, both the man and the boy looked into each other's eyes, and a healing that could almost be seen passed between them. "I'm sorry. It's kind of beat up." said the bandit.

Hakim took the bandit's hand, held it, and replied, "No amount of time can erase or damage the words of the One Who knows the secrets of our souls." The bandit grabbed Hakim in his arms and hugged him tightly.

When he released his grip, he swiftly turned toward his pack mule, took up its straps and disappeared back down the trail into the midnight world of the dark. Hakim stood still for a moment. He was no longer a boy. *"Allah is the Greatest,"* he said softly, *"There is no power and there is no might save in Allah."*

And, as he turned to go, he remembered that he never asked the bandit for his name.

KAREN ENGLISH

Karen English was born in Vallejo, California in 1947. She grew up in Los Angeles, California with her mother, stepfather, brother, and sister. She received her B.A. in Psychology from California State University at Los Angeles, as well as a teaching credential. Until recently, she taught second grade. She is the mother of four grown children and grandmother of one. She currently lives in Los Angeles. She feels blessed to be a writer and has authored 13 books. Karen says that writing makes life so much more interesting, because she sees a story in almost everything.

Awards:
- Coretta Scott King Honor Award for FRANCIE
- BABRA Award for FRANCIE
- Parent Choice for FRANCIE
- Judy Lopez Award for FRANCIE
- Jane Addams Award for HOT DAY ON ABBOTT AVENUE

YUSUF'S WIFE BY KAREN ENGLISH

Yusuf was talking to her. His voice was irritating. She was busy watching their son out the window – and Coley, that neighbor boy. Coley Bunch was a thickset boy with a short neck that implied some kind of pending, unbridled meanness when he grew into his future redneck self. Now he had Ephraim's basketball and, while Ephraim stood powerless at the side of the driveway, Coley stood at the end, making futile after futile attempt to sink the ball into the basket. It did not matter that he had no skill. His intention was to hijack Ephraim's basketball. From time to time he directed one of his fiendish grins toward her son.

Shemsia felt a familiar tension growing in the back of her neck. She leaned into the window for a better view and was dismayed to see Ephraim assuming a defeatist posture. His arms hung loosely. He kept his head bowed. He seemed to be regarding his situation apologetically. She was nearly vibrating with anger. She thought she might just run out there and snatch that ball out of Coley's hands.

"Shemsia…" Her husband's voice again.

"What *is* it, Yusuf?"

"I need to talk to you."

"In a minute." She could not help herself. She waved Yusuf's words away, grabbed the bag of laundry as a pretext, and then marched out the back door. "Give Ephraim back his ball," she hissed as she passed on the way to the garage to throw the laundry bag into the back seat of the car. Their washing machine had been broken for months.

Ephraim was too far away to hear, but Coley caught the sharp threat in her voice. He stopped mid-shot, having brought the ball to his chest to make another fruitless throw at the basket. She'd caught him off guard, and now she knew he was busy making his weasel-like calculations about whether he had to obey this small brown woman. He looked back at his house, but his house stood lifeless and silent.

"Give Ephraim back his ball," he repeated in a whiny voice, meant to mock her thick accent. He bounced the ball low and hard toward Ephraim, gathered his bike that he'd let carelessly drop at the foot of their stone steps, then gave a running start and hopped on. He sped away – chunky legs pumping.

On her way back to her kitchen, Shemsia was shaking with fury. The nerve of that little urchin to mock her when he wasn't even fit to wash her feet. She met Ephraim's level gaze and in that fraction of a second she knew she'd made a serious misstep. He'd heard her. This moment would follow him. And no matter what he achieved in his later life, even winning the regional spelling bee at the end of the month, he would always remember that it was his mother, with her unbearably thick accent, who'd had to rescue his basketball for him.

He bounced it listlessly a few times, then let it roll to a stop. He turned on it and went into the house. She followed behind him, noting the fragile shoulder blades that showed under his thin t-shirt like folded wings. How she'd like to reverse his growth until he was her babe in arms again. But that could not be done.

Shemsia walked into the kitchen and stopped short. What had Yusuf done to his hair? It now had the matte finish and unnatural color of wrought iron. It did not work against his fading complexion or his brows, which, once straight and thick and dark, were now paled by unruly gray hair. Shemsia sank into the seat across from him, feeling suddenly very tired. She inhaled deeply and offered a quick prayer for patience.

She would not mention his hair. Not yet. Sometimes, it was better to wait before pointing out Yusuf's foolishness to him. Better just to enlist his help with their son. Tell him what he must do about the Coley situation – which had some history.

"Yusuf, do you know what your son was doing while that neighbor boy was hogging his basketball? Do you know what he was doing?"

Yusuf seemed to be looking at her as if through a curtain of fog. He frowned.

"He was just standing there. Doing nothing." She stopped to discern how her husband, with his silly dyed hair, was taking this. He did not look like a man moved to action. He looked like a man barely inspired to take up for his own self, even. But then he said, "Are you ready to talk, Shemsia?"

"Yusuf, you have to do something about your son. You have to help him grow a backbone."

Yusuf closed his eyes. Shemsia waited. "I have something important to tell you, first," he said.

"Tell me, then."

"Ivan has to move in with us." There was a pause in which he seemed to be bracing himself. "He has no place to go – he has no money, and he is my brother."

"Ivan's not our problem."

"He's my brother."

Shemsia held her tongue. She had to be careful here – hold off on her objections for a bit. She didn't want to make him contrary on general principal. She brought her hand up to her mouth to hide it. It wasn't the eyes that gave people away, it was the mouth. Sometimes, Shemsia could see the approach of a smile on her friend Desta's face, when Shemsia related some personal bad news. And how many times had she seen that little pursing quiver on the mouths of drinkers as they anticipated that first drink. Now, she leaned her chin on her palm, but kept her fingers over her mouth, lest he see it thinned with recalcitrance.

Yusuf went on a bit about the importance of family and how everyone must pull together. She hated the way his eyebrows lifted in the middle when he was fixing his face in one of his hangdog looks.

I will let him talk and talk, she decided, but he will come to my conclusion on his own. Ivan could not live with them. It was out of the question. Shemsia looked at Yusuf squarely, so he would be sure he had her undivided attention – then past him at the wooden base of the cup tree, where she was dismayed to see a fine layer of dust.

Something occurred to her then, as she brought her attention back to Yusuf, something that occasionally threatened to worm its way into her consciousness and cause her even more disquiet. She shouldn't have married an American black. She married him and, by default, had married his whole maladjusted family. It hadn't been a bargain for her – not equal to what she had brought to Yusuf's life.

She was from a good family of high class. Her father had been in government service. Her brother was an engineer. Her sister had gone to school in England and married a wealthy businessman from an upperclass Egyptian family. Sure, they would have preferred he'd married someone with the complexion of cream, but they soon came around when the children began to arrive, which was usually the case.

What had Shemsia done? Her father had sent her all the way to America to a top university, and she'd fallen in love with a man because his slight Ethiopian features had reminded her of home. And now she found herself cemented into his life.

Which included his sister, Vicky, and her little Roashon. (And what kind of name was that, anyway?) Roashon's father? Gone – just as soon as the very brief sense of empowerment he'd gotten from new fatherhood had fizzled. Then into her life came Yusuf's brother, Ivan, and his "a few bad breaks." As far as Shemsia was concerned, any man who included "bad breaks" in his lexicon was a flat out loser. There were no such things as bad breaks.

Downing too many beers and running into a parked car was not a bad break. Having your wife leave you because it dawned on her one day that she was the only one paying the rent was not a bad break.

"Is Ivan working?" Shemsia asked.

"Harun has promised to find him a little something while he's here."

Harun was one of Yusuf's friends who had an inflated opinion of himself. He rarely did what he said he was going to do. "He won't," Shemsia said. "Oh, yes, he'll promise, but then you'll have to chase him down."

"What choice do I have? Ivan's my brother. Right now, he's trying to find himself."

Shemsia abandoned her earlier resolve. "Yusuf, this is not going to work. A man does not wait to age forty-three to find himself. That shows he's been wasting his life. Where is Colette?" Shemsia knew Colette, Ivan's ex-wife, had the sense to be nowhere near Ivan, but still there was a glimmer of hope that an exasperated Colette had turned into a forgiving Colette.

"Colette moved back to New York last year. Ivan doesn't even know where she is."

Shemsia felt her heart sink and something like hysteria rising. "I cannot be in my hijab in my own house, Yusuf." The slight tremor in her voice surprised her.

Yusuf looked down at his hands.

Perhaps he hadn't appreciated what she just said.

"Yusuf, listen to me. I cannot be in my head covering in my own house."

"We'll put a time limit on it," Yusuf said. "One month."

"Ya'Allah!" she said as she stumbled over Ivan's duffel bag in the hallway three mornings later. "This is not good," she said under her breath. "Not good at all. I will not move that bag. If no one moves it, it will sit right there."

She stepped over it and went into the kitchen. The kitchen was empty. Her brother-in-law was probably still asleep. Of course, he'd be. People who worked their way into these kinds of predicaments were never early risers. She looked at the closed basement door, then out the window at her driveway. Her husband was gone. Yusuf liked to get to his classroom early, then spend the bonus time puttering about, getting his brain battle-ready for the onslaught of homework excuses, fights over spots in line, and the free-floating heartbreak of his students' lives. He always dropped Ephraim off at the bus stop three blocks away before he scooted off to his separate world.

She noted the Bunch's blue pickup. Only a thin grass median separated their two driveways. One entire front bumper was covered in black primer. She'd seen the requisite nude silhouettes on the rear mud flaps. There was a rusted barbeque pit by their back porch steps, long abandoned but not yet thrown out, just taking up space, marring the landscape. I'm forced to live next door to these people, Shemsia thought. A man who carries a six-pack of beer into his house every day.

The kettle began to whistle behind her and, when she turned to tend to it, there was Ivan, standing in the doorway, tucking his chin in a false show of humility, Shemsia suspected. He looked thinner, a little unhealthy, like someone who'd been putting other indulgences ahead of diet and healthy living.

"Good morning," he said cheerfully.

Shemsia fingered the end of her hijab. "Good morning."

"Sorry about my stuff in the way. I was so tired by the time I got here, it was all I could do to make it to that bed down there." He glanced back at the basement door.

Shemsia forced a smile, but deliberately remained silent.

"Can I get some of that?" He made himself at home at the table.

Shemsia got two cups down from the shelf. She prepared the tea while he drummed the edge of the table and whistled tunelessly.

"Did Yusuf tell you about my plans?"

"A little something." She dunked her tea bag and thought about dinner.

"I'm taking up carpentry."

She stood with her back to the sink. She needed to chop onion for the alecha, but made no move to go to the refrigerator.

"So how are you doing these days, Shemsia? How's Ethiopia?"

What an odd thing to ask, she thought. As if Ethiopia was a person.

"How would I know? I haven't been there in eight years." She took a sip of tea to allow him time to make the connection between loans Yusuf had shelled out to him in the past and her long separation from her family. But in Ivan's infuriating way, he appeared not to notice.

"Carpentry. I don't know why it took me so long to realize this. It must be in my blood. Did you know that our grandfather was a cabinetmaker?"

Shemsia smiled wanly. She hadn't heard this. "Mmm."

"I'm hoping to get an apprenticeship up in Seattle." He took up his drumming again, but this time with his open hands. Then he did an odd thing. He placed his cheek close to his drumming hands, as if there was some subtle, yet remarkable rhythm that only his genius could create and appreciate. He stopped abruptly. He had a final, important point to make, she was sure. "But not just yet. I need to cool out a little bit first, get myself together."

Shemsia looked at Ivan squarely. People like Ivan always had a kind of a grandiose optimism. They always had big, big plans. And they were quick to announce these plans to whoever would listen. It was as if the announcement itself was the actual doing. She studied him as he leaned into the beat he was making on her kitchen table with eyes closed. He seemed genuinely pleased with himself. He stopped to take a sip of tea through his teeth, holding his lips out protectively. After he swallowed, he said, "But I'm doin' it. I'm takin' one step at a time, but I'm gettin' there."

Ya Allah! She thought. This was not a halfway house. She went to the refrigerator for the onion.

The day Shemsia loved most was Monday. It was her market day. She actually traveled to three markets. First, a big chain market in her neighborhood for canned goods and non-food items like paper towels and soap – then on to Whole Foods across town for her fruits and vegetables and maybe something from the deli. There she'd push her cart slowly along the aisles, stopping to read ingredients on the labels of items she had no intention of buying. She enjoyed learning about strange foods that other people had on their shelves at that very moment. Her last stop was the small market in Little Ethiopia. It was actually just one street in an area once dominated by Jewish businesses. But as the businesses went farther north, the vacuum they created was soon filled by the Ethiopians, who seemed to be waiting in the wings.

She walked through the door and immediately went over to Almaz to greet her.

"How is Ayana?" she asked, once they'd hugged. "Tell me she's coming home when the school year is over."

Almaz shrugged and lifted her eyebrows. "I cannot count on it."

Shemsia sighed in commiseration. "Well, she might surprise you, Almaz."

The store was small enough to allow them to visit while Shemsia put her few things from her list in her basket. Ingredients for spiced butter and some ber-beri for spice paste. Shemsia liked Almaz and her happy, round face and eyes that neatly closed, or seemed to, when she laughed. Almaz was always in a good mood, even when life was not treating her well. She laughed off her husband's indifference, her youngest daughter's casual attitude about her home responsibilities, and didn't seem to mind that most of the responsibility of the store fell on her shoulders. Shemsia wished she had Almaz's ease of attitude. How much more pleasant life would be if she could laugh off her woes.

Shemsia pulled into the driveway. She sat there for a few minutes, thinking of the bags of groceries in the trunk. This was the part she hated: the unloading and the unpacking. She looked toward the basement window, then at her watch. Ivan had fallen into something of a routine. When the music started up, she knew he was gathering his courage. Over the last two weeks, some of that initial enthusiasm about his life plans had dulled a bit. Of course, as Shemsia had suspected, Harun's promise had been flimsy at best. It turned out that it just wasn't a good time to take on a new hire. Simply that. Ivan's long shower usually followed – with no concern for the hot water or the water bill.

She was surprised at the quiet when she entered the kitchen with her arms loaded down with groceries. She glanced at the closed basement door, and then went back out to the car. Perhaps Ivan was out "taking care of business," as he liked to call his forays into the outside world.

Shemsia thought she heard something then – a chair scraping. With the bags still in her arms, she went and stood outside the basement door, listening. Silence. She returned to the car for the last bag of the groceries, then, just before she set them on the counter, she heard the distinct sound of a woman's laughter coming up from the basement. She froze in disbelief. Then, there it was again, full-throated laughter this time, a sound of recklessness and complete abandonment.

As Shemsia stood in her kitchen considering her options, she heard their footsteps on the stairs. The basement door opened, and Ivan stepped back to allow his guest to emerge first.

"Hey, Shemsia," Ivan said, full of good cheer.

Shemsia set the bags down slowly. She watched them in silence as Ivan followed behind this woman with his hands on her waist. "This is my lady love, Markesha," he said, as he steered Markesha to a kitchen chair. The woman giggled pointlessly. "She don't believe I'ma cook her some lunch." Markesha, looking spent for some reason, quit her giggling, and now rested her forehead on her folded arms. Ivan looked over at her and laughed a low, drawn-out laugh that sounded to Shemsia's ears more like a growl. Then he pirouetted and studied the series of cabinets before him as if he were using some kind of party trick to conjure up what each contained. She watched him search out what he needed for his (according to him) famous chili, cheese, and black olive omelet. Back at the table, Markesha had surfaced from her crossed arms and was watching him with amusement. Then she rested her chin on her palm in what she must have thought a sexy pose.

Shemsia put the perishables away and left the room.

In her bedroom, she sat on her bed and stared at the telephone. Perhaps she should call Yusuf. But call him with what? She pictured him in his classroom sitting at his desk, correcting papers. No, it was too early for that. He'd be trying to teach some lesson to his largely inattentive class. She'd heard his stories and wondered why he didn't try to get hired at a school where he would be able to teach – where most of the time allocated for the lesson wasn't taken up with discipline problems?

Thinking along these lines, it was easy to extrapolate what his response would be to his brother's thoughtless, brazen behavior. He would excuse him. Not directly. At first, he would pretend to be on board with Shemsia and, while she vented, he'd second each comment with points of his own. Though they would be milder, more open-ended, exposing another way of looking at the situation. She'd seen Yusuf do this before, especially at those times when she thought she'd detected some slight or some unfairness directed toward Ephraim by a teacher, or by the little league coach when he seemed to be giving other players more time in the field over their son.

So what was the use? She would tell him of Ivan's bad behavior, and then she'd have to listen to Yusuf's pretense of outrage. He would say the right things but, little by little, he would convince her to give Ivan another chance.

She felt completely helpless. She needed to calm down before she spoke to Yusuf. She looked at the clock and saw that it was time for her midday prayer. I will pray for guidance, she thought. She went to the bathroom to wash up. But when she came out, she sat on the bed again and thought of more of her husband's shortcomings. What a sensitive man he'd seemed when they first married, anticipating her every concern, being wholly on board with what she thought was best for their lives. Now, it was as if he'd stepped out of the room. But now she could see clearly that the man was not with her.

What would he do now? Would he throw Ivan out or would he make excuses for him until he thought she was appeased? If he threw Ivan out, there was hope. If not, she would continue as she was. She would cook, clean, and care for Ephraim and act as Yusuf's wife. They would pray together, they would attend the mosque, and she would be publicly attached to him as his wife, but in her heart she would leave him. She would get a job, save her money, go visit her family. A nice, long visit. One where she'd take an extra suitcase filled only with presents for all her family. Of course, she'd take Ephraim. Her family had only seen him twice, the last time when he was four years old. She would show him all the magnificent things about her city, Bahir Dar. The tall palms and jacarandas. Its magnificent views of Lake Tana. It was his city, too. Why shouldn't he have his life there instead of here in this shabby place? Shemsia thought.

She looked around her small room. There was a wicker trunk at the end of the bed in which she stored extra blankets. She remembered when she first saw it in the small import store she sometimes wandered into. She had imagined it sitting just where it sat now. She had thought of the convenience it would provide and the beauty. Now, she saw how all the special purchases she'd made in the past, in which she'd put such faith, soon grew familiar and old and invisible. She imagined the space empty, and somehow that appealed to her more.

Shemsia took a deep breath and actually felt calm as her plan began to take shape in her mind. The more details she added to it, the calmer she felt. She heard that woman's brazen laughter filling up her kitchen, and it was a sound that had nothing to do with her. Next door, hard rock started up, music that always sounded, to Shemsia, angry and threatening. It had nothing to do with her, as well. It could not touch her. She went to the window and looked down onto the Bunch's yard full of weeds with the old swing set that their son had long ago outgrown. Just at that moment, Coley's mother slammed out of her back door with a big black bag of trash. She yelled some-thing over her shoulder – an admonishment to that demon child of hers, no doubt. The pale woman with a cigarette dangling from her hand flicked an ash at the ground and looked up at Shemsia. At one time, Shemsia would have felt caught and would have quickly moved out of sight. This time, she looked her neighbor right in the eye, and their eyes held for two or three seconds. Shemsia smiled, but the woman looked away. No matter. Shemsia wasn't smiling at her neighbor. She was smiling at a vision of herself on an airplane, flying over the Atlantic, Ephraim by her side – far, far away from where Ivan lived in the basement, where Yusuf hid himself behind his com-fortable wall of mediocrity, and where people didn't have a clue about the life from which she had come.

Fawzia Gilani

Fawzia Gilani is the author of more than twenty children's books. She was born and raised in Walsall, England. Her passion is children's Islamic literature, which she is studying at the University of Worcester, UK. She has worked as a teacher since 1993 and as a librarian since 2005. She currently works as the principal of An-Noor Private School in Windsor, Ontario. She makes her home in Oberlin, Ohio, where she lives with her husband, Robert, and daughter, Muslimah.

Subhi's Shoes: An Eid Story by Fawzia Gilani

Subhi lived in the busy city of Baghdad. His house was next to a river. He was liked by most people. He was a kind person with a good heart. But there was one problem. Subhi's shoes. They were old and worn and patched and sewn in so many places. They were not very nice to look at, but Subhi loved them all the same.

"They're so comfortable," he would say. "And they've been with me for years!"

But everyone else felt differently. How could anyone wear such old, scruffy looking shoes!

"Someone needs to throw those shoes away!" said Sadia the hijab seller.

"Someone needs to bury those shoes!" said Asiya the spinach pie maker.

One day Subhi was walking in the bazaar in his old, patched shoes.

"Why are you wearing those old, nasty shoes?" said Tarek the falafil maker.

"They are the worst looking shoes in all of Baghdad!" yelled Abdurahman the baker.

"They must be the most awful shoes in the whole country!" said Jawad the melon seller.

It was true, even when Subhi went to the mosque to pray, his shoes, wherever he put them, were always by themselves. No one would place their shoes next to his!

The days of Eid were approaching. The neighbours decided to buy Subhi a pair of shoes as an Eid gift. They went to many shoe stalls to try and find a pair of shoes that Subhi would like. Finally, they picked a nice pair of brown shoes.

On the first day of Eid, Subhi's neighbors went to visit him.

"We have brought you a gift for Eid," they said, and they handed him a pair of new shoes.

When Subhi saw the shoes, his eyes filled with tears. He really didn't want to part with his pair of old worn shoes. He would miss them very much, and this made him quite sad.

"Ah!" said Abdurahman. "Look, Subhi is crying, he is so happy!"

Subhi hugged his friends and neighbours and thanked them for the gift. When the guests left, Subhi decided to try on the shoes. They looked very nice indeed. Subhi wasn't sure what to do.

"If I keep my old shoes, I will want to wear them. This will upset my friends and neighbors." Subhi thought and thought and thought.

"Ah yes!" cried Subhi. "I know just what to do!"

Subhi picked up his old pair of shoes and flung them from his window into the river below.

"Splash!" Subhi sighed and looked down at his feet.

The next day Firas the fisherman pulled his net out of the water. He was very angry when he saw Subhi's old tatty shoes tangled in his net. Firas marched from his boat to Subhi's house and threw the shoes on the floor.

"Don't throw your shoes in the river!" shouted Firas and left.

Subhi sighed. "My shoes," he said, "you have come back to me."

Subhi thought and thought and thought.

"How can I get rid of my shoes?" he wondered.

"Ah!" cried Subhi, "I know!"

Subhi went outside and built a small fire. He placed his soggy, wet, old worn shoes into the flames. But the shoes were so wet that they only steamed and spattered.

Subhi took the shoes out of the smoldering fire and placed them on his window ledge to dry. A cat jumped up onto his window and caused the shoes to fall. Down they went, down, down, down. Smack! They hit Sadia on the head and made her drop her Eid biscuits all over the ground.

"Ayyyyeeeee!" screamed Sadia. She looked around to see what hit her and saw Subhi's old worn-out shoes. "Throwing things on old women!" she shouted and threw them back into Subhi's open window.

"Sorry! Sorry!" called Subhi. "It was an accident."

But Sadia didn't hear; she was too angry.

Poor Subhi. He didn't know what to do. During the night he lay on his bed thinking and thinking and thinking. Suddenly, he jumped up. He had just thought of a wonderful idea!

Subhi ran to the empty bazaar and climbed a big, tall palm tree. He pushed his shoes into a cluster of dates. Subhi smiled. "Now, dear shoes," he said "you can stay here forever, and no one will ever bother you!"

The next day the bazaar was full. Sadia was selling her hijabs, Firas was selling his fish, Abdurahman was selling his bread, Tarek was shouting out, "Buy tasty falafil! Come and buy my falafil!" People crowded around Asiya to buy her tasty spinach pies, and Jawad was busy taking off melons from his donkey's side baskets.

There was a strong wind that began to blow and blow. It blew so hard that it threw Subhi's shoes out of the palm tree onto Jawad's donkey.

"Eeeyaw! Eeeyaw!" brayed the donkey kicking up his legs.

Jawad's melons flew everywhere. Pieces of broken melon were on Sadia's hijabs, on the fish, on the spinach pies, on the bread and falafil. The people were furious!

Abdurahman held up an old tatty pair of shoes.

"Subhi's shoes!" they shouted. Everyone marched off to Subhi's house.

"Here are your shoes, Subhi," they said. "We think you should keep them on your feet."

"Yes" said Subhi, "that's just where they belong!"

Subhi put away his new shoes and put on his old, worn-out shoes. Then he took a walk through the city. And guess what? No one ever made fun of his shoes again!

Gohar the Tailor — A Tale for Eid by Fawzia Gilani

Long, long ago there lived a poor young tailor. His name was Gohar. Orphaned at a young age, Gohar had worked hard for all the blessings he had. He never missed his prayers, and whatever little he had, he always shared with the poor. This is what won him the admiration of his wife to be, Farah. Gohar's wedding day was the best day of his life. He felt that he had married the kindest girl in the whole wide world.

Everyone in the town had come to celebrate Gohar's wedding. Everyone was so happy. Everyone that is, except for Rujza. Rujza was the richest man in town. He was also a staunch miser. Since he had the most wealth, he had expected tall, beautiful Farah to marry him. But Farah did not care for the miser. She wanted to marry the man that praised Allah five times a day and spent freely on the poor. Gohar was just a poor tailor, and this angered Rujza all the more. How could a penniless tailor be chosen above him? His pride was greatly wounded.

From the day that Gohar and Farah got married, Rujza plotted and schemed. He swore he would have his revenge. His evil heart bore all kinds of malice toward the sweet couple. Whenever Rujza saw Gohar walking toward the mosque, he would sneer at him and mutter terrible things.

Gohar and Farah were so constant in their remembrance of God and so busy filling their day with good deeds that they were unaware of Rujza's jealousy. During the Eids, Gohar made it his concern that all orphans and widows had new clothes to wear. As the years went by, Gohar and Farah had three little children. But the years did not make the rich Rujza lessen his hate. By and by, Gohar became richer and richer. He bought a large house with fruit trees, a beautiful garden, and a barnyard full of animals.

As Rujza's grand carriage drove past Gohar's splendid house, the rich land owner's face grew dark and menacing. One terrible day, Rujza's wicked thoughts became real. Rujza hired a tailor from another town. The new tailor began to take Gohar's customers. Gohar had less and less work, and so it became more and more difficult to pay the bills.

But Rujza's evil heart was still not content. Gohar and his family still lived in their house with a pretty garden, fruit trees, and barnyard full of animals. Rujza's devious mind set to work again. Finally, he had another evil plan. Rujza was an important town official, so he passed a law that people living in large houses had to pay one hundred pieces of gold. This was all the money that Gohar had hidden away. Times became so hard for Gohar and Farah that they had to sell their beautiful house and their animals and move into a humble little house.

This sad news delighted Rujza so much that he threw himself a party. He laughed all day and night. Meanwhile, Gohar and Farah kept strong in their faith. Gohar read the family a verse, "And bear with patient fortitude whatever befalls you."

As the months passed by, the family struggled to be clothed and fed. For two weeks, Gohar had no customers. He was forced to sell his tools and material and work for Rujza's tailor. Rujza made sure that Gohar was only paid a very small wage. Farah and the children went to work at an orchard. The family sold all their belongings. They had very little left in their tiny home. But they took comfort in the verses they read,

"And put your trust in God, for God alone is sufficient as a Guardian." (33:3)

It was Ramadan, and Gohar and his family walked to the mosque to offer the tarawih prayer. Rujza watched them. Their shoes were old and worn and their clothes faded and patched. Finally, Rujza was satisfied. He skipped and jumped around the room, seeing how low Gohar and his family had fallen.

But if Gohar and his family minded their poverty, they did not show it. Their smiles were still the same, warm and friendly. They still greeted everyone with salaam, and they never missed their prayers.

One Ramadan evening, as the family sat huddled around their tiny fire, Gohar told the children the story of Prophet Job, peace be upon him. It was a story about patience. The family took comfort in the story and thanked God for his many blessings.

Gohar's son was looking forward to the Night of Power. A blessed night that came but once a year. Farah had told her children that it was called *Layla-ul-Qadr* and that, during this night, whatever deeds were done were rewarded as if they had been done for a thousand months.

"It is as God tells us," explained Farah, "the Night of Power is better than a thousand months, and on that night the Angel Gabriel descends."

"Mother!" exclaimed Rayan, the youngest. "Wouldn't it be so wonderful if the angel came to visit us on Layla-ul-Qadr?"

Farah smiled and nodded.

During Ramadan, the family kept their fast with a piece of bread and a glass of milk and broke it with the leftover fruit from the orchard that the farmer did not want. Meanwhile, Rujza ate lavish meals all day long. Never did he once think of sharing his food with the poor.

During one of the last ten nights of Ramadan, there was a knock at the door. The family had returned from Tarawih prayer and were sitting on their prayer mats, reading Qur'an. Gohar went to the door and opened it.

"Asalaamu alaikum," said Gohar.

"Wa alaikum salaam," answered the stranger. "I need a place to rest for a while. I wonder if I can warm myself by your fire?"

"Welcome! Welcome!" cried Gohar. "Please, make yourself at home."

There was only one small log burning in the fireplace. The stranger held his hands out to the fire and rubbed them. He looked at the children and smiled.

Farah hurried to the kitchen to bring the stranger some milk and bread. But the stranger asked only to drink some water. The stranger wanted to offer some duas with the family for their kindness.

As the stranger turned to leave, he recited a verse from the Qur'an. "Remember the words of Allah," he said,

"And bear with patient fortitude whatever befalls you."

And then he took out of his pocket a small bag. "A gift for Eid," smiled the stranger and he left.

The children were eager to open the bag, but Farah reminded them that they must concentrate on their prayers, since this was one of nights of Qadr. All night long, the children prayed, sometime dozing off to sleep, but then awakening and reading more Qur'an, offering more prayers.

Tomorrow would be the day of Eid. And so Gohar spent all night sewing and stitching some Eid clothes for his children. He took one of his shirts and sewed it to fit his son. Then he took one of Farah's dresses and made two dresses from it for his daughters.

When Farah saw the clothes, she smiled. "They look like new!" she exclaimed.

When the children returned from Eid prayer, they remembered the gift of the stranger.

"Let's open the bag!" cried the children excitedly.

When Farah emptied the bag onto the table, everyone stepped back in amazement. They couldn't believe their eyes. There lay twenty sparkling and glittering diamonds.

"God sent them from heaven," whispered the youngest child, his eyes wide and shining.

"Come," said Gohar, "let us share this gift with the poor."

With the money left over, Gohar was able to buy back his tools and, once again, his business flourished. For the rest of their days, Gohar and Farah lived a comfortable life, always thanking Allah for His blessings. As for Rujza, he remained miserly and bitter for a long, long time. But they say that the older he grew, the more he changed for the better.

FROM GOD WE COME BY FAWZIA GILANI

The trees were swaying gently in the wind. It seemed like Mother Nature was comforting them. The rain had just begun to fall. It was a peaceful scene. I opened the window and a fresh gust of air and rain brushed against my face. The sprinkles made me think of wudu. Soon, it would be time to offer Dhur. I looked across at the neighbor's house. They had decorated their porch for Eid with white lights hanging from the rails and bushes. There were crescent-shaped moons dangling from the trees. It looked festive. It looked warm, inviting and happy. But there were no decorations on our house.

The last two Eids had been the same. We would stay with Aunty Farah and Uncle Gohar. Eid was always fun with Aunty Farah. She would cook a hundred different treats, and Uncle Gohar would decorate the whole house and have so many wonderful Eid games for us to play. Our cousins were so loving and kind, too. Especially Nayab – she would spend hours wrapping our gifts and hiding Eid money pouches in unusual places.

Even though we had such a wonderful time with Aunty Farah and Uncle Gohar, we still missed Eid with Mom and Dad. Last night, my twin brothers, Lute and Hud, had been reminiscing about the Eids we used to have with Mom. Their room was opposite mine, and the doors were left open so that, on some nights, I could tell them stories about our heroes, the messengers of Allah, peace be upon them…just like Mom used to do. Last night, I lay awake listening to them. They spoke in loud whispers. As I listened, the memories flooded back. My throat tightened.

It was going to be Eid in another two days. My brothers and I were packing our bags, ready to go to Aunty Farah's.

"Why doesn't Dad like Eid?" asked Lute.

"You ask me that every Eid. You know why," I answered.

I continued folding my blue khimar. Mom had bought it for me. She had bought it for Eid, the Eid the year before she died. She had bought another for herself that was grey. It was her favorite khimar. "It's so comfortable and easy to wear," she would say. I stopped my thoughts, knowing that, if I let them wander, I would soon feel a lump in my throat. Lute's mouth was still open.

"Is that hard to do?" I asked. "Holding your mouth open for so long?"

Lute whined something about Dad and Eid. I tried to look busy, straightening the clothes in my luggage carrier.

"Eid is the day that Allah ta Ala wanted Mom to come and see Him," I answered in a casual way.

"How come Allah chose Eid to call Mom? Why not another day?" asked Lute.

"Because *lilahi ma fisamawatehwa ma fil ard. To Allah belong all that is in the heavens and the earth.*(2:284) He's Allah, and He can do what He likes, and He has Wisdom and Judgment and…we don't," I said matter-of-factly.

"Doesn't seem right," mused Lute.

"*Astagfirullah,*" I said, "that sounds like such a *haraam* thing to say. *Subhan Allah*, Lute, I can't believe some of the things that come out of your mouth!"

"*La hawla wa la quwata ilabillah,*" said Hud, looking at his twin in dismay. "I'll help you ask for forgiveness, Lute," he said anxiously. They both went down to the ground.

"Sorry, Allah. *Rabana la tawa khidh na aa inna seena aw akh tana* Our Lord! Condemn us not if we forget or fall into error!" (2:286). Please forgive us. We love you. *Astaghfirullah, astaghfirullah, astaghfirullah…*" they chimed.

Hud turned his head to face me and said, "You can help too, you know."

Slowly, I slipped to the floor. I put my face down, careful that my nose and forehead touched the carpet. Softly I chanted, "Allah, please forgive us," then I added, "*astaghfiru rabakum inahu kana gafaran (* 71:10) Ask forgiveness from your Lord; for He is Oft Forgiving." The carpet was soft and smelled of lavender. After a while I sat up. The twins rolled on their backs and looked up at the ceiling. Whenever we called on Allah, we felt like Allah's Merciful Hand of Love and Protection was on us. Mom used to remind us of the verse, "When My servants ask you concerning Me, I am indeed close to them: I listen to the prayer of every suppliant when he calls on Me." (2:186). We always felt that Allah was close to us, and that He answered our prayers in the way that was best for our imaan and life.

"But Baji" continued Hud, "just because Mom is with Allah now, it doesn't mean that Dad can't do Eid with us."

I reflected on the words. Finally, I looked at Hud and said, "It's complicated…adults have complicated feelings. And life is complicated, and I suppose…it's painful for Dad. He thinks of Mom and…he feels sad. Eid is a time of joy and happiness. How can Dad feel happy if he's thinking about…"

Just then, the adhan clock began the call to prayer. We stopped our conversation and repeated the words quietly, just as Mom had taught us. After the adhan was completed, we held up our hands and made dua.

"Allahumma rabba hadhihi-d-da'awati-t-tammati wa-s-Salati-l-qa'imati, ati Muhammadan il-wasilata wa-l-fadilata wa-d-darajata-r-rafi'ati wa-b'ath-hu maqamam mahmudan illadhi wa'adtahu.

0 Allah, Lord of this most perfect call, and of the Prayer that is about to be established, grant to Muhammad the favor of nearness (to You) and excellence and a place of distinction, and exalt him to a position of glory that You have promised him."

"Do I have wudu?" asked Lute.

"I don't know," said Hud. "Did you go to the bathroom?"

"I don't know," said Lute, "I can't remember."

"Well, just do it again," advised Hud.

The twins speed-walked to the bathroom; Dad didn't allow running in the house. I went downstairs and laid out the prayer mats. Dad was reading a volume of the Qur'an. The volume was old and worn. It was Mom's wedding gift.

It seemed as if, wherever I looked, Mom's presence was there. As I stared at the book, a memory came flooding back. I remembered Dad saying, "Zaynab, your Mom didn't ask for money or jewels for her dowry; she just wanted sixteen volumes of Qur'an tafsir." Then I imagined Mom's laughter. I could hear her in my head. I smiled. She said, "What better gift for a bride than the explanations of the words of Allah?"

But Dad didn't really speak about Mom very much anymore.

Dad looked up from his book and said, "Zaynab, call the boys. It's time for *Salah.*"

"They're coming Dad; they're making *wudu*," I answered.

"Did you finish packing," asked Dad as he placed the volume back in the shelf, kissing it gently before he did.

"*Alhamdulilah*, we're almost finished, but we still have to wrap the presents for Nayab, Manal, and…erm…baby Rayan."

"Remember to take the *Eidi* envelopes," said Dad. "They're by the *adhan* clock."

"*Insha' Allah*," I said, "I'll remember."

Lute did *iqamah*, and Hud was imam. After we had finished offering *salah*, we went back to our packing. I handed the twins a checklist, so they could be sure they had everything.

"Baji, wouldn't it have made more sense to give this to us *before* we packed our cases?" asked Hud, feeling annoyed.

The phone was ringing. After two more rings, I heard Dad's voice. "*Asalaamu alaikum*. Oh, Farah, *kya haal heh*. How are you?"

There was a pause followed by Dad's usual hmms, haas, and casual comments. After a while, I heard Dad call, "Zaynab? Your aunty wants to talk with you, *Betah*."

I glided down the stairs and took the phone. Aunty Farah asked me how I was, and then she asked me if we were packed. She told me that she and Aunty Wajiya had made me a shiny grey Eid suit. She couldn't wait for me to try it on. Nayab and Manal had one just like it, too. I loved listening to Aunty Farah's voice. She sounded just like Mom, and she looked like her, too. I couldn't wait to be with her. I pressed the phone tightly to my ear and closed my eyes. I kept asking her questions so I could hear her voice. It was like listening to Mom.

After getting off the phone I wondered which khimar I could wear with the Eid suit. Then I remembered Mom's grey khimar. I went in Dad's room and looked in the large closet, but couldn't find it. Then I went through the drawers and chests. I couldn't find it anywhere. I began to feel irritable, and then desperate. I couldn't find Mom's favorite khimar. It was gone, just like Mom. My eyes filled with tears. I needed to hide. So I hurried into the bathroom and locked the door. I grabbed a towel, like I had done many times before, and suddenly huge sobs poured out. I suffocated them with the towel.

Mom always said make *wudu* when you felt upset. I turned the tap. Cold water came rushing out. I held my face close to it, feeling the spray hit against my cheek. I splashed water on my face; it felt good. It cooled my hot, swollen eyes.

I walked back into my room, hoping that no one would notice me.

"Baji, Baji," called Lute, "Can you help me zip my bag?"

"Bajo! Baji !Baaaj! Baaaaajeeeeee!"

I let out a deep sigh and followed the noise.

"Oh, there you are," he said with a scowl on his face. "I can't close it!"

I looked at the suitcase. "I think you have a little too much in here, Lute," I said, understating the fact.

He looked at me with a frown, and then his expression changed.

"Have you been crying?" he asked.

I opened Lute's suitcase. I pulled out the oversized pillow. "You can't take this, Lute," I told him.

I zipped up Lute's suitcase and went downstairs.

Dad was in the kitchen stirring a pot of soup. The vegetables for the salad had been washed and were ready to chop up.

"Shall I do the salad, Dad?" I asked.

"*Inshallah*, Betah, but be careful not to cut yourself. Cut away from your hand," he instructed. He always gave the same advice every time we had to use a knife.

As I cut the cucumber, I tried to think of ways I could ask Dad where Mom's grey khimar was. But I didn't know how to ask him. It wasn't easy to talk about Mom with Dad. It felt awkward. The cucumbers, tomatoes, onions, and lettuce were chopped.

I told myself to just say it. It would probably come out wrong anyway. So, under my breath, I began with Allah's name, *Bismillah hirama niraheem*, in the name of God most Gracious most Merciful.

"Dad?" I said. He never answered straightaway. I counted eight *SubhanAllahs*.

"Yes, Zaynab?" he replied finally.

"Aunty Farah made me a shiny grey Eid suit."

Hud had heard me count numbers one time to see how long Dad would take to answer. He told me do *tasbih* rather than numbers. "Then your angels will write them as a good deed. You'll get so much *hasanat*…and so will I for telling you! And so will Mom for telling me." He laughed.

"Nayab and Manal have a *shalwar-kameez* suit just like mine." I added.

"Yes, your Aunty Farah has always been good at sewing; she can sew even better than your…" Dad stopped. He didn't finish his sentence. He never really did when it came to talking about Mom. "I think I need to put some *garam masala* in the soup," he said.

"Dad, which *khimar* shall I wear with it?" I asked.

"Your aunty always makes a *khimar* with the suits she sews for you, doesn't she?" said Dad. He turned and looked at me and smiled. I smiled back.

"Yes...but maybe she forgot to make it this one time," I said. "And, anyway, Aunty Farah's *khimars* aren't like the ones I wear. They're nice, but they have to have a pin. Maybe there's a *khimar* in the house I could wear." I said.

Dad was taking the *routis* out of the freezer. He placed them in a sheet of foil, and then placed them in the oven.

"Dad, I was...I was looking for one in...in the closet...in your room." I waited for Dad to say something, but he didn't. So I tried again.

"Dad, I wanted to wear Mom's grey khimar for Eid." There, I thought, I finally said it. I counted twelve *Allahu Akbars*.

We didn't talk anymore. I finished doing the salad, and Dad put the food in bowls and plates. He called the twins to set the table.

We all made *dua* before we ate, and Hud added a *dua* of his own like he always did. Today, he prayed that Allah would feed all the children in the world. "Please, Allah," he begged, "don't leave a single one of them hungry." When he had finished his plea, Dad asked us if we knew what day it was tomorrow.

There was silence. Nobody spoke. Nobody ate. Dad looked at us, puzzled. "Didn't your teachers remind you what day it is tomorrow?" asked Dad.

We looked at each other. Dad raised his eyebrows – surprised. "It's *Yaum-ul-Arafah*; it's a day of fasting. Remember?" he said.

"O *Arafah*!" we all chorused, nodding at each and smiling.

"We knew that, Dad," said Hud. "The Prophet Muhammad, peace be upon him, told us that if we fast the Day of *Arafah* for the pleasure of God, then our sins for the past year and year to come will be forgiven."

"*Mashallah!*" said Dad, nodding and smiling approvingly.

I ate my meal slowly. Thoughts passed through my mind. Thoughts of Mom. My thoughts were interrupted. I looked up. "Yes Dad?" I said.

"What are you thinking?" he asked. "You've hardly eaten your food."

"Oh...nothing," I answered. "Nothing, really." Then suddenly I said, "I was thinking about Mom's grey khimar for Eid." I looked in Dad's eyes.

"Oh," said Dad, and as usual he paused for a long time. "Maybe I can help you look for it later," he added.

"*Jazak Allah khairan*, Dad," I said, trying not to sound excited. "I'll wash the dishes, *inshallah*."

"*Barak Allah fi kum*," replied Dad.

"Thanks, Baji" said Hud, "because it was my turn to do the dishes!" But I didn't mind.

The twins cleared the table, and I hurriedly washed the dishes. As I dried my hands, Dad handed me a small silver key. It was to the attic. Dad always told us not to go up there because he had important papers and things that he didn't want us to disturb. Lute and I always wanted to sneak up and take a look, but Hud would constantly recite Qur'anic passages or *hadith* reminding us to obey our parents. "*Wa wa seena al insana biwalidena husna*, I have enjoined on people kindness to parents (29:8)." Hud was like our conscience. "Do a bad thing!" he would warn us. "Go ahead! You'll bring ruin on your parent's souls! Is that what you want?" Hud was such a drama king.

"There's small chest of drawers in the attic. Maybe it's in there," said Dad without looking at me.

I hurried up the stairs. I hurried so quickly that I missed a step and fell on my stomach. I grabbed a rail to stop myself from sliding down. I made a loud thud.

"Are you okay?" yelled Dad.

"*Alhamdulilah*, I'm okay," I shouted back, trying to fake a normal voice. I sat on a step and gritted my teeth. My leg had scraped against a step, and it hurt. I sat there for a long time. I was in a lot of pain.

I climbed the last few steps slowly. There was a silver lock hanging from the door. I held it up and slipped in the key. The key turned, snapping open the lock. I removed the lock and opened the latch. My hand was sweating as I put it on the door handle. I turned it slowly. My heart was beating so loud that it almost hurt. I ran my hand along the wall to feel for a switch. I found it and flicked it up. The room lit up. It was clean, but smelled a little musty. There were boxes piled neatly in one corner, and a chest of drawers in another corner. I could tell that Aunty Farah had been here. Everything was so neat. A filing cabinet and a bookshelf were against a wall with a tiny window. A large armchair was in one corner with a small side table next to it.

I walked over to the armchair and sat in it. It was Mom's special armchair. She had always liked to sit in it, and sometimes I would sit with her. I cuddled up in the armchair and closed my eyes, trying to imagine that I was sitting in Mom's lap, and she was gently nursing my hurt leg. As I opened my eyes, I saw a photo album with Zaynab written on it. Oooooh! It was my memory book that Mom had bought me. I picked it up and sat back down in the armchair. The album was bulky. I opened the cover. Mom had taped my hospital identity bracelet in it. It said, "Bukhari, 7 lb., girl." Underneath, Mom had written notes about what times I had been asleep and awake in the hospital.

I turned the page, and there was a picture of me on Mom's lap. She was wearing a dark blue khimar. She was smiling and looking at Nani-Ama. She didn't take many pictures, she didn't really like to, and she never allowed pictures to be displayed. "The angels might get upset," she would say. "We don't want to offend them because *wal malaikatu yewsabihuwna bi hamdi rabihim wa yastagfiruna liman fil ardeh.* And the angels celebrate the praises of their lord and pray for forgiveness for all beings on earth (42:5)."

There was a copy of my birth certificate, and then some more pictures. There were pages with scribbles that I had done, and Mom had put those in there, too, and lots and lots of drawings of pretty dresses. "Oh!" Mom would say, "Oh! I never saw such a pretty dress; you couldn't possibly have drawn it!" Mom always marveled at my work.

Suddenly, I heard Dad's voice call up to me.

"Did you find it yet?" he asked.

I placed the album down and hobbled quickly to the door.

"No, Dad! I'm still looking," I answered. I waited for a few moments, listening to see if there were footsteps coming up. But it was quiet. I hobbled back to the armchair and opened up the album again. There was a golden chocolate wrapper under one sheet. Mom had written a note about how I thought it would get me into Willy Wonka's chocolate factory. I smiled. Mom's childhood friend, Aunty Somiah, had given it to me when she came to visit from England.

My baby tooth was taped there, too. Mom wrote how I had put the whole memory book under my pillow with a letter to the tooth angel. It said, "Dere Angel mi mom says I can't take out my tooth from the book so I put the book under mi pillow so you can see it." I turned another page; Mom had copied out an *ayat* from surah Nisa:

Aynama yakunu yudrikkumu al mawtuwa. Wherever you are death will find you out. (4:78)

Aladhi khalaqal mawta wal hayataliyabluma kum ayukum ahsanu amalan. He who created Death and Life, that He may try which of you is best in deed. (67:2)

Kulu nafsin dha aa ikatul mawtee thumma ilayna tur jaoon. Wala dheena amanu wa amilusaliuhati lanubawee anahum minal janati ghurafan tajree min tahti hal anharu khalidena fiha nima ajrul amileen. Aladheena sabaru wa ala rabihim yatawakaloon.

Every soul shall have a taste of death in the end to Me shall you be brought back but those who believe and work deeds of righteousness to them shall I give a home in heaven – lofty mansions beneath which flow rivers – to dwell there for yes, an excellent reward for those who do good, those who persevere in patience and put their trust in their Lord and Cherisher. (29:57-59)

When I finished the verses I whispered to Allah, "Ya Allah. It's very hard...very, very, very hard."

I looked down at the page again. Mom had written "We belong to Allah and we should love to go back to Him but know that He is the One that decides the best time until then serve Him and serve humanity."

I put the memory album away and walked over to the chest of draws. I looked through the top two, but didn't find the khimar. Then I got down on my knees and opened the lowest draw. It didn't slip out like the rest. It seemed stuck. I moved it side to side, and then it popped out.

There it was the grey khimar! The Eid khimar! My mom's Eid khimar! I held it close to me and hugged it. I smelled it, hoping to find Mom's scent in it. I immediately made *sujud* again; I thanked Allah for letting me find it. *Allahu mawlakum wa huwa khayrun nasireen.* Allah is your protector and he is the best of helpers. (3:150)

The next day, as we drove to Aunty Farah's, we were so hungry. Lute complained about his growling stomach. Dad told him that we would be going to the mosque first, since it was almost Maghrib time. "We'll break our fast there, *inshallah*," he said.

When we got out of the car at Aunty Farah's, we could smell her delicious food. Hud and Lute ran up to Uncle Gohar and gave him a big hug.

I ran inside to look for Aunty Farah. When I saw her, she already had tears in her eyes. I buried myself into her and held her for a long time. She stroked my head gently. I felt her body tremble. My throat felt so, so, so tight.

"Waji!" called Aunty Farah, trying to hide her feeling. "*Theko kitni bari haw gee.* Look how big she got."

Aunty Wajiya gently pulled me from Aunty Farah and hugged me tightly.

I wanted to cry and sob, but I knew Dad would feel bad, and I knew Aunty Farah would cry harder than me. I mustered enough strength to stay calm.

"Aunty, *bohth bukh laghi heh*," I said, trying to change the mood. It worked. Aunty Farah jumped into hostess mode. She was so funny. She already had the dining table ready with food. She kept piling things on our plates. They were such yummy things, too.

It was getting late. After offering Isha in jamaat, Dad said that he had to get back home.

"*Subha jileh jana, fajr ke baad*, leave tomorrow after fajr," said Aunty Farah.

Dad shook his head. He climbed down the porch steps. Uncle Gohar went after him. They both stood at the gate.

"*Kya masebat yar?*" said Uncle Gohar.

Their voices were low; I strained my ears to listen.

"I can't stay," said Dad. "I can't."

"You need to be with the children," said Uncle Gohar.

"Maybe next Eid," sighed Dad.

"*Yar*, that's what you said last Eid," replied Uncle Gohar. He put his hand on Dad's shoulder. Dad hung his head; he turned his face away to the street. Dad's shoulders trembled. Uncle Gohar looked like he was going to cry. I went back inside.

I looked through my bag and took out the *Eidi* envelopes for my cousins.

"What's that?" asked Nayab.

"It's your *Eidi*," I replied.

"Did you want to hide them?" asked Nayab. Her eyes were wide, and her eyebrows raised, and she had a big beautiful, happy smile on her face.

"Okay," I said, "but you have to sit outside on the porch and promise not to look."

"Do two hundred *Subhan Allahs*, and then you can come in the house," I instructed. I darted inside and began to look for places to hide the money-gift envelopes.

Aunty Wajiya motioned to me and pointed to the flour bin. "Hide it under here," she whispered. By the time Nayab was in the house, I had hidden all three envelopes.

Aunty Farah was calling from the dining room. "Who wants to put mehndi on?" she asked. Manal, Nayab, and I jostled into the dining room, hoping to be first.

"Go and use the bathroom first," said Aunty Farah in a non-negotiable tone. It was a sensible suggestion. It was a nice feeling to have mendhi on our hands. I loved the smell of the mixture, and I loved the attention. Aunty Waji and Farah would sit for a long time, drawing intricate patterns on our palms and fingers. That was something Mom never did. She didn't like to wear mendhi; she was always concerned that she might have an allergic reaction.

The worst part was the sitting down afterwards. It was so boring, and every few minutes we would ask, "Has it been on long enough now?"

All three of us were sitting in the living room with our palms facing the ceiling, and we couldn't touch a thing for fear of staining it.

Lute came in with Abdussamad, who lived next door. "Are you wearing that stinky stuff again?" he asked.

"Bradder Lute," said Abdussamad, "eeets naat stinky staff. The Prophet salalahu alai he wa salaam…" All of us chorused the peace and blessings of Allah on the Prophet.

"…used henna, too."

Abdussamad was in Nayab's class. He would always tell us about his country, Uzbekistan.

"I didn't mean to say that it was bad; it just smells weird to me," defended Lute.

"*Inala dheena amanu wa amilusalihati ula ika hum khayrul bariya.* (98:7) Doze who have fait and do rijus deeds – dey are de best of creatures," said Abdussamad.

"Just cuz they're wearing mendhi, doesn't mean they have faith and are doing righteous deeds and are the best of creatures," said Lute.

"I know," said Abdussamad. "I'm just telling you to say good tings, dat's all. So insha'Allah you can be da best crecher."

"Oh," said Lute, giving Abdussamad a smile and a pat in the back.

Dad had gone back home. I knew he was going to visit Mom at the cemetery. Dad had never taken us. But we visited Mom lots of times with Aunty Farnaz. Mom had always said that when she first saw Aunty Farnaz she thought she was an angel from Allah. When Mom started getting ill, she couldn't cook anymore. Dad had to go to work. One day, Mom started crying and saying she didn't know who was going to feed her children during the day. Dad felt so bad, he tried to cook meals, but they were always yucky, but we didn't tell him that. Then Dr. Akbar came to our home with his wife, Aunty Farnaz, and brought so much food and drink. For the next few months, until Mom got better, Aunty Farnaz would cook delicious meals and leave them in the fridge. Mom told us that Aunty Farnaz and Dr. Akbar had to be angels, because they would bring the food in the middle of winter and the dark of the night with their three sleepy children. The roads were filled with snow, ice, and gusting winds, but they still came.

Aunty Farnaz was always a great source of comfort. She would always share verses from the Qur'an or *hadith* with us that made us understand life and death, pain and sorrow as a trial from Allah. "Everything is a test; Allah wants to test us with the things we love most," she would tell us.

The story of Prophet Job, peace be upon him, gave us a wonderful sense of patience. After hearing it, Hud remarked, "We sure are lucky that Allah, *subhana wa ta ala*, didn't take away Dad, our house, our health, our money, our friends, our looks – gosh!"

I remembered the day that Mom died. I had taken a copy of the Qur'an with me to the hospital, and as soon as I opened it, it opened on *Sura Yaseen*. I remember thinking at the time *Surah Yaseen* is read to the dying. I knew then that Mom was going to die. *Mamoo* Bilal was at her bedside, reciting the verses. I thought perhaps it was Allah's way of preparing me. I stopped begging Allah to save Mom. I began begging Him to give her a spacious grave. The doctors kept telling us that Mom would pull through. But I knew she wouldn't.

When we visited Mom, we would sprinkle green leaves all over her grave. We would make *dua*. Sometimes we would cry for her, and sometimes Aunty Farnaz would, too. Sometimes we would tell her what we were doing or talk about the weather. Sometimes in dreams Mom would visit Aunty Farnaz, and sometimes she would visit us. We loved sharing our dreams. We listened to each other and asked so many questions. What did she say? Did she ask about me? What was she wearing? Did she look happy? Did she look sad? We missed Mom sooo much. "It's just a matter of time before we all see her," Aunty Farnaz comforted us. "And for your patience for living without your mom, Allah will give you a rich reward in heaven, *inshallah*."

After we had come back from offering *Salat-ul-Eid*, we played Hide and Seek *Eidi*. Hud found his envelope of money in between the pages of the Qur'an. Mine was under the towels in the closet. Lute hadn't been able to find his. All day long, people came and visited, wishing everyone Eid Mubarak. People would look at us in a we-feel-sorry-for-you way.

The evening was ruined because Uncle Gohar had to leave; his beeper went off and that meant he had to go to the hospital to help a patient. We all groaned, and then we all begged him to stay. But then he said, "*Innala dheena amanu wa amilusalihati ula ika hum khayrul bareeya*. Those who have faith and do righteous deeds – they are the best of creatures." (98:7) So we all released him and told him to help the sick and needy for the pleasure of Allah.

Two days later, Dad came to collect us. He was so glad to see us. He always took my hand and kissed it as though I were a princess, then he'd kiss my head. Lute and Hud were all over him. Dad was laughing. It was nice to hear him laugh. On our trip home, the twins talked almost nonstop about what we did at Aunty Farah's. Dad would occasionally laugh or ask a question. Hud tapped me and made a gesture with his thumb, touching each segment of his forefinger. I nodded to let him know that I was doing it, too. Whenever we went on car rides, we would always remind each other to do *tasbih* on our fingers. But it was normally always Hud who reminded us.

He was teaching himself to be a Qur'an Hafiz using cassettes. He said he wanted to surprise Mom on the Day of Judgment. "She'll wonder why she's wearing a crown, and then some angel will tell her that I memorized the Qur'an." But Hud wasn't just memorizing the Qur'an; he was memorizing the translation, too. "You have to know what you're saying. When you know the meaning of the words, your love for Allah grows!"

I wanted to ask Dad what he did while we were visiting our cousins. I don't know why asking Dad questions was always so difficult.

"Dad?" I said. I started counting *Alhamdulilahs.* I counted three.

"Yes, Zaynab?"

"What did you do for Eid?" I asked.

"I visited," answered Dad in a casual voice, "and I went to work."

I leaned up closer to him so I could hear better.

"Did you visit Mom?" I asked in as much of a casual voice as I could muster.

"I went to see your mom," said Dad almost immediately.

"Oh," I said, and then I rested back against the seat. We all exchanged looks. We all smiled at each other.

"Can we go and visit her with you, Dad?" asked Hud.

"I don't know if—" began Dad.

"But we go there all the time, Dad," said Lute.

"Go where?" asked Dad, sounding confused.

"To see Mom," answered Lute.

After a while, I recognized the roads and streets that led to the cemetery. Finally, Dad parked the car. We all climbed out of the car, except Dad.

"Dad, aren't you coming?" asked Lute.

"No, son," said Dad, "You go, and I'll wait here. I can watch you from here."

"You can come with us Dad," said Hud.

We walked to Mom's grave and sat down and began to mumble our own private *duas.*

The ground was flat now with grass grown over it. When I first came, there were big clods of earth, and the grave looked so unkempt. I remember breaking the clods with my hands as if I were making the bed covers look neat. There had been large stones and pieces of brick. I had tossed them into a nearby hedge. We sat by the graveside while Hud recited the new *surahs* he had learned.

Aunty Farnaz told us that some people believe the dead cannot hear. But we told her we didn't mind. Coming to visit Mom reminded us that, one day, we would be lying under the ground, too. It made us more aware of Allah and our duty as believers.

When it was time to go, we sprinkled green leaves on Mom's grave.

The Prophet, peace be upon him, had said that if a twig with green leaves was put on the grave, then the inhabitant would be spared any punishment for the time that the leaves stayed green.

Lute said that he wanted to plant an evergreen bush over Mom's grave. But I told him it wasn't Sunnah.

Dad was sitting under a tree a little way from the car. We walked over to him. Lute sat in his lap.

"Are you okay?" asked Dad.

"*Alhamdulilah*," we answered.

"Dad, are you okay?" asked Hud.

Dad shook his head, "Not really son," said Dad. His face wore a smile. But his eyes looked very sad. I held his hand. Hud laid his head against Dad's shoulder. And Lute put his head on Dad's chest.

"Dad," said Lute, "the pain of losing Mom will never leave us. But this is how Allah made us. We'll ask Allah to give us patience until we are with Mom again."

Dad recited a beautiful verse that brought a swell of tears to my eyes.

"*Wa adhkur abdu na aa ayuba idh naa da rabahu ani masanishaytanu binusbin wa adhabin, arkudh birijlika hadha mugh tasalunbaridun washarab.* Commemorate My servant, Job. Behold he cried to his Lord: 'The evil one has afflicted me with distress and suffering!' The command was given 'Strike with your foot. Here is water with which to wash, cool and refreshing, and water to drink.'" (38:41)

"Dad," asked Lute, "will Allah send us special water to take our pain away, like He sent for Prophet Job?"

Dad looked at Lute.

"Allah sends us 'water' every day, Lute, every day. Our water is the Qur'an. It will heal our pain through the remembrance of Allah."

We all whispered Ameen.

"Dad," said Hud, "can we spend next Eid with you?"

Dad nodded. "Inshallah," said Dad. "I promise."

We drove home. I could tell that things were going to be different. I was glad.

Masarah and the Eligible Bachelors by Fawzia Gilani

My big sister's name is Mariam, but I don't call her Mariam. I call her Baji, which means big sister. I always tell everyone that my baji is the best sister in the whole wide world. And there are lots of reasons why, but I'll just share a few of them with you, because otherwise it would take too long!

My baji is fifteen years older than me. We do everything together. We cook together, we read Qur'an together, we climb trees together, and we pray together. We share the same room. Baji even lets me wear her khimars, even her best ones! She takes me to the library, she takes me shopping, and she takes me everywhere.

Baji even helps me with my homework and listens to me read; she's very good at explaining things. Mummy says Baji has to be good at explaining things because she's a teacher. She is, too. Sometimes my Baji takes me to her school. Her students all call her Miss Naqvi or Teacher. I really like going to Baji's school. She lets me do fun things. She even lets me read a story to the children. I feel very important and grownup. Baji's like my second mom. I just can't imagine life without her.

If I'm not hanging around with my Baji, I sometimes spend time with my best friend, Helen. She lives on the same street as I do. Sometimes she comes to my home to play. We walk home together from school, which isn't very far from where I live.

One day, I was walking home with Helen, and I said, "My mom's cooking samosahs today. Would you like to stay and eat?" I knew Helen liked samosahs.

"Oooh yuuum, yes, please," said Helen, nodding at the same time.

When I walked into the house, Mummy and Dadi-Amma were in the kitchen. Dadi-Amma was reading the paper and knitting at the same time.

Dadi-Amma was Dad's mom. She lived with us. She used to be a head teacher when she lived in India. She had retired a long time ago. She was a widow now.

After I greeted everyone with salaam, I said, "Oh, Mummy, I brought Helen to try some of your samosahs."

"Come in, come in, Helen," said Mummy.

"How are you, Helen?" asked my dadi-amma.

Helen said she was fine and thanked my mom for letting her come un-invited.

"You are always invited," was my mom's usual response. Dadi-Amma particularly liked Helen. She said Helen had remarkably good manners. "She is very polite," Dadi-Amma would say. Helen always took her shoes off at the door, just like we did. We never wore outside shoes inside our home. Mummy liked that about Helen, and Dadi-Amma liked it a lot.

I heard a noise in the next room.

"Is Baji home?" I asked, thinking it was too early.

"No," said Mummy."

"Then who's in the other room?" I asked, as Mummy began to make the chapattis.

"That's your Aunty Moona," she replied, adding, "Why don't you girls wash your hands and get ready to eat?"

Helen and I washed our hands while Dadi-Amma went to her room to do her prayers. We took a long time in the bathroom, comparing the smells of the soaps. When we came downstairs, I could hear Aunty Moona talking to Mummy about Baji getting married.

Helen's eyes lit up just as mine went dim. We both froze outside the kitchen and listened.

"Well, she has to get married. It's past that time of life, and people are talking," Aunty Moona said.

At first, Mummy didn't say anything. She was clapping chapattis in her hand and slapping them down on the hot griddle. Then I heard Mummy say, "She's still young." That made me feel better. I looked at Helen and motioned her to follow.

"Asalaamu alaikum, Aunty," I said, as we walked into the kitchen and sat at the counter stools.

Aunty muttered a reply, and then continued her conversation with Mummy. There was a plate of golden, delicious samosahs. I got Helen a plate, and we both helped ourselves.

"She's twenty-five! People are saying she's over the hill!" retorted Aunty Moona.

"Finding a good match is so hard these days," said Mummy.

"For goodness sake, Farah. People have been banging your door for the past six years! Who says there aren't good boys? There are plenty of eligible bachelors, and she will have a better pick than you and I ever did!"

Mummy raised her eyebrows, but didn't say anything.

"Good, it's settled then. I have some boys in mind," said Aunty.

Mummy sighed.

When Aunty left, I looked at Mummy and shook my head. "Baji's too young to get married, Mummy," I said.

"She's twenty-five," said Mummy and slapped another chapatti in her hands.

Dadi-Amma had come back into the kitchen. She was having a conversation with Helen about clouds. My mind drifted away from how high cirrus, cumulus, and stratus were and began to focus on things that mattered in life, things that could change my life.

What if Baji were to get married? That would be devastating. I shook my head. I needed a plan – a good plan. I wanted Dadi-Amma to stop talking about clouds. Helen was looking at her watch. Her face was very pink from the hot chilies in the samosahs, and her ears were bright red, but she still liked eating them.

She told me she would see me tomorrow and thanked Mummy and Dadi-Amma.

When Helen had left, I told Dadi-Amma what Aunty Moona had said. Dadi-Amma was cross. She looked at Mummy. "Mariam is still young. Why do you want to give her more stress?" Mummy didn't say anything. "She suffers enough as a teacher. Leave her alone, leave her in peace and leave Moona to me!"

It was always good to have Dadi-Amma as a spokesperson. She didn't mince her words. She was somewhat outspoken. Mummy said Dadi-Amma didn't care about being politically correct, whatever that meant.

There had been lots of weddings. Most of Baji's friends had married when they were eighteen or nineteen. Those who had gone on to university had married when they had graduated. It seemed like Baji was the only one who hadn't married yet. I thought that was great.

It was Saturday, and a week had passed by since Aunty Moona had said her menacing words, "I have some boys in mind."

I thought Aunty Moona was very reckless. But this had caused an endless point of interest with Helen.

"What kind of boys?" said Helen.

"Ridiculously boring ones," I said.

Helen started to laugh.

"I have to come up with a plan," I said.

"Why?" asked Helen.

"Because, otherwise, some boring bachelor will marry my sister," I said.

"Is she having an arranged marriage?" asked Helen.

"If your definition of an arranged marriage is having to pick from a list of a million hopeless hopefuls, then, yes, she's having an arranged marriage."

I couldn't concentrate at school that day or, in fact, any day after that. When Mrs. Hayden asked me to answer a question, I didn't know what she was talking about.

"Sorry, Mrs. Hayden," I said, as I tightened my khimar under my chin. "My mind just went blank." I tightened my eyes to look as though I was thinking really hard. I was thinking hard, but not about my studies.

Dad had just gotten off the phone. "The guests will be here in half an hour, they lost their way," he said.

Mummy and Baji had been cleaning and preparing food all morning. Dadi-Amma and I had been shaping spicy kebab fingers that were cooking under the grill. The house was filled with the delicious aroma of kebabs, biryani, and tandoori chicken. After Aunty Moona had finished making her ras milai, she busied herself picking out what Baji should wear in front of her prospective mother-in-law.

Aunty had picked out a fancy red shalwar-kameez...the color for brides. I'd picked out something, too, a tatty brown shalwar-kameez.

"How about this, Baji?" I asked holding up the scruffy outfit.

Baji began to laugh. "Masarah! Those old clothes need to be thrown away. Where on earth did you get them?" She was right, but I tried to convince her they would do just fine. Hopefully, if she dressed like a Cinderella, her prospective mother-in-law would not be impressed.

Baji didn't wear Aunty's choice or mine. Instead, she wore her blue jilbab over her clothes. Baji was very simple when it came to fashion. She didn't wear jewelry or makeup.

"When you are in front of her, don't wear your scarf, Mariam," advised Aunty Moona. "You look prettier without it."

"Of course, she will wear her headscarf!" snapped Dadi-Amma, glaring at Aunty Moona. "My grandchild won't be paraded like a prize elephant!"

The guests had arrived. I looked outside the window to catch sight of Aunty Moona's eligible bachelor.

"Oh, Baji!" I said. "He looks like the missing link." I put my hands around my throat and scrunched up my nose.

"That's quite rude, Masarah," said Baji with a slight frown. "You mustn't speak unkindly of anyone, not even for a joke. Allah doesn't like that."

"But I wasn't joking, Take a look for yourself if you don't believe me," I said.

Baji edged over to the window and peered as discreetly as she could.

"That must be his mom in sparkly green," she said in a half whisper. "Does he look like his mom?"

"Oh, very much, more worse," I said.

Baji raised her eyebrows, "Well, then, we'll trust in the old adage – don't judge a book by its cover."

I puffed out a big fed-up sigh.

"Come on, Bubbles," said Baji, without explaining. Baji had a variety of nicknames for me, but mostly she called me Bubble Gum, because she said she loved the way I always stuck to her. It was true, and that's just how I wanted to keep it.

The men were seated in the guest room and hidden from view. Baji greeted the prospective mother-in-law. Baji's skinny figure was always hidden by the baggy-styled clothes she wore. The sparkly green lady peered at Baji. It annoyed Dadi-Amma thoroughly.

The sparkly green lady explained that her son was a doctor; he owned his own house and had two cars. Baji sat and listened. Aunty Moona listened the hardest.

"Is your son a Friday only Muslim?" asked Dadi-Amma. "Does he offer all his prayers?"

"He is a busy person; he prays when he has time," answered the sparkly green lady.

"Have some kebabs," said Mummy, trying to change the subject.

"They are very tasty. Did you make them, Mariam?" asked the lady, looking at Baji.

Before Baji could answer I said, "No, Aunty jee, Baji isn't a very good cook. In fact, she generally burns everything. Dadi-Amma made them, and I helped her."

I saw Aunty Moona roll her eyes at me.

"Would your son have a problem with my grandchild's headscarf?" asked Dadi-Amma.

There was an awkward silence.

"Well," said the sparkly lady, "no one in our family wears a headscarf; we are all educated people."

"My Mariam is also educated," said Dadi-Amma trying to sound calm. "She attended Oxford University."

"What I mean to say is that I don't mind if someone wears a scarf, but I think my son would have some reservations, because public opinion thinks that girls who wear scarves are oppressed and ignorant. My son wants a wife who doesn't give that impression."

"Yes, of course," said Dadi-Amma. "We all need to be considerate of public opinion; it's better to be sheeple than people. How do the Americans put it? Masses are asses. Perhaps you could find your son an..." but before she could end her words, Mummy interrupted. "And what part of Pakistan are you from?"

I didn't really understand what the green lady meant, but I knew she didn't like women who wore scarves. I also knew that Dadi-Amma didn't approve of her or her son.

After dinner, the family took their leave. There was lots of cleaning and washing to do.

Baji vacuumed the rooms and washed the dishes. She took a break to offer the evening prayer with me, and then went to our room. It was a big room.

"Are you tired, Baji?" I asked.

"A little," she said.

"What did you think of him," I asked.

"Well, judging from what his mother was saying, I don't think I would be a good match." Baji took out a pile of papers and did what she always seemed to be doing, marking tests.

"What kind of person would you like to marry, Baji?" I asked.

"Well, the Prophet, peace be upon him, said that people marry for four reasons – beauty, wealth, status, and piety. He said pick the pious one, or you will be the loser. Do you understand why?" asked Baji.

"Yes," I said. "If you don't pick someone who follows God's way, then he follows the way of the Dunya, and that doesn't lead to Jannah," I said.

"Correct!" said Baji.

After some time, Baji finished marking the papers and said, "Let's see what Dad thought of the guests."

Dad never spoke ill of anyone. He just said positive things generally, and if he said nothing, we knew he wasn't impressed.

When we went downstairs, all we could hear were Aunty Moona and Dadi-Amma.

"I don't appreciate you bringing such people," said Dadi-Amma. "She more or less insulted your niece! What a backward woman, disapproving of head covering! Challenging Allah! Secular Pakistanis! That's what they are! You expect my grandchild to marry someone with a mother like that?"

Baji and I looked at each other.

"I'm going to watch the news in the other room," said Baji. "It seems a little too hot in the kitchen."

"Okay, Baji," I said. "Let me get some of that leftover tandoori chicken."

The tandoori chicken was a mistake. When I went into the kitchen, Aunty Moona pounced on me.

"Young lady! What do you mean, telling strangers that your sister can't cook?"

"Sorry, Aunty," I said, looking wounded. "But you say that yourself."

"Hold your tongue!" snapped Aunty. "What I say, I keep in the family. I don't publicize it for the world. You need to learn how to be conservative with the truth!"

I lowered my eyes. I stood there and waited until Mummy told me to get what I needed and go to the other room.

"I didn't like Aunty shouting at me," I complained.

"Never mind," said Baji. "It's Aunty's way."

"But I wasn't trying to show your faults, Baji. Not for cooking, anyway. I was just being honest."

"It's okay, Bubbles," Baji said, as she nibbled on a piece of chicken. "It doesn't matter. Now," said Baji, "where's your big, big smile?"

"Oh, Baji," I moaned, "I'm double digits now!"

Only two weeks had passed. Aunty Moona had put the word out. There was another knock at the door. This time, Daddy was offended.

"For goodness sake, Moona," said Daddy. And that's all he said. He didn't shout – he very rarely did – but his words expressed his dismay.

"How was I to know?" said Aunty defending herself. "Wait till I get my hands on Razia; this is all her doing!"

"Why was Dad upset?" asked Baji.

"Baji! This time Aunty Moona's eligible bachelor was a munchkin. I saw him myself. He's way too tiny for you. He's even tinier than me, and he wore a beard that went down to his tummy. He had a chubby round face and kept playing with his beard."

"Hmmm," said Baji. "I wonder where he was from?"

"From Oz, Baji," I said.

When I told Helen, she laughed uncontrollably.

"I was worried for nothing," I said, laughing along with her. "At this rate, I don't even need a plan!"

The third eligible bachelor was the son of an ex-ambassador who was living in exile. When he was told that Baji wore hijab, he asked to meet Daddy. He arrived in a magnificent, expensive car all by himself.

"About time we had a decent candidate," exclaimed Aunty Moona.

Dadi-Amma wasn't impressed. "He is a foreigner," she said. "They have strange ways."

"He's a Khazak, Ammi," said Aunty Moona.

"That's my whole point!" snapped Dadi-Amma. "These people aren't like us. Why are you creating problems for my grandchild?"

The rich foreigner, as Dadi-Amma had labeled him, insisted on seeing Baji.

Mummy and Daddy disliked this idea, but asked Baji what she thought.

"I'll be covered, Dad," said Baji. "I'll pop in for a few moments."

Baji was hardly in the room for three minutes. When she came back into the kitchen, Mummy asked her what she thought.

"I didn't like his eyes; they unsettled me," said Baji.

"He's a very good Muslim!" interrupted Aunty. "And he is very wealthy. What more do you want?" Aunty didn't stop there. "Who looks at eyes? People look at family, occupations, age, bank accounts. When did this fashion start with eyes?"

Baji looked at Mummy, and Mummy smiled.

When I told Helen about the rich foreigner, she was mesmerized.

"Perhaps he lives in a palace?" she said.

"He's the son of an exiled ambassador," I explained. "He's not a king!"

"It seems really exciting to have all these different kinds of people come to your house," said Helen.

"You can come over and see the next one, if you want," I offered.

The next bachelor acted as though he was royalty.

Dad and Mummy didn't mind that Helen had popped over. It was part of my plan. While Dad was busy doing something in the kitchen, Helen and I introduced ourselves to the bachelor.

I asked him what he thought were the top qualities a wife should have.

"Cooking, cleaning, clothes, and coffee," he answered, as he sat back, and then tapped his hand over his mouth while he yawned. "She should cook like a chef, clean like a freak, make sure all my clothes are washed and pressed, and bring coffee at the click of my fingers."

"Well, you sound like the perfect match for my Baji, then," I said. "No wonder Mummy and Daddy were so excited to see you. My Baji does cook, but whatever she cooks is always burnt. And when it comes to cleaning, she's such a lazy slob. You should see her room; she's got stashes of mugs under her bed, dirty socks stuffed under her pillow. That's why Mummy and Daddy want to get her married off. They're fed up with her lazy, selfish ways. They think you're an excellent catch. You'll soon shape her up. Congratulations! I'll give everyone the good news."

The bachelor stood up and promptly left. Helen was mortified.

"Masarah, you'll be in the most awful trouble now."

"Stop worrying," I said. "I just did Mummy and Dad an enormous favour. Baji, too. All you have to do is be conservative with the truth. Keep your lips sealed!"

Everyone was astonished at first.

"What kind of a man comes to a house, and then leaves without even taking leave of his hosts!" Dadi-Amma had said, but lucky for me, in the end everyone put it down to Aunty Moona's strange collection of bachelors.

Baji usually wasn't home when bachelors made their calls. Dadi-Amma called this the screening process.

I actually liked the next bachelor because he kept on telling really funny jokes. But it turned out that he had trouble keeping jobs.

"Life's too short to worry about jobs," he told Dad.

"So how would you support a wife?" asked Dad.

"Oh, something will come along," he said. Then he began telling Dad more jokes.

The next bachelor was a close call. He was tall and very handsome...the type that people like to stare at or look twice at. Baji was acting very weird, which was uncommon for Baji, and it irritated me.

Mummy asked me to take him a plate of samosahs. Dad had left the room for a few moments.

"What's your name?" asked the handsome bachelor.

"Falingshisha Shishaka," I said, hoping that he would try and pronounce it and sound very silly.

He smiled a charming smile, baring his neatly arranged teeth.

"How old are you?" he said.

"I'm almost sixteen," I said. I still had six years to go, and time is a relative concept.

"Aren't you a little short for sixteen?" he said.

"Yes," I said, "and my sister is twenty-five, and she's shorter." I didn't tell him how short she was. "She's a munchkin."

"Oh," said the bachelor. He wasn't wearing his smile anymore.

Then I started faking hiccups. "Sorry," I said, "it runs in the family. I usually hiccup all night long." Then I left the room.

Needless to say, we didn't hear from the handsome bachelor again.

One day when I got home, I heard Aunty Moona on the phone.

"She never gets tired of that phone," complained Dadi-Amma.

Baji was at work when Zafar came as a prospective candidate. Dad liked him. But when Mummy heard that he intended to raise his family in Canada, she said no.

One day, a woman arrived with her two daughters. The woman was dressed in a black abaya and a black khimar. Her daughters looked like they had just flopped out of a Bollywood movie. Expensive hairdos, long fake patterned nails, high heels which, to everyone's shock, they did not remove.

The eligible bachelor was in the front room with Dad. Apart from his annoying habit of cracking his fingers, he laughed so loud and frequently that Dadi-Amma thought he was on medication.

"He's not normal! That's all I know," said Dadi-Amma, as she folded her arms, and then she commented on the "Bollywood wan-to-bees" as she called them. "It's a dysfunctional family; the evidence is in the daughters and the mother!"

Dad had known Peter for some time now. Sometimes, Peter would come to the house so he could eat Mummy's chappatis and chicken salans. He loved Indian and Pakistani food. He worked with Dad as an accountant. Helen and I were working on a project about planets when Dad was talking to Peter about fasting. I had missed some of the conversation, but heard Peter mention that he had a friend that had become Muslim and was looking to get married.

"He wants to know how he can meet a Muslim girl," said Peter.

"Muslim men don't meet Muslim girls, and Muslim girls don't meet Muslim men," said Dad.

"How do you get married then?" said Peter.

Dad explained how the process worked.

"Oh, so it's like a job interview?" laughed Peter, as he sipped on some of Mummy's cardamom chai.

"Exactly," said Dad. "That's a good analogy."

Hamza was the next hopeful. Dadi-Amma nicknamed him motor mouth.

"He talks nonstop. He's like a Duracell battery…a nonstop talking machine!" Dadi-Amma placed her hands over her ears and shook her head in disbelief.

It was Saturday, and we were drinking lassi on the porch. It was almost noon.

"Dad," said Baji, "this whole process is getting very old."

"These things do," said Dad.

"But there's been at least fifteen people," said Baji.

"No, Mariam dear, there's been far more. People have been proposing since you were seventeen."

"Dad, I just mean it's a type of pressure," said Baji.

"Your Aunty Moona has not helped. Trust in God and be patient."

About a month had passed, and my guard was completely down. I thought it would be years before the next person came along. That's when I walked in on Mummy, Dadi-Amma, and Baji sitting at a table with Raool. Raool was a lecturer at a university. Dadi-Amma seemed completely interested in him. That was not a good sign. The whole situation looked as though it could turn out to be very disastrous for me. I had to act fast. I greeted the bachelor, while Mummy introduced me.

The adults hadn't left Raool's side. Thank God for prayer times. Everyone got up. Dad said he would go to the mosque with Raool. Meanwhile, he went to get wudu. I hurried over to Raool with a damp cloth and tray to wipe the table to collect the lassi glasses.

"You'd probably like to know more about my sister," I said.

"Well, she's the reason I'm here," said Raool.

"Then I should explain some things about her," I said.

"Thank you," said Raool.

"I share my room with Baji," I said, "and she's a big snorer."

"Hmmmm," said Raool.

"She's a terrible cook, too."

"That shouldn't be too much of a problem, then," said Raool smugly, "because I love to cook."

"She still wipes her nose on her sleeve. Mummy's always scolding her about that," I said.

"I'll be sure to keep some tissues close at hand then," said Raool with a smirk.

That night, Baji didn't tell me any bedtime stories. All she could do was talk about Raool. She even repeated herself. I found this rather irritating.

"What did you think of him?" she said.

I thought she'd never ask!

"I think he's very peculiar, reminds me a little of the bachelor with a Swedish mom and Pakistani dad."

"Really?" said Baji.

"And did you notice his socks? They didn't match, and the left one had a hole in it?" I said.

"I didn't see his feet," said Baji. "He was wearing shoes. We were sitting outside."

"It's when he came in the house," I said.

"Was there anything else odd?" asked Baji.

"As a matter of fact, yes. I thought I saw him spit in the rose bush – right on Dadi-Amma's favorite rose."

"How vulgar!" said Baji.

"Well, yes, there you are, bachelors generally are vulgar," I said, trying to sound like an expert.

The next day a card and a huge bunch of flowers arrived for Baji. Guess who was coming to dinner?

I sighed and threw down my pencil and folded my arms.

Raool arrived at dinner with a box of Baji's favorite chocolate. I rolled my eyes. Which fool told him about her favorite chocolates! Who could be so foolish?

I hurried around the dining room without drawing the attention of the adults, who were in the living room. Finally, it was time to eat. I sat next to Raool. When he sat in his chair, somehow he managed to fall off. But he landed like a cat. I tutted quietly. Dadi-Amma, Mummy, and Aunty Moona fussed over him as though he was in the intensive care unit.

I offered him the salt and somehow, when he went to sprinkle it, the top came off, and a pile of salt covered his plate. He peered at me, so I smiled at him.

When he went to make wudu, I put a door stopper in front of the bathroom door. It took him forever to get out. When he finally got back to the table, he peered at me again. I raised my eyebrows and smiled at him. Finally, it was time for Raool to leave. Mummy and Dad were seeing him off at the door. He didn't make a fuss when he put his shoes on. I'd put water in them from the astinger bottle. His socks must have been quite soggy and wet.

As he drove off, I clapped my hands together. "Good riddance," I said. "We shan't be seeing you again!"

A week later, our family had been invited to Raool's home. I couldn't believe it! He lived with his mom and dad. They were a little old, but very nice. I couldn't help liking them. After chatting awhile, we were led into the dining room to eat.

"Here," said Raool, turning to me, "You can sit on this chair."

As I sat down, I fell through the chair.

"Ooops!" said Raool, as he hoisted me up. I glared at him.

"Jazak Allahu khairan," I said.

When Raool passed me the pepper, the top mysteriously fell off, and there was a pile of pepper on my plate. I looked at Raool. He smiled at me.

When I used the bathroom, the door jammed. After a long time, Raool came to the rescue.

On the drive home, it was uncomfortable sitting with wet socks. Someone had put water in my shoes. My socks were soggy and wet.

When I told Helen everything that had happened, she was quiet for a while, but then she burst out laughing. I started laughing, too. Raool sounded like a fun person.

The next time I saw Raool, he said, "Are we even now?"

I nodded.

"How about a truce then?" said Raool. "I'll marry your sister, and you can visit whenever you like?"

When Baji and Raool finally got married, I was still sad. I felt like a big, huge part of me had gone away. When I went to the kitchen, I found a gift box and a card with my name on it. I read the note and smiled. It said, "We will see you soon, Masarah. Lots of love and salaam, from your Baji and Bhaijan."

*Bhaijan means Big Brother!

*Najiyah Diane Helwani

Najiyah Diana Helwani was employed during 2008-2009 teaching English at Yarmouk University, Damascus, Syria and recently returned to her homeland, USA, where she lives with her husband and children. She is the author of the Islamic fiction novel, *Sophia's Journal: Time Warp 1857*, and is currently writing the second book for this series. You can visit her website at http://najiyahhelwani.wordpress.com and email her at najiyahhelwani@gmail.com.

*Najiyah would like to credit her daughter, Amani Helwani, for her support and contribution to the writing of the Islamic fiction short story, *Labor Intensive*.

Labor Intensive by Najiyah Diana Helwani

The gel was cold and oozy on Rebecca's swollen belly. The nurse was even colder and interrogated Rebecca without looking at her.

"What was the date of your last period?"

"Sometime in March," Rebecca replied, and then added, "I'm due next week."

"Did you smoke or drink during your pregnancy?"

"I did both before I found out I was pregnant. Then I stopped drinking. It took me about a month to quit smoking." Rebecca was proud of both these accomplishments, but the nurse just glanced up at her from the ultrasound screen and scribbled something on the chart with her other hand. Another pain seized Rebecca, this one making her gasp for breath. The nurse's eyes were still glued to the screen, and Rebecca had no one to look to, so she just panted and gulped her way through it, tangling her hands into the bedsheet and squeezing it hard.

"OK, Mom," the nurse said, meaning, 'OK, anonymous patient whose name I won't bother to remember…' "Let's get you admitted. They said you were dilated to four, and the ultrasound looks normal. Your room nurse will be here to get you in a few minutes."

Without hearing Rebecca's thanks, she turned and left. Rebecca felt a little less lonely when she walked out.

Two more contractions arrived before Rebecca's room nurse did. Rebecca could tell right away that this nurse was a much more personable breed.

"So!" she beamed as she walked in. "We're gonna have a baby tonight, huh?"

"Looks that way," answered Rebecca, glad to have conversation to distract her from the pains. Where was Amira? She'd called her when she'd left the house. Rebecca allowed herself one fleeting wish for Daniel, the baby's father, who, upon hearing of his girlfriend's pregnancy had decided that Alaska was a safe distance to parent from, and had taken off to work on a cruise boat up there. Then she dismissed him from her mind and settled it on her new reality.

The room nurse was named Charlene. When she took Rebecca to her room and began settling her in, she asked if Rebecca would like to walk around before being hooked up to the monitors. Since she was too nervous to really lie down yet, she agreed.

The corridor looked longer than it had when Rebecca had come for her tour of the hospital a month ago. She set out, exploring the waiting room plants and measuring the number of footsteps to the end of the hall, while she fretted about her new life with a baby depending on her. She tried an unmarked door just to see what was behind it and was rewarded with a lovely view of the nurses' bathroom. Just as she backed out, another contraction hit her – this one bringing with it back pain, which hadn't bothered her so far. Rebecca bent forward a little and tried to rub her own back with one hand, while clutching the mercifully cold walking rail with the other. She fought to control her breathing and was losing the battle to hyperventilation when the pain began to ease. She hightailed it back to her room and reached it just as Amira was coming down the hall.

"Sorry it took me awhile," Amira half shouted, walking toward her friend. Her flower-print headscarf billowed behind her a bit as she picked up her pace. "I had to take Salsabeel to Hakim's parents' house. How's it going so far?" Amira was Rebecca's friend from high school. At that time, they'd both been cheerleaders and boy-crazy flirts. After high school, Amanda had gone straight to UCLA, while Rebecca put in two years at the community college first. During those fateful two years, Amanda had become a Muslim and had taken the name Amira. Rebecca had been offended and standoffish in the beginning, but she soon owned that, while Rebecca did look different, ate differently, and talked a bit differently, she didn't really act any different. She didn't party anymore like the girls had done the summer after senior year, but then Rebecca didn't do as much of that anymore, either. And ever since the night Rebecca had shared the news of her unexpected states – pregnant and alone – with Amira, the two had rekindled their friendship and grown close again.

When Amira reached Rebecca at the doorway, she took her arm and steered her toward the bed.

"Well, I'm dilated to four, they said, and everything looks normal." Another contraction hit as she was getting into the bed, so she turned back around and leaned over it, relaxing into the mattress. Amira watched, not quite sure whether to jump in and hold her hand or let her work through the contraction on her own.

As the pain eased up, Rebecca straightened. "That one was all in my back! It was much worse than the others!" Rebecca climbed into the bed and struggled to turn her barrel-like form around, so she could rest against the pillows. Charlene returned and began hooking Rebecca up to the fetal monitors. As she worked, she chatted with the ladies, asking Rebecca if this was her first baby, and if she had a name picked out.

"Yes," answered Rebecca, in a way that made the nurse cock her head.

"Yes, it's my first baby, and I've picked out Emily for a girl or Jad for a boy. I haven't peeked at the sex."

Charlene was about to respond with shock, as so few people actually waited to find out the sex of their baby, but another contraction interrupted.

This one seared through Rebecca's abdomen and settled right above her tailbone, across her entire back. Amira didn't have to feel useless anymore – she was at Rebecca's side, holding her hand and urging her to breathe slowly. But Rebecca was gone – blindsided by the all-consuming pain.

Charlene seemed remarkably calm and unaffected by Rebecca's drama. As soon as the contraction ended, she began cooing about what a great job Rebecca was doing.

"Are you kidding???" Rebecca exploded with all the energy she could muster. "I'm dying! This is a million times worse than it was when I was walking around. Can I walk some more?"

"Well…" Charlene hesitated. "I'll have to call the doctor and ask him. Usually, once a patient is on the monitor, the doctors like them to stay there, so we can monitor the baby's state…" She trailed off.

"How about you go ask the doctor, and I'll stay here with Rebecca," suggested Amira.

"I'll have to leave a message for him at his service, but he's usually pretty good about calling back. I'll let you know what he says."

"Can I have something to drink?" asked Rebecca.

"Sorry, sweetie," answered Charlene. Then she brightened. "You can have ice chips, though! I'll bring you some when I come back." She typed a few more things into the computer and headed out. Just as she did, another massive contraction hit.

Amira let Rebecca squeeze her hand as her entire body tensed with the pain. When it was finished, there was sweat breaking out on Rebecca's forehead.

"I can't do this, Amira," she insisted weakly. "I wasn't ready for this in the first place. And I had no idea it would hurt this much. I don't know what kind of mom I'll even be!" Her eyes were plaintive, desperate, darting around for a way out.

"You'll be a great mom, Bec." Amira wanted to say the right thing. She wished Rebecca was a Muslim or at least believed in God, so she could know real comfort. As many times as Amira had tried to share with her friend the peace and liberation of Islam, Rebecca had just never been interested. She said she was glad it worked for Amira, but that it wasn't for her.

Another contraction. They seemed to be getting closer together. As soon as Amira had eased Rebecca through it, Charlene and a doctor, who was not Rebecca's regular OB/GYN, came dashing in.

"What's wrong?" Rebecca's face was panic-stricken now, in addition to flushed and exhausted.

"Well," the doctor said distractedly, as he looked at Rebecca's fetal monitor strip instead of her face. "The baby seems to be in some kind of distress. Its heart rate is dropping after your contractions."

Rebecca looked at Amira. "And that's bad?" she asked the doctor.

"It could be." The doctor finally looked at her. "We're going to have to insert an internal monitor, so we can keep better track of what exactly is going on with your baby. And I need you to turn over onto your left side." Charlene and Amira helped her do it. "Under normal circumstances, this wouldn't be a cause for undue alarm," the doctor explained. "We could just do an emergency cesarean now. But with your history of allergies to anesthesia, we want to do everything we can to help you have a vaginal birth. I'm going to give you some Stadol to help you with these contractions."

"No!" cried Rebecca, with more force than any of them thought she was capable of at that point. "I'd rather have the pain!" She turned to Amira. "Remember how Katie said she hallucinated when they gave her drugs?"

Amira's answer was swept away as another labor pain tore through her friend. Rebecca's brow wrinkled, her lips bared back, her breathing became sharp and irregular, and she was crushing the bones in Amira's hand.

And then it was gone. Not the contraction – Amira could tell that from the monitor – but the tension and pain in Rebecca's body. Suddenly, Rebecca was calm and still. Her eyes were open, but rolled back a bit when Amira looked at them.

The doctor hit the button on Rebecca's BP monitor, and the cuff on her arm swelled. Blood pressure and pulse were both perfectly normal. When the contraction ended, Rebecca blinked and refocused her eyes.

"What happened?" Amira asked.

"I don't know…" Rebecca replied, still a bit dazed. "I saw a beautiful soft light around my stomach…" As she faltered, another pain hit her hard. This time she didn't even tense. She just went into that same hypnotic state.

Rebecca felt as if she were floating…not floating away, just floating peacefully where she was. She saw her baby born and placed on her tummy. Without anyone saying it, Rebecca knew she was a girl. A red-faced baby girl, with softly curling eyelashes and long, thin fingers. The ivory light was hovering near the baby's head, and Rebecca heard a voice come from it.

"Allaaaaaaahu Akbar, Allaaaaaaahu Akbar…" was the first thing Rebecca's baby heard. Rebecca stroked her daughter's cheek as the white light continued its serenade. Then she was back in the hospital room with no baby, and Amira at her side.

"Amira, what is this?" she asked, bewildered. She wondered if the doctor had given her the drugs against her wishes.

"I don't know," blinked Amira, just as puzzled. "But if it's helping, just go with it!"

As the next contraction rocketed to full strength on the fetal monitor, Rebecca calmed and relaxed, all traces of anxiety and pain wiped from her face.

This time she saw her little girl alone in a hospital bed – not as the baby she was now, but as a toddler of about three. The light left the girl's shoulder and whispered in Rebecca's ear, "Say, 'La hawla wa la quwwata illa billah.'" Rebecca trusted the comforting light completely and leaned down to repeat the words into her daughter's ear. As she stroked the fine brown bangs away from her pasty face, the girl opened her eyes and smiled faintly.

This time, Rebecca didn't say anything when her contraction was over. She kept her eyes closed and waited for the next one.

She saw the light first, and then her eyes focused on her daughter. She was dressed in a pink dress and a maroon graduation gown, with a scarf like Amira's tucked carefully into the collar. Rebecca felt tears well up in her eyes as the light hovered near her precious girl and crossed the stage with her as she accepted her diploma.

When Rebecca was forced back to her hospital bed this time, she felt bustling and organized chaos around her. Amira was bent over her, stroking her arm and whispering to her. Charlene was there, too.

Rebecca was surprised to find herself hugging a strange man. When he released her with a kiss on her cheek, she turned and found her baby girl in a wedding dress, with the white light floating as usual near her head. As Rebecca put her arms around her daughter's neck, careful not to muss her pearl-studded scarf and veil, she felt engulfed by the protection and peace of the soft light. "Bismillah alaihom," the white light whispered to her.

"Thank you for protecting my daughter all these years," Rebecca stammered.

"I am sent by God, and protect her at His bidding," the light, her daughter's angel, replied.

Alarms were going off from the fetal monitor, and Rebecca was annoyed that the doctor was letting the noise go on and on. She wanted to tell Amira to make them shut it up, but as she tried to form the words, she felt the calm again.

Rebecca looked up and saw her daughter's face, glowing in the soft white light. She realized she was sitting on the floor with her knees out in front of her, her feet folded beneath her. On her head was a scarf like her daughter's. The room had people in it, but they were quiet, watching Rebecca from their own seats on the floor. Her daughter was holding a microphone to her lips, and the angel was hovering between them. "Mom," the lovely, peaceful girl said. "Repeat after me…"

The vision started to fade, but Rebecca held on to it, concentrating on every single word her daughter instructed her to say.

When she returned again to the hospital, Rebecca knew what she would find. Her daughter was in her arms, wrapped loosely in a flannel receiving blanket, a tiny knitted cap covering her hair, but that was OK; Rebecca knew it was deep brown. Her daughter's precious eyelashes were closed against the skin of her cheek, which Rebecca stroked like she had done in the vision. She looked for the light, but wasn't surprised when she didn't see it. Then she turned to look into Amira's tear-stained face.

"AsShhaddu anna La illaha il Allah, wa AsShhaddu anna Mohammad urRasoolullah," she repeated after her daughter.

Tahira Abdul-Jalil

Tahira Abdul-Jalil converted to Islam in 1974 and made Hajj in 1982. She writes for both children and adults. For children, she prefers to write stories in rhyme that teach about having a strong, Muslim character. Her adult themes are expressed in poetry and in vignettes about Muslims who are struggling to find, to strengthen, or to return to their faith in an increasingly secular world.

She has co-authored several articles in the forthcoming *Encyclopedia of Muslim-American History*, Edward E. Curtis IV, editor. She blogs at www.muslimwritings.com. She also writes for www.footstepstohajj.com, the blog for *Footsteps to Paradise*, an organization that helps Muslims make Hajj.

She has friends who are Sunni, Sufi, and Shia. She wants very much to make Hajj again. This is her first published story.

The Dream of the Door by Tahira Abdul-Jalil

This is a dream, not a story. That makes me more of a transcriber than a writer. But just because it's a dream doesn't mean it's not true. It was such a clear dream, you see. And then there were the visions. Yes, visions within the dream. I don't know abut you, but for me that is a rarity, indeed. That's why I believe the story of my dream is true. I don't know who they are, this woman and this man, but they're out there, and this dream is their story.

Nor come nigh to adultery: For it is a shameful deed and an evil, opening the road to other evils. (Qur'an 17:32)

Our company sent us out of town on business and put us up in a hotel. Once I saw my hotel room, I knew our manager, and probably others on the staff, were trying to provide encouragement to promote a relationship they thought should develop that hadn't as yet. I suppose it would have been hard to miss how well suited my colleague and I were to each other, but the fact remained that he was in a strictly monogamous marriage, and I was a single woman. And we were both Muslim.

So here I was, walking into my hotel room for the first time, only to see on the far side of the room an open door and his adjoining room just beyond. I could just imagine everyone in the office chuckling to themselves in their cleverness at helping to launch a not-so-clandestine office affair. I could just hear the explicit instructions being given when the reservations were made – "And be sure that they are in adjoining rooms and that the door is open between them when the two parties check in – or else, next time, we'll take our business elsewhere." I knew there was no convincing them that there was no way Muslims would take so lightly a matter that could end in death in this life, or worse in the next.

There was nothing more between him and me than an unspoken mutual regard, and that was confined to the workplace environment. Only courtesy. Only the finest professionalism was acknowledged between us.

After that first glance, I ignored the open door. I'd already tossed my suitcase on the bed in order to begin unpacking. But then, without thought, I moved away from my suitcase, stepped to my right, walked around the end of the bed and headed toward the open door. I moved past the bed and stopped. I was momentarily immobilized and felt suddenly, heavily, the weight of the years, of all the years I'd been single, divorced, alone. The burden of those years pressed against me, pushed against me. An intense and indescribable pressure arose within me – into my chest, my neck, and my head. The pressure was so great, it was visible in the air all around me like a fog.

Of course, I knew what I would not do, would never do. If I could just… I felt if I could just do something, some small thing to relieve the pressure, this pressure. Some small gesture, to relieve it – the pressure – like a safety valve, I thought. No more than that. Then I would be fine.

I moved toward the open door. I could see clearly, now, within. A dresser to the immediate left. Windows with long, dark drapes on the adjacent wall. On the wall across from the open door was the closet in the far right corner. And there he was, almost as if trapped in the corner at the head of the bed and on the far side of it. He was not looking at the open door at all; he was studiously hanging his clothes in the closet. His suitcase was on the bed that sat straight out from the wall to the right, an effective barrier between us.

I crossed quickly into the room. I stopped at the near side of the bed, by the foot of it. He was still on the opposite side, putting a hanger with a shirt on it into the closet. Just this small thing, I thought. I smiled at him as he bent back to his suitcase. But he looked up at me then, finally, with emotions of pain and anguish intense and raw across his face. The pity I felt for him simply stopped me. Whatever I was going to say or do just disappeared. To cover the real reason for my presence, I spoke rapidly, cheerfully. My words were light and filled with observations about the assignment we had ahead of us, nothing more.

But still I needed. I needed something. Some small thing. Just one more gesture, I thought. I took one small step and sat gently on the edge of the bed, at the foot. Then I knew I was wrong. My back was to him; I was facing the open door. I could feel that he had not moved at all behind me, but stayed near the closet, where he was. I shifted slightly and looked, not at him, but to my right. The chasm appeared in the air beside me. It was huge, taller than I was. It was lit inside from the fires of hell far below and out of view. It was full of the chaos and the confusion of so many tortured souls that seemed small, as if seen from a great distance. I saw them clinging in torment, somehow, to the chasm's sheer vertical sides. The chasm was for me. For the enormity of the thing I had approached. And even with knowing the wrongs of my actions beforehand, the chasm far surpassed any punishment I could have imagined.

I knew what I had done. I had gone too far. It signified more than a gesture. I couldn't move, and I couldn't look away. I knew my colleague was speaking to me from his corner. But I couldn't make it out. His words were too thin, too distant, and too faint against this visual cacophony of suffering. I stared, and all thought was gone. Then, slowly, my mind formed a silent Bismillah, and there formed a small dark space – ovoid, the length of my arm, the height of my hand – and firm in the air just to my right beyond the chasm. The chasm was smaller now, not much bigger than my suitcase. The dark space in midair was an opening. It contained – I could just see a shining sliver of it – a rope of Allah. I felt a rush, a deluge of joy and relief and gratitude for His Mercy. Yet those emotions were gone as soon as I felt them, because I had to pay for what I'd done.

I raised my arm toward the opening, reaching over the chasm, toward this rope of Allah. I reached, an action more difficult to bear, more difficult to sustain, than all the pressure I'd felt before. But Allah's Mercy lay within that space and, slowly, I raised my arm toward it. I closed my eyes to fight the resistance I felt in my arm. I grabbed for His rope. I felt nothing in my fingers; everything was in the effort of it. Then, just as slowly, I stood and turned slightly to squarely face the open door.

On the other side of the bed, my colleague had never moved. I am sure all that he saw was me seated for a moment, and then an odd gesture as part of an awkward, slightly belabored effort on my part to rise from the foot of his bed.

Then I saw myself from behind, walking into my own room. My back was as straight and rigid as His rope. I could see it so faintly, shining, running down my spine. I moved slowly and only with the most tremendous effort. I was immured in a fine – in an exquisite spiritual pain from the weight of my guilt and my repentance. From the weight of my submission and my obedience to His Will. Allah's Will. Allah's Will was crushing all else beneath It. Crushing me.

I knew that, from the closet, my colleague was watching me. I knew he was amazed that I had entered his room. I knew that he would only partially comprehend all that turned me away. I also knew that he would close the door, and neither one of us would ever open it again.

Irving Karchmar

Irving Karchmar has been a writer, editor, and poet for many years, and a darvish of the Nimatullahi Sufi Order since 1992. He is the author of *Master of the Jinn: A Sufi Novel*, and also writes a popular Darvish blog. He currently resides near New York City. His websites are: http://www.master-ofthejinn.com and http://darvish.wordpress.com

The Judgment of God – A Sufi Tale
by Irving Karchmar

Not so long ago, as time is counted, there came to a certain oasis far in the western desert a *faqir*. He was a *Qalandar,* a wandering *darvish*, who had walked the deserts of Africa and Arabia for many years, seeking only solitude wherein he could remember his Creator and contemplate the Divine mysteries. His virtue and faith, his submission to the will of God, had been rewarded with tranquility of spirit, and his sincerity and devotion on the path of Love was such that the Hidden had been revealed to his heart, and he had become a *Wali*, a friend of God.

Now it came to pass that the night the *faqir* wandered into this oasis and lay beneath a palm tree to rest before the midnight prayer, there was, unknown to him, another man under a nearby tree who was also making camp for the night.

But the other man was a notorious bandit, once the feared chieftain of a band of robbers who had for years plundered the spice caravans and waylaid rich merchants on their way from the coastal cities to the inland towns. The outcry against his merciless raids, however, had at last reached the ears of the Sultan, and he had ordered his soldiers to hunt down the band and destroy them. Many were caught and beheaded. Many others deserted their chief out of fear that they would share the fate of their comrades.

Eventually, this evil man found himself alone. His purse was now empty, every last coin having been spent in escape, and he was a hunted criminal with a price on his head. Even his former allies, those dishonest merchants who had bought his stolen goods, closed their doors against him. They also feared, lest the wrath of the Sultan fall upon their necks. And so he had fled for many days across the desert and come at last to the oasis where, tired and hungry, he sat beneath a tree and cursed his wretched fate.

Now I ask you, which of these two men is the greater, and which the less? Whom has God blessed and whom has He cursed? No, do not answer! You do not know the answer, for you are not their judge. The Creator alone is the judge of His creation.

Munkir and *Nakir*, however, the angels who question the dead when they are assigned to the grave, looked upon the scene of the two men and sighed. "Surely," said *Munkir*, "here at least the true gold may be seen from the false. These two may be judged, though their end is not yet come. God will have the greater, and Satan the less."

"Alas! It must be so," agreed *Nakir*. "True gold is the rarest, and therefore are the fields of heaven spacious indeed, while the halls of Hell are filled to bursting, overflowing even the deepest pits."

Now God perceived the thoughts of His servants, and spoke to the hearts of the two angels. "Verily, thou hast pronounced their just fate," He said. "Yet woe unto mankind had I created the world by justice alone. Am I not the Merciful and Compassionate? Behold! I will visit them with sleep and visions that thou shalt know the truth of My creation."

Thus the Lord sent sleep and mighty dreams to the *faqir* and the wretched thief. And lo, the *Qalandar* awoke in hell, even into the midst of the great fires of the pit. And the bandit chief arose in Paradise, where he stood among the saints before the very Throne of God.

Is it mercy to send the worst of man to heaven? Or justice to send the best of man to hell?

Ah, to cleanse the heart of judgment is to discern the Way of Love. And such was the lesson of Munkir and Nakir. For they beheld the *faqir* awaken in the very midst of Hell, and saw that most worthy of men rise up naked as the fires burned his flesh and the cries of tormented souls pierced his ears. Yet he did not feel pain at the touch of the flames, and showed neither surprise nor fear. His thought was only of his Beloved, and no affliction was great enough to sway his love. He sat among the fires and the torment as a *darvish* sits, and in a voice clear and strong he began to sing.

La Illah illa Allah! La Illaha illa Allah!

The fires blazed furiously as the song began, and then dimmed to smoldering embers; and the burning mountains trembled at the Holy Name. Now the tormented souls ceased their wailing to listen, for the name of God is not uttered in the pits. Then there was no other sound to be heard but his, and the song went on and on until the very foundations of Hell were shaken, and the damned souls began to feel a spark of forbidden hope.

Surely, Hell would have fallen into ruin had not Satan himself appeared and begged the *faqir* to depart. But the old man would not move, for he had walked many years on the Path of Love, and the Beloved's Will was his will, whether it be paradise or eternal fire.

And what of the thief? This chieftain of bandits who was once so feared and terrible, and who had fallen into wretchedness and misery, the fate of all such men in the end?

God caused the two angels to perceive his vision also, and they saw him rise and stand robed in white, trembling amidst the host of heaven, before the Throne of Almighty God. And the angel Gabriel spoke unto him. "By the mercy of the Lord, thy Creator, thy earthly deeds are forgiven thee," he said. "Come now and be at peace."

And now the truth filled his heart, and great wonder, and every veil fell from his eyes; and he saw with a clear sight the Majesty and Beauty of His Compassion, and he wept.

And the Lord God spoke unto him, and said: "*O man, fear not. For thou canst not fall so low that I cannot raise thee up.*"

Now fear left the thief. He prostrated himself before his God and wept. On and on flowed the endless tears of his wasted life, until they became the very waters of mercy and would not cease; and the feet of the saints were washed by his tears.

He would have wept for eternity had not the vision ended and the two men abruptly awakened. Then the thief saw the *faqir* as he stood, and came to him still weeping from the dream. And the *faqir* perceived all that had befallen them and embraced him, and they prayed together at the midnight hour even unto the dawn. Much befell them afterwards, for the thief became the disciple of the *faqir*, but that is all of their tale I will tell.

And Munkir and Nakir, who had witnessed but the tiniest particle of the unending Mercy of God, bowed before their Creator in submission, and in shame of their rash condemnation. For, surely, beyond the comprehension of men and angels is the Judgment of God.

Excerpt adapted from *Master of the Jinn: A Sufi Novel* by Irving Karchmar

Jamilah Kolocotronis

Jamilah Kolocotronis is the author of seven books, including the nonfiction work, *Islamic Jihad,* her first novel, *Innocent People,* and the five-book Echoes Series. *Silence,* the final installment in the Echoes Series, has been recently published.

In 1985 Jamilah earned her Ph.D. in Social Science Education. For twelve years she taught social studies to middle school and high school students at an Islamic school. She and her husband have raised six sons, and they also have two granddaughters. Jamilah lives with her family in Lexington, Kentucky.

A New Face by Jamilah Kolocotronis

Rain beats softly against the window, tapping out a gentle rhythm. I pull back the curtains and peer outside again. How long can it take to drive ten lousy miles? I pace, the rain an annoying backdrop to my brooding.

He called last Wednesday. We hadn't heard from him in almost two weeks, and I was becoming more anxious every day, imagining horrible scenarios. My phone rang just as I walked into the house after another long day of teaching.

"Hi, Mom. Assalaamu alaikum."

"Where have you been, Yousif? I've been so worried. You didn't call, and we couldn't reach you. Is everything okay?"

"You shouldn't worry." He laughed. "Everything's great. It's wonderful, even. I'm getting married."

What did he say? "You're getting married? Who is the girl?"

"She's fantastic, Mom. I know you'll love her."

"How long have you known her?" I hope she's another student from his university. What if she's Moroccan, and she's just looking for an American husband and a way to get into this country? I couldn't bear to see him hurt that way.

"Almost a month now." He laughed again. "This has been the best month of my life."

How could he say that after I poured my life into raising him? We wanted more children, but Allah granted us only him, and we gave him all the love we had. Now he's met a girl, and he acts as if we don't matter anymore. How could a strange Moroccan girl give him "the best month of his life"?

I felt like screaming at him, but I was afraid it would only make him more stubborn. He has always been very determined. I took a deep breath and thought it over. We still had time. When he came home, we would sit down together, the three of us, and discuss this. I was sure we could make him see the foolishness of his behavior. "You're planning to come home on Monday, right? We can talk about it then."

"Yes, we'll be there. She can't wait to meet you."

"She's coming with you?"

"That's why we're getting married so soon. Otherwise, her father won't let us travel together."

Taking another deep breath, I pushed out the words. "When is the wedding?"

"Tomorrow. Isn't it exciting?"

He was getting married in a country halfway around the world, and he didn't think of asking us to come? "I have to go, Yousif. We'll see you on Monday, insha Allah."

"Okay, Mom. Assalaamu alaikum."

"Walaikum assalaam." I put down the phone, threw myself on the couch, and cried.

I was still crying when my husband came home. Khalid listened patiently while, still sobbing, I told him about the phone call, and he took the news calmly. "I wish he would finish his studies first, but he is a grown man. Didn't we send him to Morocco so he could experience the world?"

"Experience is one thing, but I didn't expect him to come back with a wife."

Khalid sat next to me on the couch and put his arm around my shoulders. "You know, habibti, my mother sent me here to study. She didn't expect me to find a wife, either." He kissed my cheek.

"But that's different. We're talking about our son. And your mother has five other children. It's not the same."

He didn't argue with me, but before getting up, he said, "My mother doesn't love me less than you love Yousif. You raised him well. Now trust him."

The last five days have been tense. Sometimes, I'm grateful to Khalid for his calm. Other times, I'm infuriated with him. Why doesn't he see the problem here? I guess he'll never understand. He's not a mother.

Headlights flash through the living room window. They're here. I smooth my dress, check my face in the hall mirror, and go to the front door, ready to meet the little witch who has her claws in my Yousif.

They climb out of the van. Yousif shares an umbrella with her. She's probably one of those helpless women who expects her man to take care of her every need. Khalid walks beside them, carrying an umbrella of his own. In the thirty seconds it takes them to reach the front door, I evaluate her. Shorter than Yousif. A little thin, but not sickly. She wears glasses. Her brown cheeks, round and full, stick out beneath the lenses. Her scarf and her dress are both brown and dull. This is not the kind of girl I pictured for my son. He's much too lively to have such a dour wife. And my Yousif is gifted. He deserves someone who is extraordinary.

When they reach the front porch, I grab my son and hold him tight. He's still mine. She has to see that. "I missed you so much, Yousif."

"I missed you, too." He pulls away. "Mom, I would like you to meet my wife."

She offers her hand. "Assalaamu alaikum, Mrs. Mahmoud. I'm Sakeena. It's very nice to meet you."

I fake a smile. "Come in, please. Welcome to our home."

After they get out of their wet things, I invite them to the couch. Over refreshments we quickly dispense with the niceties about their flight and the weather. With those topics off the table, I wonder what else there is to say.

Yousif breaks the silence. "You look good, Mom. Did I tell you I missed you?" He pats my hand.

If you missed me so much, why did you decide to take a wife behind my back? "My work is going well, alhamdulillah. The school year is almost over, and two of my articles are being published next month."

"That's great." He turns to the girl. "My mother teaches full time, and she's a writer, like you."

"That's wonderful, Mrs. Mahmoud. What do you write?"

"Mostly travel articles and pieces about different cultures. Yousif's father and I hope to write a book someday about bridging the cultural gap in a marriage. You write also?"

"Yes, I'm a journalist. Some of my articles about life in Morocco have been published here in America."

I'll have to look those up. "Are you still in school?"

"No, I finished two years ago." She smiles shyly and glances at my son. "I hope you don't mind that Yousif married a slightly older woman."

She's three years older than him? That's interesting. I'm only six months older than Khalid.

"Tell me more about your travel articles," she says. "I love to travel. What are some of your most memorable trips?"

She listens without interruption while I tell her about my adventures as an exchange student in Peru, before I met Khalid, and our many trips together to Syria, as well as our family vacations throughout the United States. Finally, I pause, realizing that I have completely monopolized the conversation. "Is this your first trip outside of Morocco?"

"No," she says. "My family often vacations in Europe. You have had some wonderful experiences. Yousif told me a little about his travels, but I didn't know he had hiked in the Grand Canyon." She turns and pats his arm, smiling. "And you never said anything about your whale-sighting adventures. What else haven't you told me?"

My son just grins. He looks so sweet, like my little boy again. I can't resist. "Would you like to see his baby pictures?" I ask.

"Oh, yes. I would love to see them."

"Wait just a moment. They're on a shelf in my bedroom closet."

"I'll get them," says Khalid, who has sat quietly since coming back from the airport. "You two can keep on talking."

We sit for hours, pouring over the pictures. Khalid goes to bed. Yousif sits patiently between his new wife and me, occasionally blushing as I reveal the secrets of his childhood. At one point, finally, I glance at the clock.

"Oh, I didn't realize how late it is. I'm sure you two are tired, and I need to teach tomorrow."

"Yes, we are tired," says Sakeena. "But I have enjoyed our conversation. I'm so happy to get to know you. You are even nicer than Yousif said you are."

"Tomorrow you can tell me more about you, insha Allah. I want to hear all about your family and about Morocco, too."

They stand. Yousif puts his arm around his wife's waist and gazes at her. He does love her, doesn't he? I recognize the look. That's how Khalid looks at me.

He stifles a yawn. "Good night, Mom. We'll talk tomorrow."

I hug him. "It is so good to have you home."

He kisses me on the cheek. He hasn't kissed me since he was ten years old. "It's great to be back."

When we walk into the masjid for the Friday prayer, several of my friends approach me.

"Is it true?" asks Naima. "Jenna told me that her son told her that Yousif is married."

"He certainly is." I smile. "And I would like you to meet my new daughter-in-law. This is Sakeena."

She greets them all with the same grace and charm I first witnessed on the night we met. After the Friday prayer, I'll talk with the secretary about reserving the gym. We'll invite all of our friends to come celebrate our son's marriage. Khalid plans to go to a nearby farm and slaughter a lamb for the occasion.

The adhan will be called soon. The other sisters go back to their places. Sakeena takes my hand and walks with me to an empty spot in the third row.

When it's time to pray, we stand shoulder to shoulder, and a chill runs through me. Yousif is home, and now we have Sakeena, too. I have always wanted a daughter.

The Family Business by Jamilah Kolocotronis

When I came to this country nearly thirty years ago, I had only one suit-case of clothes and a few family pictures. My father scraped together enough money for my airfare, and my uncle, who had lived in Chicago for ten years already, put me to work in his restaurant, so I could earn my keep and pay for my tuition at the community college.

I worked hard, learned to speak English, and completed my college de-gree in business. By then, my mother had picked a girl for me to marry. A few days after my graduation, I got back on a plane, loaded down with gifts, and went to meet my wife.

She had trouble at first when I brought her to this country. She didn't speak much English, and she missed home. But the children came, and she made friends, and now you would think she was American-born. She has a busy social life and still makes time to volunteer at the soup kitchen once a month. Now that the children are grown, she's happier than ever.

My uncle kept me on at the restaurant until I was able to get my citizen-ship, which wasn't as difficult in those days. By that time, we had our two children, a boy and a girl. I decided to go into business for myself.

My uncle's restaurant did well, but he worked long hard days and barely saw his family. I wanted a simpler job, providing a basic commodity that everyone seemed to think they needed. My cousin told me about his lucra-tive venture on the South Side, and I decided to follow in his footsteps. Joe's Bar and Grill opened on September 10, 1987. Almost everyone calls me Joe, even my wife.

Every morning I leave our big house in the suburbs and drive into the city. Several years ago, I installed my own garage off the alley behind the bar so I can park my car and not have to worry about it. For the last few years, my son Sam has come with me. In five years, maybe, and not more than ten, I plan to retire and let Sam take over the bar. My wife and I will return to our country, where we have a large house waiting for us.

Sam and I keep the place sparkling. While I prepare the grill, he washes the front window or sweeps the sidewalk out front. I am very proud of my business, and it has been very good to me.

Our first customers arrive soon after we open at 11 AM. They order sandwiches, fries, and beers. Many of them have been coming for years. Julio always wants a double cheeseburger and a beer.

"How are you, my friend?" I greet him.

"Everything's good," he says. "And what about you?"

"It couldn't be better." I fry his burger while Sam gets his drink.

"Here you are, Julio," says Sam. "Let me know if there's anything else you need."

Julio laughs. "I wish my wife treated me half as well."

When Lakesha walks in, she asks for a salad, as usual.

"Why don't you try our cheeseburgers?" says Sam. "How can you live on rabbit food?"

She laughs lightly. "I need to watch my weight. Do you know how many calories are in a cheeseburger?"

I shake my head. "It's a shame, a pretty woman like you, worrying about her weight. If my wife still had a waist like yours, I would count myself very fortunate."

"She probably eats your cheeseburgers. Just give me my salad." She glances at her watch. "I have to hurry today."

Don't get me wrong. My wife is still beautiful. But we have both put on some pounds over the years. Who hasn't?

The serious drinkers start coming in at around 4 PM. The first is usually Jimmy. He walks in, puts his money on the bar, and asks for a beer. With people like Jimmy, I've learned to ask for the money up front. The last I heard, he was homeless and bumming quarters from strangers. Some of these people don't know how to manage their lives. But that's not my problem. I've got my own life to live.

Frank walks in close to five for his drink after work, something to help him face his wife. Lisa flirts with him while her old man drinks himself into oblivion. Hank orders a beer, and talks about how tomorrow he's going to stop drinking. "I mean it. This is my last drink. I'm done with the stuff."

"You say that every day."

"But this time I'm serious. This stuff is no good. I'm going to turn my life around." He shakes his head and looks down, cradling his beer.

Carl always walks in with a joke. "I have a new one for you today." He waits until some of us look at him before starting his routine. "Hey. I just flew in from New York, and boy, are my arms tired!"

I laugh, even though I've heard the joke hundreds of times before. Carl is a good paying customer, who comes here for a little company. I can give him that much.

He also has something to celebrate every day. Yesterday, it was Emma M. Nutt Day, whatever that is. Today it's V-J Day, which deserves a real celebration. After he has a few drinks under his belt, he leads the bar in song, everything from "I'll Be Seeing You" to "Mexicali Rose." He must have learned those songs from his parents. He still lives with them, even though he's only a few years from retirement.

Over in the corner, Jackie sits with her bottle and broods. She comes in here crying every time another man dumps her. Sometimes I try to give her a few words of consolation.

"He wasn't worth it. You'll find a better man."

"Where is this better man? I'm almost forty-five years old, and I still haven't found him. Sometimes I just want to die."

I shrug and walk away. That's her choice. It sounds bad, but her misery helps my business.

Sam helps me keep the drinks coming, while he banters with the customers, sings along with Carl, and laughs at every one of his jokes. I'm very proud of my boy.

This afternoon, as the lunch crowd eases up, we are visited again by some of those fundamentalist Muslims.

"Assalaamu alaikum, Brother Yusuf. We would like to talk with you about your business."

"Can't you see that I'm busy?"

"This won't take long. Do you realize what Islam says about alcohol?"

"Of course, I do. If any man says he saw me take a drink, he's a liar." I whisper. I don't want my customers to know.

"But you sell it, and that is just as bad."

I sigh and turn away. They show up every few months and lecture us about the evils of selling alcohol. They all have long beards and sad eyes.

Most of them wear their trousers up above their ankles. And they always carry those prayer beads. "Don't you have someone else you can bother?"

"We're concerned about you, Brother Yusuf. Imagine how it will be when you stand in front of Allah. How will you justify your actions to Him?"

The truth is, I feel sorry for them. They're so busy worrying about the next life that they have no idea how to enjoy this one. Sam and I nod and grunt. We've learned that's the fastest way to get rid of them. "Okay, you're right. But leave it between Allah and me. Can you do that?"

They throw out a few verses from the Qur'an and add in some sayings from our Prophet. I continue about my business. Finally, they leave to go hassle another Muslim sinner somewhere in the city.

I'm a Muslim, of course, but I'm a practical man. This bar has provided a steady income for my family. It sent Sam to college and gave my daughter, Ellen, a lavish wedding. Do you think if I were to close my doors tomorrow that these people would stop drinking? No, of course they wouldn't. They would simply take their business somewhere else and make some other guy rich. Why shouldn't I benefit? Besides, I donate money to charity every year. I go to the masjid on Fridays. During the last ten days of Ramadan, I always fast and pray. These self-righteous fanatics don't know what they're talking about, and they should leave people alone.

Hank walks in and starts complaining again. "I don't know why I come here every night. I should be home with my wife and children."

"No one is keeping you here," I point out.

"I know." He takes another sip of his beer. "So why am I here? My wife doesn't like it. She'll give me the cold treatment again tonight. My children ask where I am. My oldest, Alyssa, wants me to help her with a science project. I need to go home soon." He finishes the beer and stares at the wall.

"Would you like another before you go home?" I ask.

He shrugs. "Why not? I was never very good at science, anyway. But after this, I am going home. And you will not see me in here tomorrow."

"I know, my friend." I know.

Today's sermon at the masjid was about the evils of alcohol. Those fundamentalists must have gone to the imam. As I said, I don't drink. But what is the harm in serving my fellow man? They must need it, or else they wouldn't come.

After the prayer, I'm approached by Brother Mustafa. He pals around with the fanatics, but he doesn't act like them. "Assalaamu alaikum, Brother Yusuf."

The people at this masjid are the only ones who don't call me Joe. "Walaikum assalaam. How are you today?"

"Everything from Allah is good. How's your business?"

"You're not going to start in on me, too, are you? I thought you were an educated man." Not like those ignorant high pants wearers who keep quoting the same verses and never listen to logic.

He smiles. "What about today's sermon? Did you listen?"

"I've heard it all before, Brother. Let the imam run the masjid. I won't tell him how to do his job, and he shouldn't tell me how to do mine."

Mustafa throws his hands in the air. "You're right. We each must answer to Allah."

"I'm glad you see things my way." I pat his shoulder. "Don't spend too much time with those fanatics. It's not good for your brain."

"I'll see you next week, Yusuf. Assalaamu alaikum."

"Walaikum assalaam." We walk our separate ways. I'm glad some Muslims are still willing to listen to reason.

The regulars are all here tonight, except for Hank. Did he finally get up the nerve to stop coming? I doubt it.

We have a few new customers tonight. I worry that Carl could scare them away with his jokes. But Sam directs the banter.

"Hi, there. Welcome to Joe's Bar and Grill. Haven't I seen you in here before?"

"Hi. I'm Liz. Are you this nice to all your customers?"

Sam smiles. "Only the good-looking ones."

That's my boy.

Hank walks in much later than usual, looking like hell. His eyes are bloodshot and lifeless. His clothes are disheveled. At first, I think he must have stopped off at another bar, but when he gets closer I can see he's still stone sober.

"Hi there, Hank. I'm glad you showed up tonight. Are you ready for your beer?"

"Go ahead." He takes his seat, waves his hand, and looks down.

"Is there something I can help you with? Bartenders are good listeners, you know."

"No, you've helped enough."

He continues to look down while drinking his beers, even as the banter of our Friday night crowd grows louder. After three beers, he pays his bill and leaves.

Maybe Hank will stop coming. That's no problem for me. Liz and my other new customers will more than make up for his absence.

I haven't seen Hank all weekend, but business has been great. A new guy, Andy, led a sing-along the past two nights and the place is really picking up. If business stays this good, I can retire two or three years early.

On Monday, when Hank returns, only the regulars are here. Frank walked in first tonight and put his money on the bar. He's soused by the time Carl, Lisa, and Liz show up. Jimmy straggles in and puts some quarters on the counter. Jackie takes her place at a table in the back.

Carl takes one swig of his drink and starts with a joke. "I have a new one about the farmer's daughter," he says.

I wish Andy was here. Hopefully, he'll come back next weekend and save us from Carl's jokes. "Are there any new ones?"

"I guarantee you haven't heard this before. A salesman is driving through. The night is dark and stormy. His car hits something and won't start again so he walks up to the nearest farmhouse."

This is a new one. I'm looking at Carl and don't notice Hank walking up to the front door.

"So he knocks at the door of the farmhouse, and this lovely teenage girl answers."

The door to the bar opens, and something makes me look up, away from Carl and his story. Hank is standing in the open doorway, hands in his pockets and a scowl on his face.

"Hey, Hank, come on in. Have a beer."

Hank stomps into the bar and approaches the counter. Something is definitely bothering him.

"Have a seat, my friend. Come have a beer and listen to Carl's story. There's no problem in the world that can't be helped by a beer."

Hank pulls his right hand out of his pocket. He has a gun.

"Oh, God – settle down, Hank. Let's talk about this."

He raises the gun and a shot rings out, bringing down small pieces of my ceiling. "I'm finished talking," he says. "I'm going to kill you all." He's shouting now. "Then I'm going to kill myself."

My heart beats furiously. I must calm him down. "No, no, my friend. You don't want to do that. Whatever it is, we can talk about it. Just put the gun away."

"She left me. When I got home from work, they were gone." Hank closes his eyes and sobs a little. "I told her I would change, but she left me. I lost everything that's important to me. Now I got nothing."

"You got us, Hank. Come sit down and have a drink. It's on the house."

"It's your fault she left," he shouts, waving the gun. "You keep giving me drinks, even when I'm trying to resist. The money's gone. My wife and kids are gone. There's nothing left."

"Kill me first," shouts Jackie from her table in back. "There's nothing left for me. The men come and go. No one stays. No one ever will." She stands, holding out her arms. "Kill me. Do it now."

Hank looks at her, his hand shaking. "You don't want to die."

"Sure I do. Listen to me. Pretend I'm your wife. And you're a good-for-nothing drunk who throws away the money while your children freeze. You never take me anywhere. Your whole life is in this stinking bar. I'm leaving you, and you'll never see me or the kids again!"

Hank raises his weapon. I try to remember a prayer, but my mind is blank.

"Go ahead," says Jackie. "I dare you. But you're not man enough, are you? You're nothing but a drunk."

He raises the weapon and fires. She falls to the floor. I didn't think he would do it. I move to help her.

He brandishes the gun. "Stay back. She wanted to die. Let her die. Who's next?"

Everyone's quiet, even Carl. Hank shoots into the ceiling again. "Did you hear me? Who's next? What about you, Jimmy? Aren't you tired of living this way?"

Jimmy raises his head from the bar and peers at Hank. "You talking to me?"

"You got no home. Every day you beg for just enough to forget. What are you trying to forget, Jimmy?"

He speaks slowly, with a thick slur. "I had a nice house once. A good job, too, working in an office. People respected me. You don't believe me, do you?"

"I believe you," says Hank. "You lost it all because of this bar, didn't you?"

"I did, didn't I?"

"Do you like living this way?"

"What do you think? I got no home. People won't come near me. I spend every day panhandling quarters for another drink." He pauses. "You have another bullet in there?"

The shot is quick and clean. Jimmy's brains splatter onto the counter. "Okay. Who's next?"

"Stop this," I shout. "You're insane. Give me the gun, Hank." I take a step toward him.

"So you're my next volunteer."

"No, I don't want to die. I like my life. Just give me the gun."

"Are you happy, Joe, driving your big car and living in your big house? What have you sacrificed? Was it worth it?"

"I have my family and my business. People come here because they want to be happy for a while."

"Look around you. Does everyone here look happy? Do I look happy?"

I don't need to look around. This is the truth that haunts me some nights when the words of the fundamentalists come back to me. "Everyone's fine, Hank. Your wife will return. She knows what a good man you are. Put down the gun and relax a little."

"My wife will come back? I have more fairy tales. Jimmy will get a good job and Jackie will find the man of her dreams." He takes his eyes off me and spins around to meet Carl. "What about you, good time Charlie? Always coming in here with a joke. You're happy, right?"

"Of course, I am."

"That's why you spend your evenings here with us losers. Why don't you go celebrate something with your friends?"

"You are my friends."

"Really? That's sad. All these years, and we're all you have. You never married, did you?"

"Well, no, but I don't see what that has to do with anything."

"You never held your new baby in your arms. It's one of the greatest moments on earth, better than anything I can get from a bottle." His voice becomes softer. "I can't believe I forgot."

"No, but I have my job and my friends here."

"And you have your jokes, don't you? Jokes make it easier because they keep you from facing your life. I'm right, aren't I?"

Carl shrugs. "You could say that. I never thought of it that way."

"So even though you spend every evening laughing it up, you're just as lonely as the rest of us, aren't you?"

Carl nods slowly. "I guess I am."

While Hank concentrates on Carl, I spot Sam inching toward the store-room. We have to keep Hank busy.

I move a little closer to Carl and throw my arm around his shoulders. "We like your jokes. You tell stories, too. That's a talent."

"Maybe," he says softly.

"Is that all you want from life?" Hank asks. "Sit in a bar every night telling stories and making people laugh? There must be something more."

"I want friends," says Carl. "That's all."

"And we are your friends." I hug him to me.

"What about you?" Hank turns to Lisa.

"Honey, I'm just looking for a good time. Isn't that what life is about?"

"Is it? I don't know anymore."

"Sure it is. Forget about that woman. She wasn't good enough for you, anyway. Lisa can take care of you." She approaches him slowly, arms reaching out.

"Get away!" Hank shouts. "You come here every night, flirt with every man in the place, and yet you go home with him." Hank motions to the lifeless figure of Lisa's old man, passed out from another night of hard drinking. "What's in it for you?"

"You don't know me, honey, and you got no right telling me how to live my life."

Sam is just about to enter the storeroom. But Hank notices. He raises his gun. "Stop right there, Sammy."

Sam freezes.

"Are you happy spending your days in this bar? You went to college, and for what? Tell me, Sammy. Are you happy?"

"Leave my son alone!" I shout.

"You're forgetting who has the gun, old Joe. Answer me, Sammy, or I'll blow your head off."

"I'm happy," Sam says quietly.

"I couldn't hear you. What did you say?"

"I'm happy, okay? My father needs me to help him with the family business, and that's what I'm doing. Please don't hurt me."

"What are your dreams, Sam?" Hank speaks in a soft voice.

"It doesn't matter."

"Tell me," he coaxes.

"I always wanted to run my own import-export business. But my father needs me here."

"You're not happy, are you, Sam? You're stuck here working in this bar. No wife, no children. You live your life for your father."

"Leave him alone!" I scream.

Sam shrugs. "Is everything in life about being happy?"

"Tell your father what you want," Hank commands, still pointing his gun at my son.

"Go ahead," I say softly. If it will get Hank to leave my son alone, I must go along with him.

Sam looks at the floor. "I don't want to work here. I want my own business. And I want my own apartment, my own life. You always tell me what to do, and I've tried to be good, but I'm twenty-five years old, Dad, and it's time for me to start living my life."

"Doesn't that feel better?" Hank asks.

Sam nods, tears falling. I reach for him.

"Stay away!" yells Hank. "If you want to see your son live."

I take a step back and look at Hank, plead with him. "Tell me what you need from me. Anything you want. Just leave us alone."

"Anything? I want you to lose what is most important to you." He raises his right arm. The air explodes.

"No!" I cry out and reach for Sam, but I'm too late. Hank's shot got him in the head and my son falls to the floor. I cradle Sam in my arms and weep. "What do you want from me? Do you want to kill me, too?"

"No," says Hank. "That was enough. Carl, call the police. I'm ready to turn myself in." He stuffs the gun in his pocket and takes a seat. "Can somebody get me a beer?"

Sam is still alive, hanging by a thread. He came through the surgery, but has remained in a coma for over a week. The doctors don't know if he'll ever come out.

Last night, I returned to the bar, gathered all the bottles, and slammed them into the garbage bin in the alley. Then I went inside and took a baseball bat to the counter, the stools, and the booths. If somebody wants this place, they're welcome to it. I'm finished.

Sam's eyes flickered today. They say he may wake up soon, though they warn us he could have permanent brain damage. They don't know my son. He's strong. He'll come through this. We'll sell the house and return to our country. Sam will get better there. He must.

S. E. Jihad Levine

S. E. Jihad Levine, Sister Safiyyah, is the 2009-2010 Director of the Islamic Writers Alliance. She is primarily a freelance journalist, and has had journal articles and poems published in both online and print venues. As well, Sister Safiyyah is a professional editor. She lives in Pennsylvania with her husband and three cats, and serves as Muslim Chaplain for the Pennsylvania Department of Corrections, SCI Muncy. She blogs at http://www.shaalom2salaam.blogspot.com. Sister Safiyyah plans to publish her first book in early 2010, Insha'Allah.

Our Strength Comes From Allah by S. E. Jihad Levine

I was in my kitchen when I heard about it, putting the finishing touches on our evening meal. I went to the oven, took one last look at the lamb roast, and then called out to my teenage kids. "Samir. Lubna. Turn off that television and go tell your dad that dinner is ready."

After a minute, I still heard the voice of the evening news anchor. I was about to go into the living room and turn off the TV myself, when I heard Lubna shriek, "Mommy, come quickly. Look."

"Whoa! That's Brother Abdul-Mateen," my son yelled out to no one in particular. Lubna was now crying.

Hearing the commotion, my husband ran in from the study, where he had been reading the Qur'an. I rushed into the living room and saw my family staring at a mind-boggling sight on our TV screen. Umm Hafsa's husband, Brother Abdul-Mateen, was in handcuffs, being led away from their home by the police. Neighbors were standing around in small groups; some were hugging, others were crying. A reporter was saying something about a stabbing and a shooting. Not trusting my legs, I dropped to the sofa, where I stuffed my face into my hands and wept.

Once the details of the murder became known, no one in our little masjid could believe what had occurred. The imam himself went to the city lockup to hear it directly from the lips of the jailed husband. While most of the community battled with disbelief, we, the close friends of Umm Hafsa, dealt with a demon of our own. In hindsight, all the signs were there.

On the morning of the janaaza, we agreed to gather early in the women's area of the masjid. We needed the comfort of each other. A tearful Umm Nadia was sitting alone, saying dua, when I entered the prayer area.

"*Inna lillahi wa inna ilaihi rajioon*," she sobbed, after rising to greet me. "I feel like I can't wake up from a nightmare! I heard on the news...that he shot..." The unfinished sentence trailed off as she dug in her purse for a tissue. "And the precious children saw everything...Ya Rabb!" she wailed.

"I know, shhhh," I murmured, as she collapsed into my outstretched arms. Looking over Umm Nadia's shoulder, I saw Sister Halima arrive. There was a chorus of 'as salaamu alaikums' as we embraced each other and cried. After we sat down, we silently supplicated together for Allah to forgive the sins of Umm Hafsa, and for Him to prepare for her a spacious grave.

"I feel so guilty, may Allah forgive me," Umm Nadia confessed. "I should have heeded my gut feelings. Her husband seemed so controlling and dominating. I had a bad sense about him from the start. When I saw her with that discolored eye, I believed her when she claimed that the baby had poked her. Then there was the broken arm she explained away by saying that she tripped over her son's toy fire truck. Ya Allah! They were all excuses."

"Where's Sister Amina? I thought she was riding here with you," I asked Sister Halima.

"Hmm, speaking of controlling," Sister Halima said, chewing her bottom lip. "After waiting in front of her apartment for more than five minutes, I dialed her number. Her husband answered her cell phone and told me that *he* would bring her to the masjid. I could swear I saw her looking through the curtain."

"Maybe she's just running late," I offered, trying to change the subject.

Moments passed as we sat there, each of us swept up in the silent solitude of private thoughts and memories.

"Umm Hafsa's miscarriage!" Sister Halima exclaimed, stirring us from the stillness. "Do you think...?"

Umm Nadia related how she had attempted to reach Umm Hafsa by phone for weeks on end, to no avail. "I knew she was home. Where else would she be?" she sniffed. "Her husband wouldn't teach her how to drive or let her go anywhere without him. He was the one who would chauffeur her when it was absolutely necessary for her to go out of the house."

"That's strange," Sister Halima said. "Didn't Amina say she spoke to Umm Hafsa last week?"

"I don't know about that," I said, "but remember when Umm Hafsa came to our halaqas? Eventually, he put an end to that. What kind of husband doesn't want his wife to get together with her sisters to learn about the deen?" I asked, as I twisted in my seat.

"He was isolating her," Sister Halima explained. "He wouldn't even buy a computer for the house so she could use email and instant message. Y'all know how much she missed her mom and family overseas. He tried to keep her from everyone, but he sure enough had his own *Blackberry*."

"I remember inviting her out to lunch and an afternoon of shopping," I added. "She told me she didn't have her own money."

I hung my head and remembered the frustration I felt in trying to nurture my friendship with Umm Hafsa over the past few months. I developed a connection with her the first time I met her at the Eid prayer a year ago. She and her husband had just moved to our community. Our children were the same ages, and she reminded me of my own sister. I drifted off, remembering my gentle friend and Muslim sister. Umm Hafsa was a slim woman with warm chestnut eyes. She recited verses of Sūrah An-Nisā' with a voice so sweet, it brought tears to my eyes. My lips turned up in a smile as I recalled how we used to get together while our husbands were working. Going to the park with the kids, chatting, laughing, remembering Allah – then her husband lost his job and was home most of the time. I did go over to her house once when he was there. I started to nibble at my fingers, remembering how I could sense he didn't want me in his home. I didn't stay long that day, and it got more difficult for us to get together after that.

"What?" I said, roused from my daydream by the voice of Umm Nadia.

"You were talking about money, and I was saying that he wouldn't allow her to work outside of the home. I thought it was a shame, because she had a university education and really wanted to work as an English teacher. And they could have used the money."

Sister Halima confided to us that Umm Hafsa had once acknowledged feelings of depression and anxiety. She worried about her husband's humiliation over being unemployed.

"He was always stressed out, spending most of his day barking orders at Umm Hafsa as if he was a drill sergeant. Umm Hafsa felt crushed and helpless."

"That's no excuse," I argued. "A lot of men lose their jobs and don't abuse their wives. There was probably a lot going on that we didn't know about. I'm sure his abuse didn't just happen overnight."

"You're right," Sister Halima admitted. "I think the job loss intensified what was always there. Umm Hafsa was horrified that her husband spanked their son one day just because he dropped juice on the carpet. He never laid a hand on the boy before that."

Umm Nadia recounted a conversation she had with her own husband. She told him she had suspicions that her friend was being abused, and asked her husband to speak with Umm Hafsa's husband. Sadly, Umm Nadia's husband said he didn't want to interfere with a brother and his family problems.

"A lot of help these brothers are," Sister Halima complained. "Umm Hafsa even resorted to consulting the imam. She told him she knew a sister who was being abused by her husband, and the sister was seeking naseehah. But the imam's only counsel was for her to say dua and be patient with her husband. He advised her to trust Allah and assured her that He would soon grant her relief."

Little did he know…same old empty platitudes.

"Silence destroys Muslim families. Take us, for example. We didn't admit the truth to each other. We resisted the temptation to feed our suspicions. We absolved ourselves by claiming we were busy with our own homes and jobs. When we didn't see her or hear from her, we told ourselves we would check in 'tomorrow,' but the day never came. Why were we so afraid?"

"Okay," Sister Halima blurted out. "Allah, forgive me, but I need to say something. I think that Sister Amina's in trouble. We need to help her."

"Look!" Umm Nadia said, pointing to the stairwell. "Here she comes."

Sister Amina hesitated at the bottom of the stairs, shifting her son, Nafis, further up on her hip while trying to adjust the big diaper bag hanging from her other shoulder. When she hoisted up little Nafis, he grabbed at her niqaab. We gasped at the sight of a reddish blue mark on her cheek, and it looked like she had been crying. Sister Amina quickly adjusted her niqaab.

"Amina," I called, waving my hand so she could see us. She waited while we walked toward her. The speakers revealed the adjusting of the microphones from upstairs in the men's area. Umm Nadia took the baby from Sister Amina. I slipped the diaper bag from her shoulder and slung it over my own as I put my arm around her waist. "We need to talk to you when your husband leaves for the cemetery," I whispered in her ear.

"I...I d-don't ..." She hesitated.

I looked deeply into Amina's eyes for a moment, and then gently touched her cheek with two fingers through her niqaab. She flinched and averted her attention to the baby. "Don't worry, my husband will help," I promised, as I quickly sent him a text message. I was stunned when I read his reply: "*Leave it alone!*"

Leaning against the wall, I handed my phone to Umm Nadia. Her face fell when she read his reply. "We can't leave it alone," she whispered. "I won't face my Lord on the Last Day knowing that another one of my sisters suffered because I was afraid to do something. I'm going to ask Allah to help us. Our strength comes from Him."

After the Salat ul Janaaza, my phone vibrated. It was a text from my husband. "*Won't be going to the cemetery, meet me out front.*"

Pushing through the crowd that was waiting to leave for the burial, I found my husband pacing in front of the masjid. Amin Bey, an elderly brother from the masjid shura, was talking to him, and it looked like he was trying to calm my husband.

"I can't stop thinking about your message," my husband stammered. "Brother Abdul-Mateen is my friend and a trusted member of this community. I prayed shoulder to shoulder with him every day, and I never suspected that he was capable of abusing his family."

Kicking at the stones on the sidewalk, he continued, "Now I find out that Sister Amina's husband is doing the same thing?"

Brother Amin stepped forward and put his arm around my husband's shoulder. "Come inside," he offered. "We will talk to Sister Amina, and then meet with her husband when he returns from the cemetery."

With Every Difficulty There is Relief
by S. E. Jihad Levine

Sister Huda had been spotting heavily for weeks. But then the evening came when the bleeding turned into hemorrhaging. Roused from slumber in the middle of the night by a searing sensation in her stomach and a nauseating pungent smell, Huda flicked on the bedside lamp and illuminated a horrific scene: bed sheets saturated with blood. Unnerved by the sight and trembling with fear, she dialed downstairs to her landlord, Sarah.

"Sarah, please come quickly. Use your own key. I need you."

Huda sat on the toilet seat, shivering and bathed in sweat from the exertion of moving from her bed to the bathroom, while waiting for Sarah to come upstairs. The last thing Huda remembered before she blacked out was the sound of Sarah's key turning in the hallway lock.

When Huda regained consciousness, it took her a moment to gather her bearings. The sharp smell of disinfectant assailed her nostrils. An intravenous line was taped to her hand. Huda squinted to see a young man, with the name, *J. Eshelman, M.D.*, embroidered in green letters on the pocket of his white lab coat, towering over her.

"Hello, Huda," he said in a tone of voice reserved for comforting children. "You're okay now. You're in the hospital emergency room. Your friend, Sarah, is here with you. It's a good thing she called the ambulance. The paramedics stabilized you before you got here. I'm glad you're awake."

Huda turned her head and smiled weakly at Sarah, who was taking in the scene from the edge of her chair.

"The nurse here is going to help you get changed so I can examine you," he continued, as he turned to walk out of the cubicle. "Sarah will be right outside in the waiting room. I'll take her there and come back," he said. Sarah stood up and crossed over to Huda with concern in her eyes and gave Huda's hand a squeeze of support before the nurse moved in briskly. Then Sarah followed the doctor out.

"Are there any female doctors here?" Huda whispered to the nurse through parched lips.

"No, honey," she apologized. "He's the only gynecologist on call."

As the nurse sat her up and attempted to help her undress, Huda clasped the nurse's arm.

"Can you do it yourself?" the nurse asked, stepping back, sensing Huda's uneasiness.

"I think so. Let me try," Huda murmured, carefully lowering her legs over the side of the examination table. She quivered as she slid the amira-style hijab off her head. She slowly unbuttoned her jilbab, and then removed her blood-soaked night gown. *Night gown!* Sarah must have thrown her garb over her before the ambulance took her to the hospital. *Oh, Sarah, thank you!* Tonight was the first time Sarah had seen her uncovered since she moved into the apartment. Huda's hands trembled as she put on the flimsy hospital gown, and her legs wobbled as the nurse helped her back onto the long examination table. It seemed like an eternity before the curtains parted and J. Eshelman, M.D. returned. Even though Huda knew she was in a life-threatening situation, she still felt an intense sense of burning shame as the examination began.

The next morning Huda called Sister Basimah on the telephone and recounted what had transpired the night before. Basimah was her dearest friend and closest sister in Islam. A year ago, Huda had said Shahadah in Basimah's house.

"Why didn't you have Sarah call me?" Basimah gently scolded. "I would have met you at the hospital."

"I know. But it was very late. I didn't want to trouble your husband to bring you there."

"It's okay, he would have brought me. We wouldn't have wanted you to be there alone."

"I know. May Allah reward you, but it turned out all right. I wasn't alone. Sarah waited and brought me home."

"So what did the doctor say?"

"He said I have to follow up with my family gynecologist, and he gave me an injection to stop the hemorrhaging. I'm still bleeding, but the appointment is this afternoon. He stressed that any bleeding in post-menopausal women is very serious. I shouldn't have ignored it for so long, but I thought it would stop."

"Did you call your husband?"

"No."

"You should call him."

"Hmm…I don't know. I haven't spoken to him in weeks."

"Sister, I know this separation has been difficult for both of you, but I think he would want to know about this. After all, you're still his wife."

"We'll see. I'll decide when I come back from the appointment this afternoon. Insha Allah, I'll call you as soon as I come back."

After hanging up with Basimah, Huda swallowed the morning dose of pills given to her at the emergency room. Before dressing to face the day, Huda made a strong black coffee and settled into the antique wooden rocking chair that had belonged to her grandmother. Samir, the newest addition to her cat family, jumped up and curled into her lap. As she gently kneaded his ears and watched the steam rise from the hot mug, her thoughts turned to her husband, Abdur-Raheem.

When she converted to Islam shortly after marriage, Huda's family refused to accept her decision to apostate from Judaism. Estranged and isolated from her family, Huda became increasingly dependent on her husband. Stressed out from balancing the demands of a full-time job and participation in a master's degree program, Abdur-Raheem didn't have the patience for Huda's emotional neediness or insecurities.

To avoid confrontation with Huda, Abdur-Raheem began studying long hours at the college library. Huda recalled all the evenings and weekends spent only in the company of her cats. Her jaw tightened at the memory of endless hours spent on watch at the living room window, waiting for his car lights to shine in the driveway. Angry tears pooled in her eyes as she recollected how he went straight to bed as soon as he came home, and how he fell asleep as soon as his head hit the pillow. She remembered how he ignored her pleas for marital counseling with the imam. Frustrated with Huda's nagging, Abdur-Raheem became violent with her. Afraid of his own anger, he pronounced talaq. Because she feared that he would hit her again if she remained in his house during her period of iddat, Huda moved out. But then he called her, apologized for his behavior, begged for another chance, promised to talk with the imam, said he needed time…

"Hmm, I need time, too," Huda said aloud to Samir. Rolling over in her lap and stretching his paw in the air, Samir purred in agreement.

The women's clinic was in a health complex only two blocks from Huda's city apartment. Huda decided to walk to the appointment, since parking spaces were at a premium in her neighborhood. Besides, she figured that some fresh air would clear her head. Glancing at the bare trees that lined the sidewalk, she was reminded of the hadith, *"Whenever a Muslim is afflicted with harm from sickness or other matters, Allah drops his sins as a tree drops its leaves."*

The afternoon shadows were long when Huda left the doctor's office. She clutched in her hand prescriptions for more medication and a pre-surgery information packet. As she hurried home to prepare for Asr prayer, she toyed with the idea of calling her husband. The new knowledge of impending surgery changed her perspective. *Wasn't this a crisis, after all?* As she cinched the buckle of her coat and lowered her head against the wind, she realized that it was really only comfort and reassurance that she was seeking. *Would he come through for her if she called?* She knew he was in the middle of mid-term exams. When she got in the house, Huda settled into her grandmother's rocking chair and called Basimah.

"She said she thinks I may have uterine cancer." Huda shuddered at the sound of the word cancer coming from her own lips.

"Cancer? SubhanAllah!"

"Yes, can you believe it?" Huda sobbed.

"Why does she think that?"

"All my symptoms point to it, but she can't be 100 percent sure until she does more tests. She tried to biopsy me in the office, but my body wouldn't yield to her instruments. So she said she'll have to do it in the hospital, go through my belly button, and get the biopsy that way."

"Ya Allah," exclaimed Basimah.

"While I'm under the anesthesia, she'll also do a D&C to clean my uterus out, and we talked about the possibility of a hysterectomy. I told her I wanted to know for sure if it's cancer before I'd even consider something as drastic as a hysterectomy."

The reality of potential major surgery caused a fresh wave of tears.

"When will you go to the hospital?" Basimah asked.

"They don't have any openings until the third week of December," Huda sniffed.

"That's almost another month."

"Yes, almost a month…"

"Did you call him?"

"No. I'm afraid he'll be upset with me. I know he's already stressed out with school…we haven't met with the imam yet."

"Maybe you can call Imam Mahmoud," Basimah suggested. "He can talk to him."

"I'll think about it. I'll pray istikharah, Basimah. I know it sounds awful, but I can't cope with the stress of dealing with him right now."

The holy month of Ramadan started, and Huda endured. The medication slowed down the bleeding, but didn't stop it entirely. She went to the masjid each night for iftar and busied herself with serving the others and cleaning up afterward. While everyone was happily eating and chatting to people they hadn't seen for a long time, Huda dwelled in the background, picking up dishes and utensils, loading the dishwasher, wiping up, and putting food away. She didn't feel like joining the others, didn't want to engage in idle talk, and didn't want to pretend like everything was normal in her life.

From the security of her emotional shadows, Huda eyed her Muslim sisters with jealousy. Exotic women, beautifully garbed, wearing exquisite jewelry, smiling, surrounded by friends and family, children, seemingly not a care in the world, secure in their beautiful houses with their protective husbands who took care of them the way that Allah commanded. Stung by the pettiness of her thoughts, Huda felt ashamed. She slipped into the musallah and prayed for Allah to remove the evil from her heart. She reminded herself that her current situation was a test from Allah. Ya Allah, so many tests! Alienation from her family, marriage problems, moving alone to a small apartment, working two jobs just to survive, and now possibly cancer.

During those weeks, Huda put her life in order. She updated important documents and threw away old papers and letters that had accumulated over the years. It was her way of maintaining some semblance of control over her life. As surgery day approached, she thoroughly cleaned the house and did the last of the laundry.

On the morning of the surgery, Huda paced around her apartment waiting for Sister Basimah to show up. Before they left for the hospital, Basimah suggested they pray two rakat. Bowing in prostration, Huda beseeched Allah for protection and mercy. *If my days are not finished, dear*

Allah, heal me so I may be a better Muslim, so I may continue to serve You. On the way to the hospital, Basimah again asked Huda whether she had called her husband.

"I don't want him to be there for me out of his own guilt. I wouldn't be able to handle it when he left again."

"Sister, I'm not a doctor, but something tells me that it's not cancer that you have."

"What do you mean?"

"I think it's your emotions?"

"Emotions?"

"Yes. Feelings. Feelings due to the situation between you and your husband. Between you and your family. All the changes in your life – emotions have a powerful impact on a woman's body."

"But the doctor seems so sure that I have cancer."

"Hmm. I just had to tell you what I think. I've seen it before."

They arrived at the hospital and checked in. Huda's heart was racing as she signed all the forms, releases, and permissions.

"In my country," Basimah marveled, "you wouldn't be able to do all this without your husband's permission."

Huda didn't reply as she shuffled the forms back through the slot of the intake window. She didn't want to hurt her dear friend's feelings. *Are women and girls over there supposed to die if their husbands don't agree to medical care?* she wondered. Even she, a new convert to Islam, knew that didn't have anything to do with the religion.

They were led back to the preparation area, where Huda exchanged her own clothing for a hospital gown. This time she left her hijab on. The nurse told her that she could wear it all the way up to the operating room, where she'd have to exchange it for a paper cap. Another nurse came in and gave Huda an injection to "relax" her before the procedure. She leaned back on the gurney and watched Basimah, sitting on the chair beside her, crochet needles clicking, working on an afghan blanket. As the drugs took over, Huda felt a sweet release of all her anxiety.

"How are you doing?" Basimah inquired, looking at Huda over the top of her eyeglasses.

"Okay, but I feel a little chilly."

"Here," she said, spreading the afghan over Huda. "This will warm you up. I'll be right back. I need to call home to check on the kids."

When Basimah returned, she found Huda softly crying.

"What?

"Why are you crying?"

"Because I love you so much!" Huda sniffed between tears, "because I feel so alone, because I don't know what I would do without you."

"I love you, too, habibiti," she cooed, smiling at Huda. "But better than me, you have Allah. Now, don't cry; I think you're feeling the effects of the drugs they gave you," she teased.

Huda closed her eyes and prayed du'a until they came to get her to go into the operating room. Basimah accompanied her all the way to the doors. She stood in front of Huda to shield her from view, and removed her hijab. The nurse replaced it with the paper cap. Basimah leaned over, kissed Huda, and whispered in her ear, "Say Shahadah with me." They joined hands, and together they repeated the words that every devout Muslim says at least five times a day: *"ašhadu 'an l il ha ill -ll hu wa ašhadu 'an muhammadun-r-ras lu-ll h – I testify that there is none worthy of worship except Allah and I testify that Muhammad is the Messenger of Allah."* Basimah straightened up and took a step back. They reluctantly let go of each other's hands as an orderly wheeled Huda through the doors.

The following Friday morning, Huda returned to her gynecologist's office to get the results of the biopsy. She resolved to go to the Jumuah prayer after the appointment, no matter what the result. She sat on the examination table, swinging her legs back and forth, staring down at the tiles. So much had happened since the first time she sat in this room. The doctor entered, carrying Huda's thick file.

"Good morning, Huda."

"Good morning." Huda's voice broke as she jerked her head up and greeted the doctor.

"Well, I'll put your mind at ease first thing. The biopsy didn't show any cancer—"

Huda's heart jumped in her chest. The doctor kept talking, but she didn't hear anything else she was saying. She had heard enough. *No cancer!*

Alhamdulillah! That's all she needed to know. She noticed a peculiar look on the doctor's face.

"I'm so sorry," Huda smiled. "I was just so relieved when you said there was no cancer. I guess I stopped listening."

"That's okay." The doctor laughed. "I understand. But I was saying that we did find some small cysts on your ovary. They may have been responsible for the bleeding."

Huda's face fell.

"Oh," she said, chewing her bottom lip. "Couldn't you remove them?" she asked, after a brief moment. "One of my sisters had a larger one, and her doctor removed it," Huda said in a small voice.

"That procedure wasn't covered on the consent form, so I couldn't remove them. Anyhow, small cysts often dissolve on their own. In another month, we'll do an ultrasound to follow up. Don't worry, Huda."

"Really?" Huda asked, smiling again.

"Yes, really." The doctor grinned.

"Alhamdulillah!" Huda exclaimed.

"What?" the doctor asked.

"Alhamdulillah! It means 'All Praise be to Allah'," Huda explained.

"Yes, Praise Allah," replied the doctor.

Huda practically flew the two blocks home to her apartment. She was reminded of Allah's promise, "*With every difficulty there is relief.*" This test with her health gave her hope that the rest of her problems would be resolved by Allah's Mercy. Huda had a renewed strength that came from trusting in Allah. She hurried up the hallway steps and dialed Basimah's number as soon as she got through the door.

"As Salaamu Alaikum," she said breathlessly. "Meet me at the masjid for the Jummah prayer. I have wonderful news!"

J. Samia Mair

J. Samia Mair is a freelance writer, who has published fiction, nonfiction, and poetry in magazines, books, and scientific journals. Her writing covers a variety of topics, including Islam, public health, and law. She regularly contributes to *SISTERS* and *Hiba* magazines and has her own column, "Tea Talk," in *SISTERS*. Mair is also the Baltimore Muslim Examiner for the on-line magazine, *examiner.com*. Two children's picture books, *Amira's Totally Chocolate World* and *The Perfect Gift*, are expected to be published in 2009. She is a member of the Islamic Writers Alliance, Muslimah Writers Alliance, and National Writers Union.

The Photograph by J. Samia Mair

I try to lock the door to my apartment but I fumble with the keys in my haste. I wonder who will notice me today and how they will respond. My hijab fits uncomfortably on my head as strands of dark brown hair announce to the world that I am a novice. I have been told that I look Iranian, and several Egyptian women tell me I can pass for Egyptian. When I lived in Brazil, Brazilians thought I was Brazilian until they heard my accent. Even then, they did not think I was American, instead guessing I was from Argentina or Mexico. When I visited Spain, I passed easily as Spanish, and in France people thought I was Italian. I smile to myself, remembering how I always envied the girls with blonde hair and light eyes, ashamed of my dark features and olive skin, angry that my Italian heritage dominated the Irish. I have come to realize, though, that I miss blending in.

The door finally locks. I take a deep breath before turning around to face the familiar yet alien world. I remember a conversation with my atheist father years ago when he discovered I was attending church. He was disappointed, ashamed of my weakness, decidedly embarrassed that I could actually believe. Although I was an adult by then, his disapproval hurt me deeply. But pain, like all else in this world, is fleeting, and the pain of that memory has long since faded. My father learned to tolerate my Christian beliefs, but he will never accept a Muslim daughter. He hopes for what will never be.

I walk to my car along the crowded street and notice the stares. Expressions of curiosity or even disapproval no longer bother me, but the faces of pity I cannot forget. It is as if I am afflicted with some horrible disease, a slow-moving cancer for which they have found the cure that I refuse to take. They want to reach out and free me from my prison. I, too, feel the bars, yet I am not the captive.

On the drive to my office, a police car to my left refuses to pass although I travel under the speed limit and the road ahead is clear. Other cars form an impatient line behind him. I make a right turn, and the police car follows. All I see is the officer's cold stare in the rear view mirror. I have broken no laws, but my heart thumps loudly. Not long ago, I felt safe when the police were near. How strange that a thin piece of cloth holds so much power.

Without warning, the police car speeds away. I have heard Muslim women described as invisible, but ironically not here in the melting pot I call home.

I park my car and walk to a beautiful old stone building behind the church on the corner. Initially, my coworkers seemed to take the news of my conversion fairly well. Soon, though, conversations became unexpectedly awkward. When I began covering a few weeks ago, the change was palpable. They could no longer pretend that I was not the person whom I professed to be. I assumed relationships would stay the same. I, like my father, want the impossible. My old self lingers like faint perfume in an empty room.

I walk in the front door and exchange pleasant greetings with my coworkers, chatting over morning coffee. I do not join them. I sit down at my desk, prepared to read through the email that accumulated overnight. Before I log in, my boss calls me to his office. He shuts the door and motions me to sit down in the chair across from him. I recognize his expression. It is not good news.

"Sarah, you know that I have supported your decision to accept Islam. After all, religion is a personal choice."

I respectfully remain silent. He would not understand if I told him that Islam chose me.

"I also understand that you feel wearing that, um, that scarf is a religious obligation, but, well…well, under the circumstances, it is starting to raise questions – questions I am having trouble answering."

I immediately respond, hoping to assuage his concerns. "I realize many people have difficulty with covering at first but—"

"Sarah, please, let me finish my thought."

I quietly sit back noticing distress in his eyes, so unlike his usual easygoing manner.

"In a different place, this wouldn't be a problem, but it has become one here. Certainly, you must have anticipated it yourself."

"I guess I thought it wouldn't be too much of a problem, as we are involved in so many interfaith activities. In fact, I thought it could eventually be viewed as a good thing."

"But didn't you consider that other people would think it was a little strange that you work here?" He hesitates momentarily, but then jumps abruptly to the point. "You have been a great employee, no complaints whatsoever, but...I...I...just don't think it's a good fit anymore."

"Are you firing me?" I ask in a voice revealing surprise more than anything else.

"I don't think it has to come to that, Sarah. I think that once we talk this over, you will agree with me that it is best for everyone."

He stops speaking and waits for my response. I remain silent, not quite sure what to say.

"Sarah, it's not personal, but your beliefs are somewhat at odds with our mission."

"But Father—"

"Sarah, this is a Catholic church, you work for the priest in the rectory, and everything we do is in the name of Jesus Christ."

Father Paul's last few words ring loudly in my ears like church bells on a Sunday morning. The mention of Jesus Christ, peace be upon him, triggers a memory of my Jewish friend's visit to the church. When the service was over, I asked her what she thought. She told me that it was nice, and at times uplifting, but found it distracting to hear the name "Jesus Christ" mentioned so often. "Why not just use 'God' instead?" she asked. That little exchange began my long journey to Islam. I would like to see more of my friend, but the hijab is a veil between us as well.

"Sarah, Sarah," Father Paul gently brings me back to our conversation. "I will give you a great recommendation. I even printed out some job openings that might interest you. Of course, we will help you financially. I thought two month's pay is fair. If you need to apply for unemployment, I will help you with that as well. With your skills, though, I suspect that won't be necessary."

Father Paul continues to speak. I find myself a dispassionate observer in the conversation. It occurs to me that it never occurred to me that my employment would be in jeopardy so soon. I suddenly find myself replying to a question I cannot recall being asked.

"Father, I can probably get my work in order in a week or two. Do you know who will be taking over my responsibilities?"

"I don't expect it will take that long," Father Paul responds quickly. He looks away from me for the first time. "Just write a short memo of where you are in your work and what needs to be done next. That should take only an hour or two."

"Are you sure, Father? I'd feel better if I tied up loose ends."

"Positive. I think it is best that you leave as soon as possible."

As soon as possible! I think to myself. *How disruptive can I possibly be?* The image of the middle-aged parishioner who wears short skirts and plunging necklines creeps into my mind.

My situation begins to sink in, and in the muddled haze of my racing thoughts I head back to my desk, unaware of how the conversation exactly ended.

Stares can be revealing, but their absence may tell you more. My co-workers are uncharacteristically busy, heads buried intently in their work. An empty cardboard box sits on the floor at the side of my desk. Apparently, I am the last to learn of my departure.

I finish the memo and survey the room. A picture of Jesus and Mary hangs crookedly on the wall in front of me. Small crucifixes dangle from desk lamps and computer monitors. A miniature statue of Angel Gabriel sits on the front desk, his wings brilliant white against the dark brown of his flowing porcelain robe. I catch my reflection in the large window on my right. On top, there is a scene of the crucifixion in expensive stained glass. I am suddenly uncomfortable. Poor Father Paul, what a good soul. For months, he has waited patiently for me to leave.

I pick up the box at my feet and begin to empty my desk of personal belongings. I have not accumulated much over the years – a few letters, a list of books to buy and read, numerous scraps of paper with messily written telephone numbers, and a small journal with some quotes I found particularly inspiring.

Stuck between two desk drawers in the back, I find a photograph that I took while living in Brazil. It is a picture of three very distinct sun rays breaking through the dense forest canopy, shining light on a magnificent, iridescent blue butterfly hovering between the trees. The photograph reminds me of Tupa; it always reminded him of home.

Tupa is one of those rare individuals whom you immediately know you will never forget. I met him in the unusually sterile city of Brasilia at a protest against the deforestation of indigenous lands. Tupa was less than five feet tall with a stocky build. He had golden brown skin and jet black hair that glistened like the oil beneath the forest. His gentle dark eyes dominated his otherwise strong, chiseled face. He was beautiful both to eye and heart.

Tupa told me the most amazing story – the story of his life. He was born deep in the Brazilian Amazon in a year that was remembered more for death than life. He belonged to a tribe that, until recently, had no contact with the outside world, living as they had for thousands of years. His village was built on a large patch of cleared forest near the banks of a winding river. He laughed when I told him that I had come all the way to Brazil to venture into the rainforest, whereas he exerted a great effort to get out. He explained that the forest was a dangerous place. He spent most of his time near or in the river, unconcerned with the piranhas and the other creatures that inhabit those murky waters.

When he was about twelve years old, an anthropologist from the United States began living with his tribe for the next several years. The contact changed his life forever. She grew especially fond of him and offered to send him to nursing school in Brasilia. Tupa accepted the invitation despite the disapproval of his father, the tribe's only medicine man. After Tupa graduated, he visited the anthropologist in the United States and traveled across the country with some of her students. In just a few short years, Tupa went from living a primitive existence in a remote village deep in the Amazon basin to gallivanting around one of the most technologically advanced countries in the world. That is a story for the movies.

Tupa showed me the documentary that the anthropologist had filmed of his tribe. He kept interrupting the narration, pointing enthusiastically at the screen and proudly shouting out when family members appeared. During the film, Tupa often looked over at me. The twinkle in his eyes suggested that he eagerly awaited my reaction to the upcoming scene. I recall one scene in particular. His cousin was sitting on a log behind her young boy. She would methodically pick a louse from the child's hair, examine it, plop it into her mouth, and do the same thing over and over again. I must have had a funny expression on my face because Tupa was laughing loudly when I looked back at him. He told me in the butchered Portuguese we spoke to each other that when I visited his tribe, I, too, would have to eat lice. I informed Tupa quite emphatically that this vegetarian from the hills of Western Pennsylvania was not going to be eating lice anytime soon. Tupa said nothing, but his smirk suggested that he had other plans for me.

The loud ringing of church bells brings me back to the present. I place the photograph on top of the pile in my cardboard box. I wonder what Tupa would think of me now. I see the faces of those friends and family who mourn the loss of the person I was and fear the person they believe I have become. I wish I could find Tupa. He would understand. He, more than anyone, understands change.

The last time I heard from Tupa was in a letter telling me that he was back living with his tribe. His father was now very proud of his nursing degree, proud that he had carried on the tradition of healers in the family. Tupa shyly boasted that he even saved a boy's life with antibiotics that he had brought back to the forest. I miss my friend, whose heart glows like the sun rising on the river he calls home.

I stare at the photograph one more time, remembering what Tupa told me about butterflies. While in the chrysalis, the caterpillar's body dissolves into a gooey soup that feeds the few remaining cells that become the butterfly. I close the lid to the cardboard box and smile. Tupa's healing presence embraces me in the knowledge that transformation cannot occur without loss.

BALQEES MOHAMMED

Balqees Mohammed – An American convert to Islam since 1979, Balqees Mohammed draws from her past experiences as a Christian in the west while also drawing upon her ongoing experiences as a Muslim living in Saudi Arabia to relay her message to her readers. Whether using the genre of fiction or nonfiction, she addresses the many social challenges she sees in the world about her, in an effort to enlighten people to how Islam addresses such challenges, all in an artistic effort to entertain while at the same time drive home an important Islamic moral.

She is also a regular contributor with inspirational articles that expel an Islamic lesson to a website for one of the local chapters of the Islamic Education Centers, which are spread throughout Saudi Arabia and come under the supervision of the Ministry of Islamic Affairs. You can view a collection of some of her articles previously published on this site at her blog: www.life-islam.blogspot.com; or log onto www.islamunveiled.org to read her articles (posted under the name Om Mohammed) and much more.

TA'IBAH AND THE ANTS BY BALQEES MOHAMMED

It had been a long day at school for Ta'ibah, and the walk home in the mid-afternoon August humidity of coastal central Florida made it all that much longer. Not a long walk at two miles, but stretched out longer by the long end-of-summer days of August, compounded only by the great load of books the new school year threatened her with daily. Not one to shun her assignments, though, Ta'ibah carried her burden of books to and from school. She couldn't afford to be lazy this year, this last year of high school, if she was truly serious in her intentions to get into Harvard – not an easy feat for any high school graduate, compounded only by the fact that she was a 'covering Muslimah'. Yes, one of *those*. Against her own parents' directives, she opted to obey her God and stick to the rules of her religion, Islam, which, she said, dictated that she (and all other believing females) cover her head on down to the shoulder region. Yes, she had some extra outside forces going against her in her quest toward a better future, beginning with college, but she was determined to overcome the darkness that threatened to keep her in the dark.

She needed every extra point she could get, and of course could not afford to lose anything off of her regular curriculum.

As she walked in the glass sliding door from the porch, Ta'ibah noticed her mother spraying toward something on the floor at the opposite end of the family room. In fact, she had been led to this back yard door of the house by the acrid piercing stench of the bug spray. It was her usual routine to come in the side door after school to avoid dirtying up the main entrance-way to the house. Years of her mother complaining about her tracking in dirt when she came home from school had taught her that going in the side door, where she could conveniently leave her dirty shoes in the coat closet, was a good way to avoid engaging her mother's anger. Besides, the side door was closer to her room than both the front and back doors.

But when she approached the side entrance, a strong smell of bug spray came lingering out to her, almost sweeping her toward the source with its acrid hand. As if pulled by some invisible magnet, she followed the smell around to the back yard, almost choking on the stench as she came in closer and closer to the back door entrance. Suzanne motioned her to stay at the glass door, but Ta'ibah insisted to see what the terrible vermin was that her mother was so intent on killing.

"The bug spray must not be working so well, Mom," Ta'ibah said, as she noticed her mom stomping frantically right and left – first one leg, then the other.

Afraid for her daughter, Suzanne ordered, "Get back, Ta'ibah – don't want these things getting in your hair and clothes, too. I'm enough. I'll get them even if I have to stomp on every last one!"

And with that, Suzanne returned to her simultaneous spraying, stomp-ing, and flinging her arms every which way in an effort to fight them off from every angle, trying desperately to get the invasive things out of her hair mass.

"Mom! What is it?" cried Ta'ibah in despair at viewing her mother in such an angered state. Then, as she came in closer to her mother's side, her eyes grew wide with frightful surprise at the sight: ANTS! Lots and lots of big, fat, black jumbo ants with wings, and lots of half-sized red ants. Also with wings. But they didn't go about in normal fashion as one normally sees ants – searching for tidbits of food to carry innocently and ceremoniously home to their nest. No, they were going round in circles, every which way, apparently ganging up on her mom with a vengeful force. When aggravated, these winged ants took to jumping their opponent with frightfully vicious speed and in a quite unpredictable manner, jumping in a direction totally alien to their physical stance. What made matters worse, at this present stage, was their immense numbers. The white floor had turned black and red with their dense presence.

It was only with a second of thought and remembrance of the lessons she had learned from Sheikh Mahmud a year earlier that Ta'ibah was able to suppress her reflex reaction to scream at the sight of the multitudes of ants seizing in on her mother, replacing it with a valiant remembrance of God's name and a meaningful heartfelt declaration of her faith. *"Bismillah! Ashhadu an laa ilaha illa-llah, wa ash-hadu anna Muhammadan rasul Allah!"*

Noticing her mother freezing with fright at the impending attacks upon her by the millions of ants, she then attempted to instruct her mother as calmly as possible. "Mom! First thing is you gotta stop stomping everywhere. Just stand still a moment, and say '*Bismillah*'."

Her fright taking over, making her lose her sense of understanding and reason, Suzanne argued, "But they're everywhere, Ta'ibah. Can't you see them flying and jumping onto me? God! Is that one in my hair now?!"

Although she herself was scared, Ta'ibah realized that her mom needed calming in order to take a firm grip on the situation. Silently praying to Allah in an attempt to summon up the strength she needed, Ta'ibah inhaled a deep breath while uttering *Bismillah*, and then she proceeded to advise her now hysterical mother once more.

"Mom…it *is* frightening, for sure. But when you remember Allah, turn to Him in repentance, and seek His help, He will then give you the strength to face the most dangerous opponent, not just a colony or two of ants."

Her fright still getting the best of her, Suzanne stuttered, "B…b…b… but…"

Not giving her mother the chance to continue in her hysterical tirade, Ta'ibah went on instructing her, and Suzanne repeated after her, as if she were the child, and Ta'ibah the mother.

"OK, Mom, now repeat after me. Say, '*Bismillah illadhi laa yadharu ma' asmahi shay'un fil-ardhi wala fi-as-samaa' wa huwa as-sami' al-alim*.' Repeat it three times, mother dear."

Obediently repeating her daughter's guiding and reassuring words, Suzanne's voice became calmer and stronger with the utterance of each word.

Going on before her mother could slip back into her frightful state, Ta'ibah went on instructing her on what to say for protection and strength: *"Aoudhu bi-kalimaati-llahi min sharri ma khalaq.* Again, mother, repeat these words three times."

Once more following her daughter's wise instructions, Suzanne's confidence built with each word, as she noticed the ants that were upon her retreating to the floor, and those on the floor no longer coming her way, but merely going 'round in directionless circles.

Not wanting to give the ants one moment's rest to return in their attack, Ta'ibah immediately continued when her mother finished the previous recitation.

"Now, mother dear, begin with saying Allah's name, and then seeking refuge with Him from Satan, and then recite surat al-Fatihah once only. When you've said that, then recite ayat-al-kursi. You *do* know ayat al-kursi, don't you, Mom?"

Quickly glancing at her daughter with a mixture of surprise and anger at this insinuation, Suzanne answered her question with a perfect and meaningfully strong recitation of surat-al-Fatihah followed by ayat al-kursi. When finished, Suzanne piped in before giving Ta'ibah a chance to go on with her instructions. "Who do you think taught you those verses in the first place, dearie? Or have you forgotten your mother's hard work all those years to learn in order to coach and teach you? You may have gained a lot of knowledge through the years, my dear, even surpassing me by a long shot, but I might just surprise you with a few things that I know."

A bit embarrassed and rightfully ashamed of her accusing insinuation of her mother's intellect, Ta'ibah found it hard to lift her eyes up to even meet her mother's once she had finally found her voice. "Ehem...ehem..." Something seemed to be stuck in Ta'ibah's throat, but she finally was able to clear it enough to speak her mind and apologize properly to her dear mother. "Ehem...aw, Mom...I'm sorry. I really didn't mean it that way. I know it sounded bad. Gee...I really didn't mean it like that. But, hey, look! See? The ants are going away, Mom! You did it! You have convinced them that this is certainly not the right place for them by your reciting of Allah's words and the remembrance of His name."

A little embarrassed herself, Suzanne answered, "No, dear, *you* did it. You calmed me with your faithful and persistent reminders. You calmed me and strengthened me with your own calm and strength. It was as if you were my mother, and I was your child. I couldn't control my fear. I lost it. But you guided me back into sanity and security."

"Aw, Mom…it wasn't me that had the strength. You stayed right where you were, even chased me out for my safety. You were the brave one. And it was Allah who gave us both the strength and descended upon us His magnificent and merciful tranquility at a time we dearly needed it."

"Yes, indeed, my darling daughter. Such a wise one for a teenager."

Smiling while hugging her mother in a never-let-go hold, Ta'ibah said, "I had a good teacher. You taught me all the basics, you guided me throughout my years, and you were the one who put me on the right track to begin with. May Allah be pleased with you, mother dear, for raising me in the manner you did."

Not able to control her tears, Suzanne replied, "And may Allah be pleased with you, my darling Ta'ibah."

TROUBLED WATERS CAN BE SAILABLE
BY BALQEES MOHAMMED

Dhafer was late once again for dinner. Sara had been waiting all day. After cleaning the house and cooking his favorite dish, she sat to watch the news before he was due to come home after work.

As the news program finished, Sara began to impatiently switch the channels, trying to get her mind off of steaming at his being late again – third time this week. It didn't so much bother her that he was so late. But, she thought, at least he could call, couldn't he? Shouldn't he? Why did he so inconsiderately leave her hanging in waiting all day long? Didn't he think of her? Didn't he have any concern for her having to wait like this all day with no explanation? If it were his daily schedule, it wouldn't have bothered her so much. But his daily schedule was that he was home at 1:30 PM, latest, for the meal. And today – well, it was now past 6:00 PM – the salad had wilted, the stew was cold, and the bread stale – and still not even a word from him. She would have been worried that perhaps he'd had an accident, but his previous similar performances had taught her that he was just simply late and didn't think to call. Par for the course. Meetings. Hmmph. Indeed.

By the time Dhafer walked through the door at 6:45 PM, Sara had built up enough steam to blow up the tea kettle, much less make it come to a boil. He came in ever so cautiously, so as to hopefully avoid her fury at his first entrance. To his surprise, almost even dread, she was almost deathly quiet as he walked in the door. She went to heat up the stew and served up the dinner table – all to his amazement at her composure. Yet, through it all, it was obvious that she was terribly stressed out. The quiet before the storm.

Although she could feel the pressure rising from her gut through her chest, and then pressing its way up through her head – almost popping her ears – she ever so wisely waited until Dhafer was on his fruit before making any effort at small talk through dinner. She cautiously kept her mouth shut tight, out of the fear that she would not be able to control herself if she began. When she did finally begin, she proved her fears right. Halfway through his apple, she could no longer hold it in. She began to let the steam loose, before she had a real breakdown and eventual blowup.

"How many times are you going to do this?"

"What?" Dhafer replied, rolling his innocent-looking wide eyes her way.

"You know perfectly well 'what'!" she answered in impatient disgust. With uncontrollably rising anger, Sara continued, "This is the third time this week – the tenth this month – that you've ruined dinner. I want a divorce."

"What?"

"Is that all you can say...what?! You heard me – I want a divorce."

"You've gotta be kidding! Because I'm late for dinner?"

"Dhafer – it's not that exactly, or on its own, at least. You know that. You don't have the courtesy to call me and tell me that you'll be late. It's so disrespectful, you know, thoughtless of my hard work trying to please you and keep our home nice. I'm tired of this treatment. I want out. I would rather live out the rest of my life on my own than have to put up with this disrespect. I want a divorce."

"OK, dear. Let's just sleep on it tonight – OK? You'll feel better tomorrow, I'm sure. I have to go check up on my parents now. We'll talk more when I get home later."

"No, Dhafer. I don't want to talk anymore. Not now, and certainly not later. Divorce me – now."

A few moments of silence passed by as Dhafer thought through his options. To Sara, it seemed as if hours had passed before he began his reply.

"All right, Sara, if you insist. What I'll do is – I'll go out for a while, and then send you your paper shortly." With that, Dhafer left Sara alone to wallow in her sorrow at her own impatience, pouting ever more about her lot in life. No sooner had he shut the door, but what she flung herself at the bed in a rage of fury – at Dhafer for his non-caring for her, at herself for her own impatience, at her lot in general.

After a period of two hours had passed, Dhafer came home once again, for a shorter yet quieter period this time. As he made his way to his closet to pack a few things for an overnight stay at his parents', he gently put the sealed envelope on the bedspread beside the now sleeping Sara. No need to wake her for this, he thought. She will find it when she wakes. It's better that way. He knew that if he needed more clothes later, he could always come by another time for some more, or he could even go shopping so as to avoid any more conflict. But for tonight, they had both had enough. It was best just to leave things in this manner, in hopeful quiet and a sense of peace. After putting all his things together and leaving the envelope beside Sara, he stood at the doorway to their bedroom one more time to take another silent and longing look at his bride of only six months earlier. In sad reflection, he began to think – what happened to those happy honeymoon days? What happened to our excitement and thrill at being married?

In thoughtful response to his reflection, he answered himself his own questions: Life is what happened to us. The honeymoon ended, and we began to live the reality of life. Working, exhaustion, bills, tensions – life in general. Well, he thought, as he turned to continue his way out of the apartment, Sara now has what she's been asking for. Let's wait and see her response – if this finally makes her happy.

When Sara woke groggy from her unrestful slumber, she could hardly pull herself up on her elbows to look around and acquaint herself once again with her surroundings. Was it real? she thought to herself. Did all of that really happen? Did I really go overboard this time in asking for a divorce… just because he was late for dinner again? Looking around her bedroom and noticing no telltale signs of Dhafer's presence – his shoes were not where he put them when he was at home, his ghutra and cap worn under it were not on the chair beside the door, his keys were not hanging on the wooden key box – she realized that he must have left. This time, perhaps for good. Then, as she turned her head even farther to the right and a bit downwards, she saw it…there it was, lying right beside her on the bed…a sealed envelope with only her first name written on it: Sara. Now she just knew he had left for good. Isn't that what she was asking for, anyway?

As soon as she noticed it, she just knew instinctively what it was. Her divorce, just as she had requested. Why, wasn't she the one who asked for it with such immaturity and bad manners? Wasn't she the one who picked the fight in the first place? Wasn't she the one who was ranting and raving in uncontrollable rage? As she played the previous evening over and over again in her head like a run-down video tape, it made her literally sick to her stomach to remember how she had acted and spoken to her beloved Dhafer.

Sure, he had been thoughtless of her, making her wait with dinner all that time without even calling to let her know he'd be late. But did it really constitute or deserve such an outrage of reaction? Surely, there was more to their relationship that would help them through such rough waters. But was there?

Realizing the painful fact that she had now lost him, she once again disintegrated into a limp slump on the bed, crying until she almost had no tears anymore, until her voice went rough and hoarse with her painful cries of sorrow. She was sure that nothing could bring back, once again, what once was. Time had passed by mercifully, letting her fall into a restless slumber. She awoke only to a terribly disturbing bell ringing off somewhere in the distant hills. But what distant hills? They lived in the middle of the desert! No, the disturbing incessant ringing was coming from some barrel somewhere. Then, as she pried her swollen eyes open ever so slightly, she realized that the ringing was coming from her bedside phone. Reaching over to pick the receiver off the hook, she barely made it in time before the caller hung up…again. The caller on the other end, almost losing all sense of control over the fact of her not answering, was startled by the quiet on Sara's end when she picked up. Sara began to waken more when she realized that her mother was there on the other end, and she was apparently terribly worried or angry, or something.

"Sara…Sara…are you there? Why don't you answer, dear? Why did it take you so long to answer the phone?" said Maya, Sara's mother.

Remembering more now, as she came almost to full consciousness, Sara sprang into her uncontrollable crying once more. She could not disguise her pain and her sorrow, but her mother on the other end could only hear her crying. She had no idea what was the cause of her crying. Not able to say one audible word, the only thing Sara could do was to sob her throbbing sobs into the phone's receiver, worrying her mother even more.

"Sara…Sara…what's wrong?! Please talk! Take a deep breath…and talk, dear!"

But every time Sara made motion to begin speaking, the only thing that would come out of her mouth were even more sobs, the hot tears burning her cheeks as they rolled unchecked down her face from her already swollen eyes.

"Sara, dear…I'm on my way. Don't hang up. Stay on the line. I'll be there in a few moments. I'm close already. And I've texted your father to come and bring your brother, Mohsen, with him, as well."

Sara fell once more in the limp slump on the bed, phone receiver still in hand, but no longer at her ear. She couldn't bring herself to talk to anyone.

Not her Mum, not her Dad, not her brother...no one. She didn't deserve to live. In fact, she felt that life was no longer worth living. She had had it all...a wonderful and loving husband, a nice new home, a promising future...and she threw it all out the door with her selfish and immature impatience and fury. Why couldn't I have been more patient and adult about things? Why did I have to be so childish in asking for divorce at the first sign of a problem? Why couldn't I have simply asked him why he hadn't called, or even told him how it made me feel...without pressing for divorce? And why did he have to respond to my stupid insistence at divorce?

All the rhetorical questions and what ifs and why nots would never help her now, and she knew it well. In fact, this manner of beating herself up made her realize the wisdom in the Islamic advice to not reflect on the past in this manner by asking or demanding of yourself what if or why or why not. She realized, for sure, that what had happened was in the past, and if she were destined to live with it and to live any sensible life afterwards, she would simply need to make the best of what was to come because of it.

Arriving at the same time in Sara's driveway, Maya and Hassan met each other with worried glances. In answer to her husband's unspoken question, Maya prompted, "I have no idea what is going on. She wouldn't...she couldn't...say anything on the phone. All I know is that she is still alive...I can hear her breathing...and her sobbing. In fact, she hasn't stopped sobbing since she first picked up the phone."

Goading his parents on, Mohsen wisely said, "Well, then, we'd better get in there and tend to our dear Sara. God forbid, perhaps she's had an accident, or someone broke in and attacked her." No sooner had Mohsen finished those words, but they were all three entering into her bedroom, cautiously tiptoeing from room to room, in case the alleged invader was still in the house. But as they came closer toward her, they all three realized at the same time that there was nothing terribly wrong here, at least nothing physically. All they could see was that Sara was lying on the bed, consumed in her uncontrollable tears and sobs, and beside her was an unopened envelope with her name on it: Sara. Not able to retain herself, Maya bent over to hold her daughter in a comforting hug. "Sara...Sara...come out of it, dear. What's wrong? You can tell your Mum."

Sitting up, with her mother propping her, Sara looked up to see her father and her brother, Mohsen, standing above her, as well as her mother now sitting at her side on the bed. Trying to contain herself enough to explain, but finding that she could not, she broke into yet another fit of uncontrollable sobs and the hottest tears yet. "Oh…Mum!! Dad!! What h…h…have I done?" Then she could say no more, only sobbing more and more, shaking in her mother's tight grasp.

Trying to take control of the situation, Sara's father said, "What's this here beside you, Sara? It looks like a letter of some kind. The envelope has only your first name on it: Sara." Picking up the envelope as he simultaneously put the phone's receiver back on the hook, Hassan continued before Sara could answer. Looking over his reading glasses at his daughter, he gave her the undeniable sign that he was about to read the contents of the mysterious envelope. Sara closed her eyes, just knowing what was to come next. Exhausted with her previous sobbing to the extent of almost fainting, all she could manage now was the incessant stream of hot tears rolling down her cheeks, reddened already from the overflow of the salty tears.

Coughing slightly to clear his throat, Hassan began to read the note addressed to his daughter: "My dearly beloved wife, Sara. After such a short time of marriage, we have encountered some rough waters that not all couples encounter. But we have crossed over them so far with what I had assumed understanding and tolerance. Perhaps I was wrong. Perhaps you were acting. And perhaps I simply misunderstood the signs. The only thing I can say is to ask for your forgiveness if I have somehow been intolerant of your feelings and needs. You should know…you need to know…that since the first day that we met before our engagement, I have loved you. And then, as we came to know each other better before the marriage and afterwards, I have grown to love you only more and more. You are everything to me in this life, second only to Allah and His Apostle. My parents are gone. I have no sisters or brothers. And we have not yet been blessed to have any children in our short time together. Just remember that marriage is a two-way street. It takes two to make it, and it takes two to break it. And even though you have asked…no, demanded…in your hour of impatience…for divorce…I am sorry to tell you that I cannot be the second to join in on the breaking of this marriage. So, for now at least, I am not divorcing you. And I ask you humbly to reconsider seriously your previous request. I will grant you all the time you feel you need to recuperate and nourish your soul and heart. Then, whenever you are ready for us to make a new start, I am here for you whenever you shall call me. You know where I am, and you know my number. I will be waiting ever so patiently and lovingly for your call. I miss your voice, your touch, and your company. Let's both try harder now to make a new and fresh start. Signed: Your loving partner, Dhafer."

His mother and father now speechless from this beautiful love letter, Mohsen spoke up to break the silence. In his usual teasing manner, his prodding of his sister gave a light air to the heavy load obviously lifting from her shoulders. "Tsk tsk…my, my, my, dear sister. You certainly do have him wrapped around your finger, eh? What did you do to deserve such a letter?"

Only now able to begin to control her sobs to a slight whimper, Sara began to find her voice to explain the whole situation to her family, embarrassing as it was. "…We…we…we had a fight."

Almost overcome with anger at what she was beginning to understand of her daughter's impatience and apparent insistence at divorce, Maya could no longer hold her tongue. "Yes…I think we all understand that now. What on earth about? My goodness, Sara. Dhafer is such a good man. And he's been so good to you. You should be ashamed of yourself…asking for a divorce…and after only six months of marriage!"

Making a move to usher his wife out of the room, Hassan insisted that she either retain her comments or leave. "Hush, Maya. Leave the girl speak. It is obvious that she's had a hard time. Like Dhafer so wisely put it in his own letter…it takes two to make it, and two to break it. As with any problem in any marriage, there has obviously been two contributors. Neither one should ever be put to shoulder the whole blame. Let her go on." Looking toward Sara and nodding to her in a gesture to go on, Hassan said, "Go on, dear…do tell us the rest."

Still fighting off the tears, but able to control her sobs finally, Sara continued. "We had a fight. It began actually a long time ago. But the last straw was last night. He came home late for dinner…terribly late. He didn't call to tell me he'd be late or to apologize. He simply came home late. By the time he came home, I was fuming. Obviously. Kept myself quiet until the last course of the fruit…then I couldn't bear it any longer. Let the dam flow, as they say. And flow it did. I ended up asking for a divorce. Of course, he objected at first…but I kept on insisting. Finally, he got quiet. Frighteningly quiet. He just left. Without saying one more word. Then he came back couple hours later…laid this envelope on the bed beside me, and left once more…never to come back. I of course assumed…that it was my divorce. Now you've read it, Dad…you've all heard it…my gosh…I'm so embarrassed. From all of you, from myself, from Dhafer…from Allah. Ya…Allah…why did I have to get so impatient in asking for divorce? Why couldn't I see through the red madness and notice Dhafer's kindness and loving?"

Interrupting Sara's tirade of what ifs and why nots, Maya felt the need to attempt to guide her daughter as to how to renew her relationship with Dhafer. Noticing the look on Maya's face, obvious that she was about to begin speaking, Hassan gave her a stern look of warning to remind her to be kind and loving with their daughter, even though she had been wrong to so impatiently ask for a divorce over such a simple problem. Not letting him even speak a word, but realizing the meaning of his look all the same, Maya began by reassuring him of her stance and intentions. "Don't worry, Hassan, I know what to say, and how to handle this. Just let me do my job as a mother."

Maya then began to advise and guide her daughter as to how to begin renewing her relationship with her husband. "Sara, dear, we all have misunderstandings. That is part of human nature and our makeup as males and females. Why, even our beloved prophet Mohammed had misunderstandings from time to time with his wives. But neither did he nor his wives let those misunderstandings end up in needless and tragic divorce. Allah has mercifully provided for us a way out of every bad situation, including a dysfunctional marriage. But, my dear, a misunderstanding such as what you have just described does not really qualify as dysfunctional. It is simply a misunderstanding…which has blown out of proportion. Don't let it get the best of you, and don't let it destroy what you have and what you can have with this loving man."

Back to sobbing again, but not so uncontrollably as earlier, Sara managed a few words before she lost control once again: "Yes, Mum…I know all that. I was stupid. I was immature. But…I asked for…no, demanded for… divorce. And now…this…this…love letter from him. What am I to do now? I'm so embarrassed."

Almost laughing, while gently wiping away her daughter's tears, Maya said, "Yes, my dear, you were indeed stupid and immature in your request. But I think that perhaps you have learned your lesson now. And to add icing onto the cake...your husband has proved that he has his head set square on his shoulders, and he is loving and kind enough to be so patient so as to offer you some time to yourself for your own healing, while humbly asking your forgiveness and for a second chance for the two of you. Such a wise man, something very rare in today's world, my dear. Don't let this opportunity pass you by."

Going on, not letting her daughter or anyone else speak yet, Maya said, "Do, now, as your loving husband has so wisely advised and requested of you...take the time that you need. But I strongly advise you...don't take too long. Then, once you are ready, make that call to him...I'm sure you will find him waiting...and anxiously willing to return to your home to begin once again, almost as fresh as you were on your wedding day. Let what is in the past remain there, and start anew with a new clean page. Kind of like when Allah has promised us a clean slate as we begin our new lives as reborn Muslims. So you should also make a new start with your marriage, putting the past behind you, not bringing up old harps, and looking toward a new and brighter future, having both of you learned the hard lessons from this experience. Remember that Allah is oft-forgiving...He so mercifully forgives all of our sins, as long as we humbly approach Him in seeking His divine forgiveness. Now, your husband has asked your forgiveness. Don't be silly and stubborn in refusing it to him. You, also, need to seek his forgiveness, and both of you need to put all of this behind you to begin fresh and new."

Surprised that Sara had so quickly come round with this short session of advice, Maya, Hassan, and Mohsen were all taken by her next move. With her eyes still flowing with tears, this time tears of hope and inspiration mixed with a tinge of fear of rejection, Sara made her way across the bed once more to the phone, this time to make a call rather than answering. She dialed the number almost burned into her memory, Dhafer's mobile number. It rang only once, and she could hear his low, almost frightened voice on the other end. The fight of the previous night had been so strenuous and burning, he was afraid of anything that might come next. Answering his low and tender voice, she said: "Assalaamu alaikum, Dhafer. Dear. I'm...I'm...

I'm...so sooorry." Interrupting her apologies, he said on the other end, only she could hear now, "No, dear...I'm sorry..." Not letting him continue, she went on,"I'm so sorry, dear. How can you ever forgive me? Yes...I'm ready, if you are. OK...I'm here. I'll be here."

With that, and with tears still stringing down her cheeks, she hung up the phone. Making their way to the door, her mother turned round once more to her daughter. "Are you sure you're ready, dear? Have you really had enough time?"

Realizing her mistakes and the need for their healing together, Sara replied, "Yes, mother. Thank you...thanks to all of you...for everything. But yes, I'm ready. We both are ready. It's time, as you said, to put the past behind us. If I remain here alone, I'll only go over things again and again, and maybe I will once again blow everything out of proportion, without hearing his side of it. That is what caused this whole thing in the first place, you know...I didn't give him the chance...didn't even ask...for his side of things. Didn't ask why he was late. Didn't ask why he didn't call me. All I did was impatiently ask for divorce. You know, Mother, maybe this is why Allah didn't give the free and open choice to women for divorce. Only in extenuating circumstances of dysfunctional marriage can she apply for annulment or separation. And, surely, as you have already pointed out, Mother, our marriage certainly is not dysfunctional – maybe a few problems here and there, but certainly not dysfunctional. I think...at least I hope...I've learned my lesson. And I thank Allah sincerely that I have such a loving and understanding husband who will stand beside me at such a horrific time. I only hope that he can forgive me."

All of them looked at Sara one last time before they left, their combined sense of reassurance that things would work out right showing on their bright faces. Hassan said one parting word of fatherly advice as he was the last to walk out the door. "Just remember, Sara, not everything is always as it may seem to be at first. Give the other person the chance to explain his or her standpoint, and only then should you begin to judge your reaction. I'm sure you will tread more carefully from now on. You have a fine husband. Take care of him, and he will surely take care of you. It is obvious that he already is. Both of you together...take care of your marriage."

With silent tears of remorse for her past impatience combined with hope for the future, Sara reassured her father. "Yes, Father, I will indeed take care of him, as he is taking care of me, and together we shall take care of our marriage. Thank you for coming."

Several days later, Dhafer called Hassan to invite them all for a family dinner to publicly announce their official reunion. It was a most happy occasion, perhaps even happier than the original marriage itself. They had been through some tough waters, but they weathered the storm together, and perhaps they were now stronger because of it.

Years later, after many years of blissful marriage and many children, Sara lovingly reflected on those long past days when Dhafer so patiently rejected her immature request for a divorce. By then she was able to laugh at herself and had learned her lesson well. She emphatically passed on to many the importance of the lessons both she and Dhafer learned from the whole experience.

ENITH MORILLO

Enith Morillo is a revert from Venezuela. Enith is an engineer by profession and a writer by passion. Her writing spans from poetry and short fiction, to career-related articles, to essays about women in science and technology. A lover of reading and the written word, she aspires to become a published poet and author, and to contribute to the spread of Islam by translating Islamic works to Spanish. Enith enjoys photography, nature hikes, and learning.

THE BLESSING OF HOPE BY ENITH MORILLO

4 down, 1 to go! My husband and I hurried through the logistics of making time for each other on this cold Saturday evening. Okay, so one is in bed asleep, two are watching TV, the older one is playing video games while babysitting the younger three, and the oldest one is at work until 11 PM, at which time he will need a ride back home. Let's go!

At the speed of light, we left the house and got in the car, driving in no particular direction, while voting on whether an hour and a half was better spent indulging in a rich, calorie-packed dessert at the Cheesecake Factory, or browsing through the latest books at Barnes & Noble. Although secretly my soul craved for the written word, we decided cheesecake was better than books. Fortunately, the waiting time at the Cheesecake Factory was 45 minutes, so we ended up at the bookstore, my haven, alhamdulillah.

As we sampled the variety of titles available in the Religious section, skimming through the intoxicating poems of Rumi and the controversial *The Problem with Islam Today*, our quality time (more like my communion with books) was quickly interrupted by a familiar greeting. "As-salaamu-alaikum."

Needless to say, the greeting of peace I usually long for brought frustration instead. "What? You mean to tell me that after finally getting a minute to ourselves following an arduous week of work and chores, someone wants to engage in conversation." I sternly turned in the direction of the voice, and my aggravation immediately dissolved at the sight of this young, college-student-looking sister smiling at me. "Alaikum salaam," I answered.

And so began my journey into the past!

The sister, whose name turned out to be Amal, enthusiastically introduced herself as a recent convert who did not wear the scarf, but knew she would someday. To prove it, she showed us her latest scarf purchase in her shopping bag. She was heading home after working at the mall's chocolatier when her heart called out to the Islamic books' section of Barnes & Noble. Her hesitation to approach us banished the minute her lips burst out our greeting. I, looking at the young sister in amazement, couldn't help being transported fourteen years back to when, as a teenager on a semester abroad, I raced through the streets of Venice at the sight of a Muslim couple. Their skepticism seemed now well-founded as I thought of my eager "As-salaamu-alaikum" while in my shorts and tank.

Amal, who in appearance seemed to have roots anywhere from Morocco to Philippines, was an American college student. She had accepted Islam no more than a few months ago, at the hands of another student in her campus: a Saudi sister who had recently gone back to her homeland. The Saudi sister had not only introduced Amal to Islam, but to the beauty of real sisterhood, being by her side as she learned how to pray and navigated the rough waters of telling your family you have decided to embrace Islam. Her return to Saudi Arabia had left Amal with a hard void to fill. Yet Amal persevered in drawing closer to Allah in prayer and patience, and with frequent "Alhamdulillahs" and calls to her Saudi sister, she pressed on.

Rewind to the early '90s, to find myself in college, surrounded by Muslim students from all over the world thinking that this "Alhamdulillah" concept was very cool. "Oh, I failed my thermodynamics test, Alhamdulillah." "Man, I have to work the whole spring break, Alhamdulillah." "I got a call last night about my uncle's passing, Alhamdulillah." I could not comprehend how seemingly catastrophic events could all be suffixed with this word "Alhamdulillah" and a scary calmness. Whatever the word meant, I wanted to own it. I wanted to be able to end my sentences, worries, and sadness with this amazing word.

After having accepted Islam, Amal's family, with the exception of her mother, had agreed that Islam would protect her from the evils of society. They supported her decision to wear modest clothes and not drink, date, or gamble. Her mother, on the other hand, took Amal's acceptance of Islam as a slap on the face. "How dare you go and get a religion of your own! Wasn't what I taught you good enough?" Through prayer, Amal worked on smoothing out these rough edges of her conversion. She was already replacing her so-called Muslim guy roommates with Muslim gals, making frequent visits to the local masjid, and brushing off with grace the constant harassment at the university's cafeteria by the same ignorant attendant.

I found it hard to focus on Amal's story and not draw parallels with my own. After accepting Islam, my mother had been my strongest opponent (now my closest supporter), and I had given an ultimatum to my "Muslim" boyfriend that we had to get married. Nonchalantly, he had declined by sharing with me he was a descendent of the prophet Muhammad (saw) and that he was only allowed to marry other descendants. I recall wondering how he wanted to honor his ancestry by not marrying me, while still disgracing himself by disobeying Allah's command. The heartbreak didn't last as long as the astonishment of the irony of it all.

Amal happily continued to tell us her story. Along her path, she had met a fierce sister who instilled in her fear of even touching our blessed book. With severe warnings of hell, punishment, and hypocrisy, the sister had left out the balance between fear and hope, and had made Amal withdraw from Allah's call for a short while. Luckily, Allah chooses and guides whom He pleases, and Amal soon realized that sister possibly had good intentions but a terrible approach to teaching Islam. Amal put her fear aside and courageously went back to reading the Qur'an and making her prayers. Alhamdulillah.

Fast forward through one divorce, a saga with an imam secretly marrying and divorcing sisters a.k.a. a "serial-marriager," and finally to the blessing of my husband and our blended family of five children. As I stood there listening to this lively sister, I couldn't help but think what her future would bring. Would she survive the heartache of learning that Muslims and Islam are not interchangeable words? Would she be able to live through the disappointment of some sisters' ill behavior in the masjid? Would Allah test her with a marriage gone wrong?

With these thoughts racing through my head, my Muslim mother and teacher came to mind. She had taken me under her wing, and helped me grow in Islam and through life. She had sheltered me from misguidance by always encouraging me to read and to think. "Use your mind!" she would tell me. "And what I do for you, you do for someone else." Looking at Amal I knew what my responsibility would be.

Suddenly, this night seemed a marvel and blessing from Allah. What had started off as a date with my husband had turned out to be a call to duty. I no longer resented Amal for interrupting our quality time away from the children, but felt humbled and grateful for having crossed paths with her. Time ran out too soon, and we had to head out to pick up our oldest child from work. Swiftly we exchanged numbers, hugs, and greetings of peace, and agreed to meet again.

On our way home, with a takeout order of cheesecake, all I could happily utter was "Alhamdulillah," for the blessing of hope.

SABAH NEGASH

Sabah Negash was born and raised in Southern California. She is from a family of teachers and enjoys traveling and experiencing new things. Her 15-year teaching career has given her the wonderful opportunity to live and work abroad. It was through her teaching that she came to love writing and story-telling to encourage good morals and character in her students. Her love for teaching and her mother's constant support, love, and guidance have encouraged her to continue her education in the field of Early Childhood Education.

A LETTER TO JEDDAH BY SABAH NEGASH

"Can I see Jeddah now?" I asked Daddy for the fifth time. I had been sitting in the waiting room all morning and wanted a chance to see her. Daddy paced back and forth as doctors rushed in and out of Jeddah's hospital room, taking tests and asking Daddy and my aunties questions. No one noticed me sitting and waiting; no one would tell me what was going on or when I could go see my Jeddah.

"Your grandmother is very ill, Najah," Daddy said, his voice tense and his brows scrunched at the center of his head, frowning at me. "She needs her rest."

I sat back in my chair, staring at the floor and holding my knees for comfort. Daddy stopped pacing. He looked at me, wide-eyed and teary. He sat in the chair next to me, placed his arm around me and held me close. No longer frowning, he tried to smile, but his eyes still glistened as he tried to fight back his tears.

"I'm sorry Najah, I should not have snapped at you."

Jeddah's illness had been sudden. She was visiting in Malaysia when Daddy got a call that she was coming home right away. I could see in his face he was worried as he spoke into the phone. His voice and hand shook as he handed me my breakfast. I knew something was wrong when he would not let me speak to Jeddah, saying, "She is too sick to speak right now." Jeddah never called without speaking to me. She always made time, even if she was tired or busy. She always made time for me.

As I sat in thought, I remembered the fun times I had with Jeddah, even before I met her. Jeddah loved to travel. When I was born, she was teaching in China with my aunties. Daddy always showed me pictures of them together. Jeddah was tall and had a kind smile.

When I could talk, I would speak to her on the phone. Once, when I did not want to go to bed, Daddy let me call Jeddah. She sang me songs and told me a bedtime story to help me go to sleep. I loved talking to Jeddah because she always listened to me.

She always sent me pictures and presents from the different countries she visited, like my pink Chinese dress and panda bear from China, or the gold necklace she bought for me when she visited Sudan, and a picture of my aunties climbing the Great Wall in China. When I was four, I got a big surprise. Jeddah was coming back to the States, just to meet me. I was so excited, but a little worried. "Is Jeddah going to like me?" I asked Daddy.

"Of course, she is." He laughed. "She is going to love you, just as she already does now."

Daddy had been right. Jeddah and I got along very well. We did everything together – playing, gardening, reading, shopping, and even cooking. Jeddah always knew the right answer to everything. When there was a problem, she knew how to fix it. Like the time she helped my Mommy and Daddy find me a good Muslim school. Or the time a cat scratched me as I petted it, she chased the cat away, then she cleaned the scratch and put a Band-Aid on it. My daddy and aunties always say that Allah answers Jeddah's duas because she is a good Muslim. That's why they always ask her to pray and make dua for them when they have problems. When I got sick once, Jeddah made dua for me, cared for me, and stayed with me until I got better. But now Jeddah was really sick, and the doctors didn't know how to make her better.

I unfolded my legs and climbed into my daddy's chair and curled up in his lap.

"Well, when can I see her, Daddy?" I asked, wiping away my tears.

"Insha Allah...soon, baby, soon," he answered. "If God wills it."

A man in a white coat and a long face entered the waiting room. "We have the results back in," he said to my Daddy. They walked toward the door of the waiting room. I could barely hear what he was saying. "I'm sorry to say that your mother has terminal stage cancer. We have tried everything, but her body is not responding to treatment. All we can do now is to make her comfortable."

Daddy lowered his head. "From Allah we come, and to Him we return," he whispered in grief.

With a gentle pat on the back, the doctor said, "You may go in and see your mother now. Your sisters are already with her." Then he bade Daddy goodbye. Finally, I could go in and see Jeddah!

Daddy took my hand and led me to Jeddah's room. Her eyes were closed. My aunties were sitting next to her bed, holding her hands. I thought she was sleeping, but when I entered the room, she opened her eyes and smiled. In a weak and hoarse voice, not at all her own, she whispered, "As Salaamu Alaikum, Honey Pie, how are you today?"

A tear fell as I gazed at Jeddah, weak but still strong. She embarrassed me with a warm and gentle hug, the kind that only grandmothers can give. "Don't be afraid, baby cakes," she whispered. "Everyone must return to Allah – it is just my time." Jeddah smiled, gently stroking my head. "Everything will be all right."

The next week, Jeddah came home. Night after night, I prayed and prayed. Jeddah always told me to pray to Allah, to make dua. But Jeddah only got weaker and sicker. "Is Jeddah going to die?" I tearfully whispered to Auntie Zakiyyah as she read the Qur'an to Jeddah while she rested in bed.

Auntie slowly closed the Qur'an. She picked me up and held me tight. "It is possible. I don't know for sure, but Jeddah is very sick. Her body can no longer fight the cancer."

"But I've been praying and praying," I said.

Auntie smiled and kissed me on the head. She hugged me as I buried my face into her scarf. "Mommy," she said gently, she always called me 'mommy' when she wanted to explain something important to me, "Allah has decreed death for everyone. We will all die one day and return to Allah. Some people die old, some die young. Some die healthy, while others die from sickness. But when Allah calls a man, woman, or child to return to Him, no one can change it," she said.

That night, I kissed Jeddah gently on the cheek. Her breath was slow and gentle, but weak. "Insha Allah, see you tomorrow," I whispered as she slept.

The next day, the sun was gray, and the birds did not sing. Daddy entered my room with tears in his eyes. He picked me up and hugged me tight. "Jeddah has returned to Allah."

I cried that morning, noon, and night. Why did she have to die? I thought. My Mommy tried to comfort me, she held me tight. I cried and cried some more. I missed Jeddah so much. All the times we shared, all the fun we had, and everything she taught me. Who would teach me now?

Days, weeks, and months soon passed. I sat next to Auntie one day at the kitchen table. "Do you miss Jeddah?" I asked.

Auntie smiled. "Of course, I do, and I always will. That is why I pray and make dua for her every day," she answered.

"I miss her, too," I said, "and it makes me very sad that I can't talk to her anymore." I laid my head on the table and closed my eyes.

Auntie put down her pen and papers, then folded her hands. "You know," she said softly, "you can still 'talk' to Jeddah. Even though Jeddah is not here, you can keep her memory alive. What was your favorite activity you and Jeddah did together?" she asked.

Hmm, I thought, we did so much together, and I loved all of it. I thought long and hard. "I really liked writing letters to Jeddah," I smiled. When Jeddah was in the hospital, my mommy would help me write letters and cards to Jeddah. She said it would make Jeddah happy and feel better. Sometimes, Jeddah would write me back when she wasn't too sick.

Auntie smiled. "Okay, then, you can still write letters to her, even if she can't read them."

Write a letter to Jeddah…that seemed a bit weird, but I could give it a try anyway. In the privacy of my room, I switched on my night light. I stared at my paper and pen. What will I say? Where do I begin? I lifted my pen.

Dear Jeddah,
As Salaamu Alaikum, Jeddah. I really miss you.

CONFLICT BY SABAH NEGASH

"Subhan Allah, I'm late. I've got 20 minutes to get ready," the young girl murmured. If there was one thing she hated, it was being late. Being on time was a quality she was known for; people who didn't have respect for time annoyed her. She rushed about the room trying to get ready.

"What's the rush?" Her companion yawned. "Now where are you off to; it's not even noon yet," she asked, while the young girl bustled to and fro.

"Where else would I be going on a Friday at noon," she answered, annoyed at the stupidity of the question.

Ever since she started praying and wearing hijab, the young girl had never missed a Friday prayer. She always found peace, guidance, and strength in the sermons. She even stayed for the lectures held after the prayers. She had learned so much about her deen.

Her companion frowned. "You know, for once, have a little fun. Let's go to the mall or something, maybe grab a movie with some friends?"

The young girl did not respond. She was busy trying to decide whether to wear her blue abaya or black one. Her companion grew agitated. "Besides, it's not even mandatory for women to go. It's not like you are going to go to hell if you miss one or two."

Silence. The young girl did love to socialize; that's what she enjoyed most about the lectures after prayer. She got to meet so many wonderful and knowledgeable sisters.

Her companion thought a bit and smiled. "I hear Samia's having a party today. We could go. It's going to be a blast – great music, great food, cool crowd and—"

"What?" she interrupted. "You want me to miss my prayer just to go to some lame party, no doubt there will be all kinds of fitnah and haraam activities. Are you nuts?" she asked, disgusted at the thought. A year ago, the young girl would have jumped at the opportunity; she was known to be a party girl. But things had changed; she had changed. She turned to the mirror and began brushing back her hair. "No, thanks. Unlike you, I fear Allah (swt) and the last day."

"Oh, come on," her companion replied. "It wouldn't be that bad. No one is asking you to do anything haraam, just have a little fun, that's all. There will be other Muslims there, as well – Dana and Tahir."

The young girl ignored her and continued to get ready. Her companion watched in horror as she changed from her attractive, slim-cut blue abaya to a looser-fitting black one. "It's hot as hell today. Why don't you wear that lovely white sundress Anise got you last week?" she suggested. "It's a lot prettier and cooler than that black blanket."

"It's not a blanket," the young girl protested. "And no, that dress doesn't cover properly."

Her companion sneered. "You are going to look like an old lady in that. Why can't you dress fashionably like the other girls at your school? What about a cute skirt and tunic, or a pair of pants and a nice top? Girl, you have one heck of a figure. Don't hide it, flaunt it!"

Silence. Her companion continued, "You act as if you are still in the old country. Wake up, you are in the west now, you are—"

"I know, I know, I'm FREE!" the young girl shouted in frustration. "If there is so much freedom here, then why do you and everyone else insist that I take off my Islamic covering and dress like unrespectable women of the night?" she asked furiously. Her companion did not answer. "I'm happy with my dress and being modest," she added. "You should be, too. We are respected as Muslim women when we observe proper covering." The young girl had hoped to convince her companion but, as usual, her silence was her way of blocking out naseeha. She sighed; there was just no persuading her.

The young girl looked in her purse to make sure she had everything: wallet, pocket Qur'an, electronic address book, keys, and cell phone. She had three messages, all from the same person. "You know who *that* is, don't you?" her companion asked slyly.

"No, should I?"

"He's been trying to talk to you for the past week, haven't you noticed?"

"Who?"

"Derek: the cutest and most popular guy in school. He seriously has the hots for you."

The young girl frowned. "Derek Anderson?"

Her companion was beyond disbelief. "I can't believe you haven't noticed him. It's because you keep your nose in your Qur'an or your school books," she said in an accusing voice. "Anyways, I hear he's going to Samia's party. He really wants to meet you," she said with a scheming smile, cocking her head to the side.

"Why would I want to get involved with a ruffian like him? He changes girls every week, sleeps in class, has no respect for law or authority, drinks, and God knows what else." The young girl angrily erased the messages.

"What? You didn't even read what he had to say," her companion cried.

"I don't have anything to say to him; he is not even a Muslim. There is no reason for me to get involved with him," she answered sternly. "I did not give him my number. When I find the person who did, I'm going to strangle them. I bet it was Samia," the young girl added angrily, throwing her phone into her purse. She had had enough of this conversation, which wasn't going anywhere. "Leave me alone." She glared at her companion in her chestnut vanity mirror, and she turned away. "You are making me late." The young girl grabbed the rest of her things and left out quickly before the first adhan of Jummah.

Camilla Sayf

Camilla Sayf is a haiku poet, freelance writer, and the author of *Lebanese Chronicles*. She is a former language teacher who finds her conversion to Islam to be her greatest inspiration. Her work has been published in MuslimHeritage.com, *Qalam*, *MuslimWakeUp*, *DaralslamLive* and *Breakthrough*. Some of her writing, including *Lebanese Chronicles* and *Innocent Heart*, have been translated and published in other languages.

Salt Of The Earth by Camilla Sayf

Oh Allah, oh Allah…

On that early morning, Hassan Becker kept calling his God without realizing he'd been up all night. He then raised his head and looked up at a huge clock on the wall. Visitation hours at Faulkner Hospital would begin soon, he thought, kneeling down again and prostrating himself on the floor.

Ar-Rahman ar-Raheem Maaliki yaumid Deen…

He felt that his head was spinning and his heart was agonizing in pain. If only he had known this before, he would have been better prepared. He then immediately dismissed these thoughts, understanding that there was no need in exhausting his already tired mind with this fruitless talk to himself. Upon finishing his prayer, he stood up, carefully rolled his rug, took off his robe and put it all in the drawer. His wife made it a habit of keeping prayer attributes accurately stored to preserve them clean.

He couldn't eat. A chill spread along his body, his legs felt numb and his head light as he took his car keys and rushed out of the door. That early morning, Hassan Becker headed toward the hospital with a hopeful heart, pushing fear away and trying to stay calm while driving the highway.

"Please, where can I see Ameena Becker? She arrived yesterday." He pulled a passing by nurse by her sleeve, completely forgetting how inappropriate this gesture might be.

"Are you family, sir?" She was calm and wore a purple robe. Purple is nice, he thought, my wife's favorite color.

"Yes, yes, I'm her husband." His breathing suddenly became strangely heavy as he introduced himself.

"Here, I'll show you the way."

Ameena lay in bed, covered up in white sheets. He had no flowers, no sweets, nothing to cheer her up. He tried to be quiet, but she heard him entering the room and opened her eyes. She recognized him and smiled, trying to free her hand from under the sheets to wave at him, but she was too weak to move. Tied up to the machines among the white bedsheets and tubes, she seemed so small and so fragile. His heart broke. Realization of the harm done to her health shook him to the core. She couldn't talk, not even whisper. He never imagined that, one day, he would be standing there alone, helpless, and not knowing what to do next. Over the past year, Ameena had become his best source concerning all matters in life, his guide and the only one who believed firmly in his ability to change and become a better person. She taught him everything he needed to know, and he relied on her at all times. But not today. Hassan sat in a chair next to her bed and nearly broke into tears. He struggled with his emotions for a few moments, hoping she didn't see his grim face. He lifted his head and smiled at his wife. She will be okay. *They* will be okay. He had to believe that this trial would be over soon, and she would be back home, healthy and sound as she always was.

"Hassan…Qur'an…read…" Her voice didn't belong to her as she breathed those three short words out.

He hadn't brought the Qur'an with him! Absolutely ashamed of himself for not thinking straight and forgetting the most important and life-saving attribute of their existence, he turned red and covered his face with his hands. What could he do? There was little time till the end of the visitation hours. He knew a few chapters by heart, the ones he used to recite during his prayers. Giving a quick glance at his wife, he suddenly felt overwhelmed with warmth and decided to recite *Al-Fatiha* to her. His voice trembled as he softly began the first lines of his favorite Qur'anic verses; it was a formula that he adhered to, and he had memorized it, never, ever to let it vanish from his mind.

"Ghairil maghduubi' alaihim waladaaleen."

A tear fell down Ameena's cheek. She couldn't move her body, but her soul was moving toward her husband to embrace him for being what she thought he would become prior to their marriage in the Jamaa mosque. God had a special plan for them. Ameena closed her eyes. *Oh Allah, praise be to Thee, guide us through this ordeal!* Her mind was active, though her body was injured and motionless and, as her husband finished his recitation, she was able to vocalize a soft shokran to him.

Hassan Becker stood near the hospital window and watched the mix of colors that Fall had brought that year: breathtaking bright blue sky, trees hiding in clouds of yellow and orange, tidy alleys. He had missed Boston, though he preferred to have a different reason than his wife's illness for visiting the city. He had to work, yet he was too worried. No matter how hard he tried, he couldn't push this feeling away. His wife meant everything to him. He could take good care of her. His IT job payed well, and they could afford a house, which secured their comfort and tranquility. Yet when it came to *other* terms, she was his mentor; she was the one who knew where to find the answers. And now she was weakened, and he was searching for a way to hang on. He knew so little and never realized it till today.

"Henry Becker?" He didn't quite recognize the voice.

"Yes?"

"I am your wife's doctor." The voice that spoke from above a white robe came from a rather short, aging man, who smiled at him, while firmly shaking his hand.

"Doctor..." Hassan couldn't find words for an endless number of chaotic thoughts crossing his mind at the moment.

"She will be all right, if that's what you want to know. But we need to operate, and soon."

That's what he was afraid of. The idea of cutting up her body seemed so alien to him. His precious Ameena would be opened up, and then stitched?! He didn't fully comprehend the scale of her illness, but he knew one thing for sure, that with every trial, God would also send a solution. If surgery was their solution, they had to take it. Taking a deep breath, he signed all required forms and left the hospital. Ameena was already sleeping and he had to work.

The next morning brought good news with it. Ameena's doctor scheduled her surgery for the afternoon, giving Hassan enough time to say a prayer at his wife's bed before the operation. This time he took the Qur'an with him and read from it till Ameena was taken to another location. He thanked Allah for the transcription of the Arabic verses in the book, making it possible for him to have read to his wife. Today, he thought they both felt stronger than the day before. Even though Ameena's face was unusually pale, and her body seemed weaker, Hassan knew somewhere deep in his heart that she would be fine. He also felt an increasing belief that her time hadn't come yet. He was not sure where this feeling came from or whether he could fully believe that feeling, but he knew God would never abandon them. These thoughts and feelings are what made him stay strong. He gave his wife a goodbye kiss as she was taken by nurses out of the room. For some time, he remained, looking out the window at the Fall colors in the hospital garden.

He was a new convert to Islam, and no one had expected Ameena to marry him or for him to decide he wanted to marry her. They were so different. Ameena was raised by Muslim parents and was a practicing Muslimah. She was a Palestinian by birth, and a graduate of the Abou Noor University. He wondered if Ameena had anticipated that her young American husband would grow a beard and become her soul mate. He was overwhelmed that she would love him so strongly and passionately. He recalled a scene from last year's picnic and smiled. She definitely knew she would love him from the very beginning, there was no doubt about it.

As he watched birds making their way through the bright blue sky, a sharp thought crossed his mind. Why didn't she mention it before? Did she leave it for him to remember, or maybe she was not strong enough to think of it herself? Panicking, he ran out of the hospital, got in his car and drove home. It had occurred to him that *she missed her prayers* during those few days in the hospital. At other times, she would be the one to tell him what the rule for this situation was, and where to find the appropriate guidance. But she wasn't there to tell him. He felt alone in the busy, chaotic city with his questions. He felt desperate to find the answers.

Books! He needed to find the book that could tell him what to do! When he got home he went to the bookshelves filled with Islamic books. His fingers ran through the titles as he searched. Here, maybe this one? He opened the *Fiqh-us-Sunnah* that he had never found time to read before, looked through the index, but couldn't concentrate. His vision was blurred, and his eyes were red-rimmed and tired. He needed someone to explain things to him in simple terms, like his wife used to do every time they dealt with certain issues. *Oh Allah, help me with this!* Hassan switched on his computer and typed in a search engine what he was looking for. As he surfed through the web, briefly scanning texts, he kept telling himself how inconsiderate and reckless he had been.

Always relying on Ameena had been convenient. During their one year of marriage, he never had to worry. All he needed to do was ask her to explain about something Islamic. She was always available for his needs, be it emotional, pleasures, or spiritual necessities. Now, in the time when her health took away her availability, he felt lost. His mind was in agony because he had been thoughtless and had not recognized his wife's needs.At that momment, he felt worthless. He had been selfish, and now he could barely stand himself. He had been childish, so irresponsible!

His eye stumbled upon a few words that immediately grasped his attention. As he ran through the lines, he realized that he had found the answer he needed by himself. His religion once again proved to be gracious and powerful, powerful enough to break through the minds of the most resistant sceptics and gracious enough to teach about love. He switched his computer off. Hassan had been worried for no reason. When a Muslim is ill or injured, prayers can be made up. Islam is the religion of ease! All praise be to God! Hassan Becker was now a changed man.

Ameena loved purple. A day after the surgery, she wore a purple scarf and laughed when he joked about it. That day, he bought her a bouquet of lavender with a genuine desire to please her. The doctor said it would be a few more days for her to stay in the hospital and continue to recover from the surgery. Ameena was already showing remarkable signs of recovery, and her wounds were healing beautifully. She couldn't sit up yet, but was already able to talk. The nurse allowed him to place a bucket with water next to her bed and wipe Ameena's face, arms, and feet. Hassan did everything with great accuracy, for he loved his wife, and it was time for him to take care of her needs. Now he would lead his wife in prayer. He had his God to thank for his wonderful wife and life.

Mahasin Shamsid-Deen

Mahasin Shamsid-Deen is a second generation American Muslimah with degrees in international marketing and public programs. She has been married since 1986 and has three children.

Active in the Muslim community, she runs an Islamic school, organizes programs for local masajid, and often serves as a public speaker, conducting educational workshops for organizations. A writer since childhood, Mahasin has collected data and written technical journals for businesses and schools, handbooks, educational papers, business reports, proposals, grants, and even ghost writing. In addition, she has written and/or contributed writing to pamphlets and brochures on Islam, Muslim women, public policy, economics, voting rights, domestic violence, and Mohammed Schools.

As a poet and published playwright, her first play, "One God," was translated into three languages and presented in special audience before the King of Saudi Arabia. Currently, with her own theatre company, her plays are much sought after commodities for Islamic programs and fundraisers. Mahasin's goals are to Impact! Expand! Inspire! Writing the unique history and culture of American Muslims so it may be preserved as a legacy for all to enjoy and learn!

Her Household by Mahasin Shamsid-Deen

Qadirah looked out the kitchen window, enjoying the view of her large lawn and beautiful flower bed. She learned forward slightly to see if she could see her husband's car approaching. Aziz would be back shortly, and she and the children were ready. The children were sitting content in the den watching cartoons. Sister Rita had done her hair earlier, so it felt light on the head. Qadirah had insisted she only oil it lightly, so as not to stain her new khimar. As she turned from the window, she looked around the room, satisfied that the house was clean, the dinner was precooked, the children were dressed, and there was nothing left to do but go. For a moment, she felt dizzy. Alarmed briefly, she shook it off, assuming it was nothing.

When Aziz arrived, he had bought some soda, and the children came to life, running to him. They were always so excited whenever their father was around. Aziz both loved and craved the attention. Qadirah was glad to share the responsibility with the kids. They all piled in the car, happy and chattering.

As they entered the courtyard of the masjid, people turned to look at them. The El-Amin's were a respected family in the community. Aziz and his two sons carried two pans of food to the table for the brothers, while Qadirah took her young daughter to the women's section.

"As Salaamu Alaikum," everyone said back and forth to each other in greeting. Sister Tauheedah came forward to hug Qadirah and her daughter. "I have someone for you to meet," she said, gesturing to a woman behind her. Qadirah looked toward a young, short, slim sister with a round face. "This is Wilmona," Tauheedah announced.

"Oh – my name is Imani now!" interjected the young woman before Qadirah could respond or Tauheedah could finish.

"I didn't realize you had changed your name," said Tauheedah apologetically.

"I changed it in the eyes of Allah!" the girl exclaimed.

"Oh," Tauheedah responded, glancing at Qadirah. "Well, um," she continued, "I thought you might like to meet Sister Qadirah here. She is a Social Worker, and many of the members of this masjid call on her for advice and assistance."

"Good," said Imani quickly. "I'm destitute, and I need a place to stay."

"Don't you have any family here?" Qadirah quizzed.

"Nobody. I came here from New Jersey by myself," Imani answered flatly.

Qadirah was not discouraged; she knew she could help. "I'll get back with you by the end of the night," she promised.

"My things are in the bathroom," explained Imani. "I stayed in a shelter last night. I can do it again."

"I wouldn't dream of such a thing," Qadirah insisted emphatically. "May I ask, though, how it came to be that you are displaced?"

"I don't have any money," answered Imani.

"Oh, but I mean, why did you come here?" asked Qadirah.

"I had to," Imani finished. Qadirah asked no further questions.

Qadirah had asked seven ladies before she found someone in a position to help. She found Auntie Nena Karim, a widow in her late sixties, who was willing to take in the young convert. Auntie Nena was an extremely kind and patient woman. Qadirah explained that she could not vouch for Imani, but would use her resources to help the young sister get on her feet. She left feeling that everything was in order.

Three days later, Qadirah found her home in an uproar. She had scolded the children, but found that her impatience had to do with her own exhaustion. She had made home visits that day to her clients, which was always draining. Mainly, she was tired of seeing people in the same condition with broken promises they had made to themselves. She had visited a woman from Samoa, who was cooking some kind of dish that had left her feeling dizzy and nauseated for the rest of the day.

"Mamma, Auntie Nena is on the phone," her son announced, just as she was giving in to a slight doze.

"Sister El-Amin," Auntie Nena started without greeting. "I do not think having this Imani sister here with me is going to work out!"

"What's wrong?" Qadirah asked, concerned.

"Everything!" Auntie Nena snapped. "We clash! I ain't one to spread slander, but—"

"Don't worry about me!" came another voice on the phone that Qadirah recognized was Imani's. "I have a place to stay already. Sister Huda has welcomed me into her home."

"Don't you know better than to barge into other people's conversations?" Auntie Nena scolded. "Well, I guess you can see what the problem is, Qadirah, can't you?" finished Auntie Nena.

Qadirah was silent. She was skeptical of the new arrangement, since Huda was young, married to a man from Yemen, and prone to irrational behavior. She belonged to another congregation, so to speak, so Qadirah only had limited experience with her. "Come by the office tomorrow, Imani, and I can see about what other services are available to help you get settled," Qadirah offered.

The next day, Qadirah found that she was just too sick to go into work. The flu or something like it had ahold of her and wouldn't let go. Still, she sent out the laundry and cleaned lightly. She had shopped for an easy to fix means for dinner, not quite TV dinner, but nearly. She usually chopped vegetables and froze them in plastics bags of a cup each on the weekends. She revised her weekly menu and left a message for a co-worker to help Imani – Wilmona – when she came in.

It was two days before she was able to return to work, a Saturday, no less, and on a day when she was scheduled to attend a Muslim women's conference. Her short absence had either made her really behind, or she was getting slower and slower getting her work done. Either way, Qadirah found it hard to hurry as she wanted. She still planned to get to the conference by midday. She had been to the doctor the day before and had taken a pregnancy test. Qadirah knew that was unnecessary. She was thirty-eight and already had three children. Her daughter was seven years old, and those baby days were gone. Still, the possibility had distracted her.

By the time she arrived at the conference, the ladies had already had lunch and were in the second series of workshops. Qadirah sat down when she arrived, as stomach cramps seemed to overwhelm her.

"Salaam Alaikum," came a voice from behind. Qadirah looked up to see a figure completely shrouded in black standing before her.

"It's me. Imani."

Qadirah smiled. "Wa Alaikum Salaam. How are you?"

To Qadirah's surprise, Imani answered with a paragraph of Arabic words that were beautiful to hear, but did not make a coherent comment. Qadirah immediately recognized the 'second stage' of the convert. First, being the enthusiasm, second, being the 'adopting' of the cultural dress and affectations of an immigrant in an attempt to be 'Islamically correct.'

"I'm more settled now. I'm trying to find work that will tide me over until I find a husband," said Imani.

Qadirah sat forward. "Are you looking for a husband?" There were a number of rumors out there already about that Imani sister and her unrelenting and often inappropriate search for a man.

"Oh, yes – actively" Imani exclaimed. "I have a Wali, a Brother Muhsin."

Qadirah frowned slightly, not familiar with a man by that name.

"He has tried to set me up with a couple of guys, but…" Qadirah waited for her to finish. Imani sat down to speak intimately. "He thinks that, because I'm nineteen, that I should be like the women from his country. I wasn't born in this religion, so naturally I'm experienced. I don't want to marry someone under false pretenses. The brothers he keeps setting me up with hardly even speak English, and kind of act like I'm beneath them or something. He keeps telling them – she's not like other American women, she's a good girl."

Qadirah paused, choosing her words carefully. "I would suggest waiting before you get married. Sometimes, brothers who have migrated here from other parts of the world are only looking for a green card situation, which is unfair to you and haraam for him, since it is a muta – temporary marriage. I would suggest, first, really studying Islam and getting a handle on this new way of life you have adopted."

"I've been Muslim a good number of months now. How long ago did you convert?" Imani quizzed.

"I grew up in Islam," said Qadirah.

"You guys barely knew what it was like being a Muslim back them," said Imani.

"It was different, for sure," Qadirah explained. "It was a simpler time, when the community was more unified. Muslims were more monolithic with the same social and political agenda."

"Well, you guys grew up to embrace everybody's politics now, right?" Imani quizzed.

"Not really," Qadirah answered quickly. "Just because I practice the same faith as someone from Asia, doesn't mean that their struggles are my own. I try to be moderate."

"You mean passive," Imani quipped.

"No, I mean what I say," Qadirah answered again, feeling the pain in her side rise quickly.

"Well, you need to get with it. Why don't you wear niqab? How fluent are you in Arabic? Why do you work for the kuffar?"

"Sister, over time your understanding and perspective will evolve," said Qadirah, starting to rise – something had to be done about the pain.

"Maybe it will, maybe it won't. But Sister, wait," said Imani. "Before you go, I just want to say that I don't have to be in twenty-five years to know this religion. Believe me, I know what I am doing. Besides, getting married completes half your faith."

Qadirah nodded, feeling the pain and thus not wanting to argue further. She barely made it to the hospital before the flow began. So she was pregnant after all, and now she had lost it. Qadirah sat in the hospital, feeling sorry for herself. Aziz had gone to bring the car around. She was weak, since she had bled so much, but mainly numb – mentally. A new baby would have been welcome, but disruptive. Qadirah felt her life was complete. She was happy with her life. Her husband was faithful and attentive, her children smart, obedient, and in good health, and she had a career that made a difference in other people's lives. Overall, she felt very blessed that her family was held in high esteem by all who knew. Now, she had to sit at home for a while and recuperate. Her pregnancy had been dangerous, and they had to operate. The doctor recommended six weeks rest with at least two weeks being mandatory. Aziz reappeared with the nurse and wheelchair to take her home. The nurse offered some pain medication as she was signed out, and Qadirah was glad to have it.

When Qadirah woke from her doze, she found her husband sitting next to her on the bed. She had been so tired, she barely remembered arriving home. He kissed her gently on the lips. Qadirah knew he had to be disappointed about the pregnancy and the subsequent loss of her reproductive organs. He was a religious man, so she knew he would seek solace in prayer. He would see it as the Qadar of Allah and most likely leave it there. Still... Qadirah shook her own misgivings off.

"I have done something I think you will like," he said, as he pulled away from their kiss. "I have hired someone to be here temporary to help with the house and the children."

Qadirah was surprised, but pleased.

"I already cleaned the basement and set it up like an apartment. It already has its own entrance. The sister says she has experience working as an aide, and she said she knows you. She was really insistent that I hire her. I told her I would wait for your approval," Aziz explained.

"Well, who is she?"

"She says her name is Imani Fareed."

"I don't know her," Qadirah responded.

"Well, she's kind of young, wears niqab, but said she took her shahadah at our masjid."

Qadirah slowly realized who Aziz was speaking of. She wondered if that sister Imani was capable of taking care of her children when she was so young herself.

"She said that, since she was displaced from her home, she could live and eat here in exchange for the work as your assistant. The best thing is that you will have someone here all the time to make sure you stay off your feet and recover."

Qadirah looked at her husband's face. He was so enthusiastic and proud of how he handled the situation. She hadn't the heart to tell him that she preferred not to have this young lady in her happy home.

It took four days before the conversation between Qadirah and Imani was not polite small talk. They argued over a point in the Qur'an. Qadirah was surprised that Imani had such strong opinions. This began their daily exchange of heated discourse. At first, Qadirah was stressed out with Imani's argumentative ways, but then found that she actually enjoyed the challenge. Imani served Qadirah in bed and really did do a good job getting the children off to school, fed, and to bed. She was well-mannered enough to leave the room whenever Aziz came home from work. People called on Qadirah to see how she was recuperating. Nobody approved of her letting Imani live with her, even in the capacity of a home health aide. Many tried to convince Qadirah that young, streetwise converts like Imani often joined the faith as a fad or to stand out as different. Qadirah had to admit that Imani was an aggressive, but sincere new convert. She often found herself defending Imani to her friends and reprimanding them for not trusting or believing in their young sister in the deen.

Before she knew it, the six weeks had passed, and it was time for her to return to work. She felt up to it physically, but mentally it was another matter. As she sat by the window in her bedroom, enjoying the beautiful scenery below, Qadirah was suddenly filled with intense sadness. Suddenly, she could no longer see her garden, the trees, or the intense rose bush Aziz had planted for her. She could only see herself. It was one thing to decide for oneself that your family was complete, and you really didn't want to have any more children, and quite another for that option to be taken away. She feared Aziz would find her beauty diminished. This was the first time in her marriage that she actually felt vulnerable. She looked up as Imani entered and approached her unbidden. Qadirah's tears began to flow unexpectedly as Imani soothed her fears.

Two weeks on the job, and Qadirah no longer had time for melancholy.

She was feeling better and things at home had returned pretty much to their normal routine. She was, however, more devout in her religious studies and prayer, mainly due to Imani's bidding. Imani had stayed on, even though she was no longer needed as an aide. To Qadirah's surprise, she and Imani had slowly become friends. This was an unexpected, yet pleasant development. Imani had different ways of looking at things, but her observations made Qadirah think as she defended her position or conceded that Imani's view was worthwhile.

"Surprise!" Qadirah was completely startled as she entered her home. There was Aziz, her children, Imani, and three other families from the masjid.

"It's a spouse party," announced Sister Tauheedah. Spouse parties were usually only celebrated during anniversaries, when couples got together and shared stories of marriage and wishes for continued success. She realized immediately what Aziz was trying to do as he presented her with a single rose.

"Wow," exclaimed Imani. "That's the kind of husband I want."

"You would indeed be blessed if you had him," Qadirah answered.

A month later, Qadirah found herself speaking with Maryum Ali over the phone. She and Qadirah were not close, but they were sisters in the faith. "Um, Sister. I'm sure you are wondering why I called."

"No, not at all," Qadirah said quickly. "I am pleased to hear your voice. We so seldom talk. Well, that's true. I'm busy, you're busy..." she trailed off.

"Sister Qadirah, I'm going to get right to it. I really called to speak to you about that sister Imani."

Qadirah stiffened slightly at the reference 'that sister Imani.' She had already heard many comments from people concerning the length of Imani's stay, her aggressiveness, character, and on and on. Imani had become a harmonious part of her household. Besides, one of the main reasons she seldom spoke to Maryum was because she was known to spread elaborate stories.

"I think that sister is doing something that she shouldn't, and you shouldn't be naïve," Maryum blurted.

"I'm sure I don't know what you mean," said Qadirah.

"Don't trust her. Don't turn your back on her, and get her out of your house!"

"Well sister, you seem so..." Now, Qadirah was the one trailing off.

"That sister is man hungry, and she wants it satisfied."

Qadirah was startled. Imani had put the husband hunt on the back burner to the best of her knowledge. "You know sister, Imani is a good sister, striving on the right path. I think you are just back biting, and I don't want to hear it," Qadirah reprimanded.

"Okay, then," said Maryum quickly. "You want to defend her, then let's wait and see who gets bit here."

Qadirah was going to speak to Imani about the incident, but she had started an evening class that took her out of the house most evenings, including weekends, when she worked with a study group. Qadirah had other things to worry about, anyway. Aziz had suddenly gone into business with someone. Qadirah did not know him, and Aziz seemed to be quite elusive about his time. The problem was that it was a financial drain on the family.

Aziz had finished the basement apartment for Imani, and it was now semi-permanent. He had become Imani's Wali by default. Months ago, he and Imani had often spoken at length about what she wanted in a husband. In recent weeks, though, his search for a husband seemed to have slowed. Qadirah didn't blame him, since she had to admit that Imani's strong personality and opinions were intimidating to the average Muslim brother. However, the gossip in the community was that Imani was seeing someone secretly. Since she was seldom home, even Qadirah was beginning to get suspicious that perhaps Imani had met someone at school. She had tried to introduce her to brother Jamil, a young brother in college, but was thoroughly rebuked by Imani.

"You should want a man who is strong in his faith, able to provide a good home, and of good character," she pleaded.

Imani had stood before her and sucked in her breath. "I only like older men," she answered.

"But you are young! Leave the old men to the old women," Qadirah quipped. "With a young man, you can grow and explore life together. An old man is set in his ways."

"Well, I like the older man's ways," Imani answered. "I know Jamil is handsome, educated, and nice, but what I mostly know is that he is 'your' choice – not mine."

Qadirah was unsure of what to say next. She could only assume that Imani was torn between her faith and her libido right now. As her sister in the faith, she wanted to save her from making a mistake that would embarrass her.

Qadirah didn't know when she knew, but it was clear suddenly that Imani was getting fat. She was of such a small build, anyway, that the least little bit of weight gain would show, even in big flowing clothes. Before she really knew, Qadirah had suggested walks on the weekend. But the rumors in the community were that Imani was definitely involved with a brother. Her midsection weight gain confirmed the truth. The fact that she was not open about the relationship indicated that there was a problem. Qadirah knew Imani was in over her head, but Imani completely avoided her now. Qadirah wanted to let Imani know she would be there for her and fight for her reputation in the community. Someone had taken advantage of this child, and it was unfair. But Imani had closed the door to all conversation. This was disruptive to the peace that Qadirah maintained in her home. Even without seeing Imani physically on a daily basis now, this problem was still there.

And it did not help things that Aziz was in very poor spirits. The week before, when taking the children to the County Fair, Qadirah had found herself short of monies and short of a husband accompanying her, since he called off at the last minute. The bills in the house continued to climb, but Aziz had taken a macho stance now that Qadirah had spoken to him about it and had even told her it was his right to do with the money what he felt. This was a new attitude, never before seen in the marriage. Qadirah knew that whatever financial fiasco Aziz had been drawn into was worrying him, and he was obviously embarrassed about his inability to resolve it. Aziz was the type of man who would force success. His very name meant mighty and powerful. Qadirah had always found him to be so. When they first met, Aziz thought that her name and his meant there was a sign pointing them to each other. In the past, they had worked as a team in these matters. Qadirah decided the best course of action was to wait it out. He would eventually come to her, so they could resolve this new challenge together. She just wanted to make sure he knew that whatever mistake he had made that so impacted the household was already forgiven by her.

Qadirah's sister set her in motion. Her call to Qadirah reprimanding her for allowing a scandal to develop right under her nose in her house had put Qadirah on edge. The situation had to be handled now in the same way that she handled clients at work – firmly and with a detached professionalism. There really was no explanation as to how a six-week job turned into a year's living arrangement with Imani. It just happened gradually. Strangely enough, Imani actually seemed part of her household over time. But the pregnancy situation had to be addressed and resolved – now. Imani was easily a good six months or more pregnant. Qadirah could ask around and find someone to marry her if the father didn't or wouldn't. She could even find a couple of 'older' brothers who wouldn't mind a young wife. The key was getting Imani to talk; she had been so rude lately the few times Qadirah was able to see her.

Qadirah waited in the basement for Imani to arrive. It was well past 11 o'clock when she heard the key in the door.

"What are you doing here?" Imani demanded as soon as she saw her.

Qadirah stood slightly irritated. "Well, for one, this is my house. Second, I came to speak with you."

Imani slammed the door. "About what!" she demanded.

"About the obvious situation," Qadirah said soothingly.

"What situation are you talking about?" Imani answered flippantly.

"Er – your pregnancy," Qadirah responded again, growing a bit irritated.

"Oh, that's not your concern," Imani said, sitting down and attempting to obviously ignore Qadirah.

"Well, I think it is, Imani. What do you plan to do?"

"That's between me and Aziz," Imani answered quietly.

Qadirah blinked. How was Aziz involved? Was he looking for or trying to force the brother to marry her? Had he already set up some sort of adoption for the baby?

As if on cue, Aziz came through the basement door. Qadirah looked from one to the other. Why was Aziz entering the home through this entrance instead of the one upstairs? As he moved to stand next to Imani and placed his hands on her shoulder, Qadirah slowly began to take in the full import of the situation. "Imani fit so nice here, I made her my second wife," he said.

Qadirah looked out the window of her bedroom, this time not really seeing her beautiful yard. She had confined herself to her bedroom. Everyone had something to say. "The brother has the right to take on a second wife, especially a destitute woman."

"The two of them are best friends, anyway."

"The brother wants more children; it's not like Qadirah can give him any."

"Sisters always grow in the deen from this type of experience."

Qadirah heard it all, but listened to none. "One was best – if you only knew!" These words from Allah in the Qur'an were not a suggestion, but a commandment. Sisters of the faith should be just that – sisters! But 'that sister Imani' only sat greedily seeking to reap the benefits of another sister's fifteen years of work. That sister was so guided by her own selfish desires to disrupt not only Qadirah's life, but her children as well. Somehow, she had to show Aziz that she found the whole thing unfair.

The women sat by her hospital bed, chanting from the Qur'an. "Why did she jump?"

"I should have been more supportive."

"I can't bear to see her in this full body cast!"

"Most sisters have a hard time accepting this at first."

"What do you think Brother El-Amin is going to do now?"

Qadirah was silent. Speech came no more, tears fell no longer, and even anger and disbelief seemed to be slowly evaporating. The only thing that remained was a sad resignation that her household would never be in order again and, to her surprise, a stark and intense wavering of faith.

Umm Junayd

Umm Junayd - Hailing from West Africa, Umm Junayd uses her love of the written word to relay and convey the array of beautiful colours Islam holds. She does a great deal of reflecting, and her non-fiction articles, poetry, and short fiction works are usually results of such reflection.

Umm Junayd is the Director of An-Najm Publishers - the UK's first Muslim retailer to specialize in Islamic fiction - and has a regular column in *Sisters* magazine. She has also had her works appear in various publications online and in print, and continues to write on a freelance basis. She currently resides in London, UK, with her husband and two children and can be found blogging at: www.UmmJunayd.info.

Heat of Entice by Umm Junayd

I knew you were lying in wait for me again that day, watching from a distance, analyzing my every move. I can only imagine your glee as I drove past him – you were probably excited at the prospect of me being knocked to my knees again, slipping as I naïvely slithered toward the invisibly marked danger zone.

You knew that day was like the others, as I drove the 30-minute journey to Grandma's home. I slowed down at the narrow junction that branched onto a one-way street, proceeding cautiously over the speed bumps. It was a 20-miles-per-hour driving zone, but I slowed further to 15. The orange brick terraced houses that lined the streets boasted their vigor, despite their age. Pristine evergreen foliage decorated the outskirts of each block, adding a hint of spring even during the harshest winter months. I made a mental note of the alleys that separated each five-house block. They were oddly placed, probably for the convenience of the architect, but at the peril of the residents who were left with no choice but to endure the sight of another block only a few meters from their front door.

"Block one, block two," I muttered just above a whisper, as I passed the blocks before Saleem's, paying particular attention to the road ahead. I stole a rushed glance in the direction of his house, taking care to keep my head still – not the slightest indication of where my eyes strayed.

It would be unacceptable to be seen looking at him, if he were to be watching out of his window the moment I drove by. His was the one at the very top of the three-floored house, the one facing the street. The lace curtains that skirted the windows were those his mother had picked from Clapham's bustling market. Laced flowers danced in an elegant pattern, with a fine stitch of leaves above. I'd skimmed my fingers over the edges once, intertwining them between my fingers in a smooth, drawn-out motion. Then, I wondered what had made his mother choose such an elaborate design for someone she knew would pay no attention to it. Saleem had no care for such, but she had bought it all the same.

When I had passed his house, there were no obvious signs of him. I continued to scan the almost deserted street in the hope that he would be strolling along it lazily, so that I might catch a glimpse of him. Every tall man with even a hint of his airbrushed brown skin caused my heart to thump. My hands would develop pinpricked beads of sweat as I gripped the steering wheel tighter, pretending not to look.

Grandma is such a sweet lady, ladled with jokes that could lift the spirits of the most depressed. I visited her once a fortnight to keep her company and renew her supply of groceries. I had always insisted that I visit her once a week – you suggested that idea – but Grandma refused, lamenting about how bad she feels for dragging me out each week.

"You don't drag me out, Ma," I said, as I sat on a low wooden stool. I preferred the stool to her spongy cream sofa. I liked to look up into her eyes. I stroked the back of her hand with my right hand while she clasped onto my other. Each row of aged skin on her honey-basked hand told a different story of her seventy years previous. "I enjoy the time I spend with you."

"Ah, my child. You are so good to me."

"How is that, Ma? Is it not my duty to the mother who bore my mother? I love coming to see you."

I had to keep seeing her.

"Maymuno, you are a precious gift wrapped in your scarf. Look at you." There were no mirrors in her spacious living room, but she guided her hand along my face in soft, wispy strokes as if to illustrate her thoughts.

"I remember when your Mama was to deliver you. I told her to stay at home, that I could deliver you myself as I delivered your cousins, Tawfiq and

Abbas. She bluntly refused. 'I want my child to be safe, Mama, I've waited too long to have her. I can't now lose her in this Nigerian heat.' See, you were precious before you were even born, Maymuno."

I blushed silently, and my heart thanked the One who Created me with a mellow brown complexion.

"Thank you, Ma. Your words are too kind. I wish to live up to the way you think of me."

"Yes, Maymuno, stay precious. Do not allow any man to peck at your heart. Keep it whole and devoted to Allah. When a man pecks away at you, he'll not return the pieces he stole, so let him earn it in a noble way."

She reached down and held my chin, lifting it slightly to examine my face; it was as if she were searching for any blemishes that might ruin my value.

"Yes, Ma," I whispered. I felt exposed, faint with anxiety. It was as though she had cross-examined my heart – like she knew of the secrets I kept there, wrapped with guilt and bundled to the bottom. She had a way of reaching to the depths of my consciousness, although I worked hard to ensure my tongue and actions wore the perfect mask.

I thought about the words of Grandma while I strapped myself into my car that warm evening, adjusting the mirrors before I set off home. The sun had yet to retreat behind the horizon, tucking itself away to make way for the moon. Grandma had said that I'm precious, and no man should be allowed to peck at my heart. But what sort do I have left after years of allowing the thought of Saleem to occupy it? Each trip to Grandma's caused me to grasp onto the hope of seeing him again.

I had envisioned the scene many times. Our eyes would meet and remain transfixed; a bulb of recognition would immediately be switched on in his head. I had become almost unrecognizable to those who once knew me without the head-covering, and the donning of the face veil further concealed my identity. But Saleem would know me.

I wouldn't call out his name, nor would he call mine as he had once done. "Maymunah," in the deep airy way I remembered his voice to be. No, he wouldn't call me like that when he saw me, he would simply allow for his chocolate-specked eyes to be immersed in mine, without the need for words to flutter from our lips. What could be said, anyway? What words could be uttered to express what we both wanted, but had placed a barrier between? Was it I who was too self-righteous, or he who was too laid-back?

You could have easily pulled me from the abyss of my dream, but you allowed me to inch closer, cling on evermore.

I had to grasp onto my chest as I reached the adjoining street to his. I had taken a different route from Grandma's and, if I were the betting type, I would have banked on the unlikelihood of crossing Saleem's path. The sight of a man – tall, brown-skinned, and broad-nosed – made my hands shed water in excess. I squinted, scolding myself for not wearing my contact lenses that afternoon in my rush to leave the house.

I exhaled when I realized it wasn't him, the renewed oxygen that I inhaled sent a rush to my head, and I reminded myself to breathe. *Is this what it will be like?* I didn't get to answer my own question, as I was plummeted into the firing line before I could review my strategy.

There he was. Another squint, and it was confirmed. I looked straight into his eyes, allowing my gaze to linger as he stopped abruptly in the middle of a loud laugh. I suppose the guy he was with had said something funny a few moments before my car emerged into sight. His hearty laugh was drowned out by that of the man's on the radio. I should have turned the volume down. I should have wound my window lower, so that I could hear Saleem's laugh, hear if it was the same as when we used to joke together. You fueled my 'I should haves'.

I'm still unable to decipher the expression he displayed when our eyes locked. Was it a look of recognition that emerged? Or was the slight squint an effort to gain recollection? My gaze was abandoned by my need to keep my eyes on the road, but you wasted no time in allowing arrows to be shot, piercing me deep once again. I shouldn't have let down my guard; my eyes should have been battered down as I grew hot from shame. *Is this how you should act, Maymunah? Shame on you!* I heard your reply loud and clear, justifying my actions as a way to fulfill my need for closure. And as I stared at him in my rear-view mirror – how he had stopped walking and was watching the taillights of my Corsa disappear – I knew you wouldn't allow him to want it to be closure. You'll forever lie in wait for an opportunity to entice us into the danger zone, as unmarked, yet clear as it is.

Umm Juwayriyah

Umm Juwayriyah, also known as Veiled Writer, is an American born and raised Muslim in her late twenties. She has an A.S. in Communications and is currently completing her BA in English at BayPath College in Massachusetts. Umm Juwayriyah has been writing and performing Islamic-inspired poetry and fiction for a number of years. She is the former assistant director and website creator for the Islamic Writers Alliance, and currently the editor for the New England Muslim Sisters' Association. Um Juwayriyah's first Urban Islamic fiction novel, *The Size of a Mustard Seed,* was published in July 2009. She intends to make this book the first one in an Urban Islamic fiction series.

Mother Wit by Umm Juwayriyah

You know, old folks are good for a lot of things. Talking has got be one – if not their best attribute. That's why they usually call everything that they say wisdom. Simple one or two lines are common, like, "two wrongs don't make a right," or "every shut eye ain't sleep," or "nothing beats a failure but a try." Old folks – grandmamas, madears, nanas, and grannies – have been prescribing the sayings all over the world in different languages and ways, but the meaning never changes. And you know what's really funny is, whether us young folks ask for it or not, you know when you're around the old folk, you're always gonna get a dose or two to swallow. Sometimes, it goes down smooth – other times not.

My great Aunt Lily Mae is good for dishing out mother wit. Over the years, I've come to terms with being one of her favorite targets whenever we're in the same room, to be shot one thing or another. So I stand quietly and listen each and every time. When she finishes, I shake my head, grin, kiss the palm of her hand, and move on. Nothing else I really can do. Aunt Lily Mae is eighty-three years old, in good health, and my late grandmother's older sister. She's bona fide old folk in our family, and honorary. The protocol is, when she speaks, whether you like what she has to say or whether what she has to say makes sense or not, you listen, or – well, haven't nobody ever tried crossing her in this family. But Aunt Lily Mae got a bunch of stories about folks who have, and I can tell you, it was never pretty or nice how she handled them. And you know how I can tell her stories are true is that major details never change over time. If Aunt Lily Mae says she delivered Uncle Eugene's wife's twins in the hurricane of '65 single-handedly, then that's how that went down each time she tells it.

So I guess you can say Aunt Lily Mae and me have history. I trust her, though, that's for sure. At thirty-five, with two divorces under my belt and countless other failed attempts, my two boys and I try to keep a low profile at most family gatherings – especially if my two sisters are there on display. Even though I'm the oldest, Debora and Felicia live seemingly perfect lives, while mine is like a cracked mirror at the circus. Not to mention, I reverted to Islam seven years ago. I guess they still haven't gotten used to me being a Muslim, 'cause they use it against me whenever they can. It hurts, but I stay busy working full time at the Post Office, and my boys play just about every sport before and after school, but that's not always good enough.

Sometimes, I got to come around for my parents' sake. When I do, I do my best to be brief, until I run into Aunt Lily Mae, that is. Her ramblings don't bother me anymore. In Islam, we are supposed to honor the elder, plus Aunt Lily Mae is family. My sisters, on the other hand, can't stand it. They take offense to everything she says, 'cause they think they got it going on too much with their perfect husbands and jobs and kids. Aunt Lily Mae knows better, though. She doesn't care how high you put your nose in the air, she's never afraid to call a spade a spade. It's funny, too, so I laugh right along with her when she gets on them. Felicia gets so mad. She shoots me a look of pure evil, like I'm the dirt under her nails. She's never thought much of me nohow, so I don't let it bother me. But it makes her furious, and she retaliates at me instead of Aunt Lily Mae, 'cause she can't do Aunt Lily Mae like she do me.

"Latifah, I know you, of all people, ain't tryna laugh at nobody! You got mountains to climb, girl – you hear me? mountains – before you can even take a glance in my back yard."

I guess that's one of the good things that Allah has blessed me with over my sisters: I don't mind hearing the truth. It stings at first, but it always ends up healing its wounds. It's for that same reason that I started to go hang with Aunt Lily Mae every Saturday night after I get off of work. We play scrabble, eat, I talk, she talks, I cry, she cries. I learn, and she appreciates.

Yesterday and Today by Umm Juwayriyah

Huda el Sayyed rushed into her hotel room like a bolt of lightning and slammed the door behind her. Before her, all of her strength drained, and she dropped down to her knees. Uncontrollable sobs rocked through her body, and she knew then that she had failed. She'd done what she came to Jordan to do – stop Hamood Burghouti's wedding – but the outcome wasn't anything like the dream she had: Hamood's eyes falling lovingly on her and instantly realizing that he was marrying the wrong woman, and then rushing off to marry Huda, the right woman. No, her fairytale dream had been just that – a dream. Now Huda was falling apart, and she had no idea how she could go on.

"Why...how could he? It's me he's loved all of these years. Me!" she yelled, while tearing off the delicate silk headscarf. She pulled her hair back behind her ears, and then grabbed the phone off its cradle and frantically dialed her parents' home.

As Huda held the phone, she willed herself to stop crying. She couldn't let her father hear her like this.

"Hello? Na'am, wa alykum salam. *Hatha ana* – Huda."

"Huda! Alhamdulee'lah! Again, we hear from you! Are you coming to the village to see us?"

"No, Baba. I'm here in Amman, at the Marriot. I...I went to Hamood. I know you told me not to, but I went to stop him from marrying Marwa!" Huda hurriedly said, even though she knew her father would be angry with her confession.

"You did what? *Ya elahi!* Huda, you have not learned how to listen in thirty-five years! God protect you."

"Baba, I'm sorry. But how could I listen to words that provided no comfort for my heart? I love Hamood. I should be his wife! I had to try. Didn't I?" The pain was quickly rising in Huda's throat again. She fell onto the plush, queen-sized bed and sobbed into the receiver.

Upon hearing his daughter's wails, Hussein's own contempt subsided. He hated that Huda, his only child, was suffering. He'd forbidden Huda from going near the wedding. But his stubborn daughter hadn't listened. He, too, secretly wished that Hamood would've had a change of heart. Although he knew that wasn't going to happen. Things were different between

Hamood and Huda. Hussein was reminded of the village elders as he sat on his patio under the darkening blue sky, listening to the faraway call for the evening prayer with one ear and his daughter's sobs with the other. The elders would always say, "Yesterday will never be today." Huda would learn this one day, he prayed.

Yesterday, for Huda and Hamood, was twelve years ago. It was during Huda's time at the University of Jordan in Amman that her childhood crush for Hamood blossomed into a mature admiration. It had been a perfect time, filled with daily outings with his family to coffee houses, exquisite dinners, showings at the Baladna Art Gallery, and trips to the Royal Cultural Center. Hamood took pleasure in spoiling Huda with her every heart's desire, and Huda had many. She never would have been able to do those things back in her village, only minutes away from the Bedouin city of Safawi.

Hamood's family was from the capital, and they were highly respected, well-known professionals. Huda's family was mostly farmers, a much lower social class. But, as Allah would have it, they'd met. When he was just a small boy of nine, Hamood came to her village with his nanny.

His nanny was Huda's mother's best friend, Wafa. Wafa introduced the young boy to Huda and had her take him outside to their patio, while she and Huda's mother, Yasmeen, socialized. The two children instantly took to one another. At nine, Hamood was able to recognize Huda's charm. She was a brown-skinned child with an oval face, hazel brown eyes, and a thin frame. She was spirited and a tough competitor. Hamood had never met any girl in the capital like her.

Huda also enjoyed their first meeting. Unlike the old-acting children in her village, Hamood was fun. Never once did he seem displeased by her tomboyish ways.

Hamood stood tall for his age, with shiny dark hair, broad shoulders, and a sturdy build. He spoke with the best Arabic, and his smile was endearing. Huda prayed silently right then for Hamood to be her husband in this life and in the hereafter. Every month, when Aunt Wafa came back to the village to visit, Hamood was with her.

As time passed, Huda and Hamood's friendship grew stronger. Soon, Huda and Hamood were both top students in college and had matured into young adults. It was no longer appropriate for them to hang out, but she came to see his parents as much as she could. When they did have opportunities to talk, they would often discuss their longing for graduation, so that they could apply for school in America. In America, they'd planned to finish their advanced studies, and then marry. But when Huda received her acceptance letter to New York University and brought it to Amman to show Hamood's family, she was shocked to find out that Hamood had not received one, too.

"There must have been some sort of mix up! Hamood's brilliant," she said, turning to him as the family sat in their living room. "Abu Hamood, you must call and demand an investigation." Huda pleaded with Hamood's father, but Hamood just held up his hand.

"Huda, there's been no mix up. I did not apply."

"What? Hamood! Why would you not apply? We made these plans together to go to America."

"Things have changed. I did not want to speak too soon. Huda, I've accepted a job with the university here, and it's good pay," Hamood said proudly, as he glanced over at his father. "Here, in *our* country, I can serve *our* people better. You, too. Together we can work for real change in Jordan, Enshallah."

"But…but what about New York University, Hamood? And then our plans to get married?"

"That's the best part – we can marry now! Next month even, if you want."

"How? On your professor's salary?" Huda gasped at the idea. "Hamood, have you forgotten our plans for us to earn great jobs? And what about our living well in New York City?"

"Huda, I've earned my job, and I've not lived badly in Amman. I love it here. You, too, once loved it here. We can do well with hard work, Enshallah. Please, stay in Jordan with me. Become my wife now, as you've always dreamed of doing."

Huda was furious. She couldn't believe the intelligent man she loved was capable of making such a foolish decision.

"No!" Huda said repeatedly after only seconds of deliberation. "I can't – won't stay here, Hamood. I deserve to go. I won't stay here and end up a professor's wife with no life except children and cooking. I deserve to go, and you do, too. Please, rethink—"

"About what, Huda? Love? Have you thought about love? I love it here. I love to teach. And soon, my father and uncles will need my knowledge to assist with the family business."

"But what about me, Hamood?" Huda sobbed.

"Huda, I eagerly invite you be my wife – to join our family with honor. As soon as I join my father's company, I can give you a job – a wonderful job."

"But I don't want that. I want to earn a job on my own merits," she shouted angrily, while she roughly wiped her tears away with her hand. Why didn't Hamood understand her anymore, when just days ago they seemed so in sync? Huda didn't know, but she would not give in. She'd already chosen.

"Huda, you're upset. Mother will get you some tea. Let's just—"

"No. I have to go," she said, standing and hugging Hamood's mother. "I know what I must do, with or without you."

"Please, I'm begging you to stay."

"And I beg you to come, but you won't. Masallamah, Hamood."

Huda left Jordan at the end of the month with a broken heart, but her will intact. She tackled New York City as she always dreamed she would – head on. Soon, with hard work, she'd received her MBA and gone to work for a major advertising company in Times Square.

Years later, Huda acquired the merit and wealth she'd always wanted. She'd never returned to Jordan in all the time she'd been in New York. Instead, she opted to pay for her parents' yearly trip to visit her. Over time, Huda's mother, Yasmeen, became weak from illness and could no longer travel. Still, Huda couldn't return to Jordan. She couldn't face Hamood.

She'd met many men through the years. Many of them were Arab, some not, although all had been of her same faith. Yet none of them had come close to replacing her deep admiration for Hamood. Where Hamood was kind, the men she'd met were all selfishly into their careers; where Hamood was jolly, the other men were stiff; and where Hamood was spiritual, the others were void. Huda wasn't as religious as she had been, but she prayed faithfully, gave charity as much as she could, and always fasted during the month of Ramadhan. She was determined not to settle for less. But, at thirty-five, Huda was still single and very lonely.

Often, her Baba would call her with news of her family and friends, although never would he mention Hamood. Huda was grateful for his respect. But one particular late fall night while they talked, curiosity got the best of Huda.

"Kayfa Hamood, Baba?" she asked shyly.

"Why do you ask now, Huda?"

"I don't know. I guess I need to know. I'm ready now," she admitted. "Is he well? Is he still working for the University? Please, tell me, Baba."

"Na'am, he is well. He is a board director at the Jordan University of Science and Technology, but mostly he oversees a chain of literacy programs for young mothers here in our village."

"Wonderful," Huda said softly, as she lay in her bed twirling the phone cord. She breathed in deeply before she continued.

"Does he have a spouse?" she asked, while a single tear escaped her eye.

"Laa...but soon, Enshallah. You remember Wafa's daughter, Marwa?"

"Yes, but I thought she married years ago."

"She did. Her husband died a few months ago in a car accident. Marwa was devastated."

"So now Hamood will marry her? When?"

"Four days, Enshallah."

Huda and her father talked some more, and then they ended their call. Huda couldn't fall asleep, though. She tossed and turned in her bed until her head was spinning. Hamood wasn't married. He must have been waiting for her, she thought. Now, Marwa was going to steal her last chance with Hamood. It wasn't fair; it wasn't Hamood's fault Marwa's husband died. She had to go to him. She had to go to Jordan. Huda called her travel agent, and by morning she was on her plane.

Huda made it to Hamood's wedding with ease. The only son to the Burghouti fortune was finally marrying, and many in Amman were celebrating. Huda followed the crowd. Dressed conservatively, she supplicated silently as she waited for Hamood to arrive. When Hamood entered the banquet hall, dressed eloquently in traditional clothing, she lost all composure.

He still looked the same, but more of everything now. As he walked through the hall, Huda stood, hoping he would see her. But he passed by her without so much as a second glance in her direction. Bravely, Huda stood and called out for him in front of everyone. He turned in mid-stride, immediately recognizing in disbelief the voice belonging to the woman he once loved.

"Hamoodi! It's me!" she said, walking quickly toward him with a tender smile.

"Why are you here?" Hamood asked curtly, trying hard not to show his discomfort. "You shouldn't be here, Huda."

Huda's smile turned to a confused frown. She didn't understand his frustration. She'd hoped he would see her and be filled with grateful tears.

"I wanted to see you, to tell you what an awful mistake I've made. I'm very sorry. Please, talk with me."

"Do you not realize I am marrying?"

"I came because I was wrong to leave Jordan, wrong to leave our people behind, Hamood."

"What about my heart, Huda? You threw it away!" he yelled angrily.

"No, I would never. I have kept it with me. Right here," she said placing her hands over her heart. "Please, I beg you to reconsider this marriage."

"I cannot do that, Huda. I don't feel for you what I used to," he said, shaking his head hard, trying to convince himself. "Go spend your time in Jordan with your parents!"

Embarrassed and hurt, Huda ran out of the hall furiously, as her tears splattered every which way, to return to her hotel. Presently, she lay upon her bed, wailing into the phone, and she asked her father again, "Didn't I have to try? Didn't I?"

"No, my love, you did not! Hamood has moved on." Her father revealed after moments of thought, "Had you examined his words years ago, you would have been married to him by now. But you put yourself first, and received what you have."

Huda cried harder as she tried to speak. "And what do I have, Baba?"

"You have you, Huda al Azeezah. You have you, and you have God. Yesterday and today will never be the same, but tomorrow will come, enshallah, and you must live it for all it's worth."

IWA Artist and Illustrator

Uzma Mirza

Uzma Mirza contributed the beautiful book cover artwork for *Many Voices, One Faith II - Islamic Fiction Stories.*

Uzma Mirza is a registered and licensed Architect, LEED certified with the US Green Building Council. She originally hails from Canada, a graduate of Carleton University in Ottawa. She has been practicing for 14 years in the USA, with three internationally distinct firms. She is a member of Green Roofs for Healthy Cities, the AIA, NCARB and the US Green building Council.

Presently, she is principal and founder of a Sustainable and green Architecture practice called, AYN Architect. She is also president and founder of the non-profit, The Pen and Inkpot Foundation. In addition she is an artist and a writer. Her art is called Pen and Inkpot: a Spiritual Art. Her art and architecture are compliments, of each other with the thread of philanthropy and written work the constancy. All her work celebrates, as she phrases: 'the stitching of a sustainable human'.

She is a Muslim woman business owner, building a social entrepreneurship with the environment, people and spirituality, in mind. She has spoken at various events and has been interviewed through a Radio podcast in Cairo, Egypt and IU, in Bloomington, Indiana. Presently, she's working on a Library for the Lost Boys of South Sudan and various sustainable designs.

IWA Artist and Illustrator

Brandy AZ Chase

Brandy AZ Chase contributed the creative illustrations included in *Many Voices, One Faith II - Islamic Fiction Stories.*

Brandy AZ Chase was born and raised in sunny Tucson, Arizona, USA. She converted to Islam at seventeen from Atheism and goes by the Islamic name of Aminah-Zahira. She lived in Lebanon for four years before moving to Al-Ain, United Arab Emirates, where she currently resides with her Lebanese husband and two children.

She has been writing poetry, sci-fi, fantasy, romance, and historical novels since she was twelve. Also she has been studying art and drawing with different mediums. Recently discovering the genre of Islamic Fiction, she has written many short stories and poems. In addition to writing she does home schooling, art work, interior and landscape designing, and blogging at http://www.brandyachase.blogspot.com/.

She created an All Muslimah Blog Directory at http://www.allmuslimah. blogspot.com/ and can be reached through her e-mail BrandyAZChase@ gmail.com.

Of the things in life she loves are books, sword fighting, wooden ships, tiger-lilies, delving into the realms of imagination, and above all Allah and all the great things Islam has brought to her life.

Islamic Writers Alliance Inc. (IWA)

The Islamic Writers Alliance Inc. is a USA based, professional organization for Muslims involved in the literary arts and includes published and aspiring authors, novelists, poets, essayists, publishers, editors, translators, illustrators, journalists, spoken word artists, bloggers, and playwrights. We support one another in our goals as writers, whether it be honing our craft, seeking publication opportunities, or promoting our published works to both the Muslim and non-Muslim world. We are dedicated to writing about, presenting, and supporting positive Islamic fiction and non-fiction reading materials, in all genres, for all ages.

The IWA is an inclusive organization and welcomes Muslim men and women of all races, ethnicities, linguistic backgrounds, abilities, and creeds.

The IWA's Goals

1. To promote Alliance members' works to the public, both Muslim and non-Muslim, and to book distributors and retailers.

2. To support unpublished authors in their efforts to seek publication, and promote their works to Islamic publishers.

3. To promote reading and writing creative Islamic fiction among Muslim children, the future authors of Islamic literature.

4. To make regular donations of quality Islamic books to Islamic schools and libraries.

www.ingramcontent.com/pod-product-compliance
Lightning Source LLC
Chambersburg PA
CBHW050038180626
46810CB00002B/782